Prai

MW01234022

The Roads Left Behind Us

5 star, 5 star, 5 star...did I like this story...yes! The writing is beautifully filled with so much emotion and intelligent dialog, I was sad when it ended. The environment is academia which makes the content of many conversations slightly elevated over other romance novels. Yet very understandable and warm. The characters are real, interesting, and distinct. I liked all of them. I highly recommend this story.

-Cheryl S., *NetGalley*

That was some marvelous writing; the vocabulary alone was spellbinding. The two MC's and every single supporting character are so well fleshed out that you feel as if you stepped into a room full of your friends and are catching up on all the gossip. The "will they, won't they" makes quite a pull at your heartstrings, but the end result makes the shipwreck all the more survivable. Their love story is charming, it's refreshing, it's as stormy as it is placid, and you will find yourself smiling hard at the MC's antics throughout. A play at the Student/Professor fantasy, but you'll find these two are on equal footing in the PhD program where a delicious age-gap and big, beautiful brains war to find shelter.

-Alice G., *NetGalley*

Across the Hall

I loved Kat Jackson's first book, *Begin Again*, and I've been not-very-patiently awaiting the release of her second. I was not in any way disappointed! If you're looking for a layered tale of wonderfully flawed people, look no further. What enchanted me so much about *Begin Again*, and what runs through *Across the Hall* is one of the things that makes humans so interesting is that we are not perfect.

Mallory and Caitlin are complex characters with great depth, who I alternately wanted to hug and shake. Their stories are carefully crafted, and I am so thrilled to hear that Lina is getting her own book!

-Orlando J., *NetGalley*

Kat Jackson's *Begin Again* was an incredible debut and she became my favorite new author of 2020. Needless to say I was really looking forward to this sophomore effort. It didn't disappoint.

It's a workplace romance featuring two mains with a lot of baggage to bring to a fledging relationship. This story is really told in third person from Caitlin's POV, so we don't really know what's going on in Mallory's head. I really enjoyed following the ups and downs of the relationship and it was hard to tell where it was going. I started reading and next thing I knew, I was finished. That's what I love about a book.

-Karen R., *NetGalley*

I completely enjoyed this book from start to finish. I thought Caitlin was super charming and I really felt for her when she was trying to get back on the dating horse. Of course she picks a woman who's a bit of an ice queen! They are always the hot ones!! What I loved even more, though, was that Mallory was actually a great equal to Caitlin. I really felt the ying/yang and their chemistry.

I don't want to spoil it, but there is a bit of angst between the two that I wasn't expecting, but it made it that much more entertaining. And go Caitlin for calling Mallory out when she was, in part, being led on. I may have cheered a little.

Overall, a very fun read with great characters, excellent chemistry, and just the right amount of story. Can't wait for the next one from Kat Jackson.

-T. Geist, *NetGalley*

Begin Again

This debut novel was well written, with a good pace, and I could sympathize with the characters.

Begin Again is one of the most beautiful, heartrending, and thought-provoking books I've read. Kat Jackson manages the rare feat of making a lesfic novel that toys with infidelity meaningful and elegant. While this all might sound a bit grim, it does have plenty of lighthearted moments too.

Begin Again is one of the most thought-provoking, honest, emotional and heartrending books I've ever read. How the author managed to get the real, raw emotions (that I could believe and feel) down on paper and into words is amazing. If you read the blurb you will know, sort of what this story is about. But it's much more than that. As other reviewers have stated, it's not a comfy read but was totally riveting. I read it in a day, I just couldn't put it down. Definitely one of the best books I've read and if I could give it more stars I would for sure! Superbly written. Totally recommend.

Golden Hour

KAT JACKSON

Other Bella Books by Kat Jackson

Begin Again
Across the Hall
The Roads Left Behind Us

About the Author

Kat Jackson is a collector of feelings, words, and typewriters. She's a teacher/behavior coach living in Pennsylvania, where she enjoys all four seasons in the span of a single week. Kat's been consumed with words and language for essentially her whole life, and continues to spend entirely too much time overthinking anything that's ever been said to her (this is a joke, kind of, but not completely). Running is her #1 coping mechanism, followed closely by sitting in the sun with a good book and/or losing herself in a true crime podcast.

Golden Hour

KAT JACKSON

BELLA
BOOKS
2022

Bella Books, Inc.
P.O. Box 10543
Tallahassee, FL 32302

First Edition - 2022

Editor: Alissa McGowan
Cover Designer: Heather Honeywell

ISBN: 978-1-64247-397-1

Acknowledgments

First and foremost, thank you to everyone at Bella for providing the space and opportunity for writers like me to bring their dream stories to life. I'm grateful and still a little stunned every day that I get to do this.

Alissa, I swear one day you won't have to comma-check me. Thank you for all of your work on *Golden Hour*; I knew Lina's story would flourish in your hands.

JC, thank you for your willingness to give this book a much-needed once-over, and for pairing suggestions with compliments (A+ work). Also, thanks for being an overall wonderful sounding board/fellow nerd brain.

VLS, I wish you were here to see this one. Lina couldn't exist without you.

Dedication

For anyone who needs a reminder
to *give up the ghost*

CHAPTER ONE

Kitty Hawk, North Carolina, present day

Misty air hangs over the quiet, nearly deserted street. Every so often, a seagull squawks loudly overhead on its way to the shoreline. Sand splays out onto the pavement, creating treacherous spots for the dedicated runners and bikers that share the road with the few cars out this early. The sun may have risen over an hour ago, but there remains a persistent cling of clouds and haze that seem determined not to burn off just yet.

It is a golden hour—not *the* golden hour, of course, but one that Lina Ragelis claims as her own. Maybe rose gold hour is a better descriptor, since the sun is desperately hanging on to a pink stretch of sky over the water, refusing to submit completely to the dawn of a new day. *Relatable*, Lina thinks. As she coasts along Beach Road, Lina glances to her right each time the houses give way to dunes and wind-worn fences. She can't see the ocean from her Jeep, but she can hear it quietly pounding the sand, pulling in and out with its secretive rhythm.

As a soldier who spent time overseas, Lina knows she's a bit of an anomaly in the fact that her deployments into deserts didn't destroy her love for the beach. Sure, sand sucks a little more than it did when she was a kid, but the beach still calms her in a way that nothing else can. Especially now, when the streets are practically barren and the houses around her are mostly empty.

She likes it that way: empty.

No, really. She does.

Lina slows as she reaches the house in Kitty Hawk. She can't bring herself to refer to it as "her house," or even "home," though it is for the next eleven months. Her Jeep slides into the tiny driveway and Lina hops out, looking up at the cottage before her. It's a dream home of the smallest variety and Lina loves it.

Set on stilts and crafted with the touch of someone who clearly understood the historical cottage look of Old Nags Head homes, the house is wooden with a cedar-shingle roof. The prop-shuttered windows were recently painted a bright green that pops against the worn dark wood siding. A thin porch crawls across the back of the house before jutting out into a sizable deck on the right side, then attaching itself to another long porch at the front of the home. It seems weird to call this spot, the part of the house that faces the road, the back, but once Lina walked through the home and stepped onto the other porch for the first time, she understood why the beach side could only be called the front of the house.

Stuffing her keys and phone into the pockets of her shorts, Lina reaches behind the driver's seat and picks up the lone bag of groceries. She grabs her iced coffee from the center console before heading up to the house.

Inside, the weathered look of the cottage all but disappears. For the most part anyway. Years of rentals have taken a toll on the paint and floors that span the three-bedroom home. That's part of Lina's job while she's here: glorified handywoman and interior decorator. Agreeing to take on the necessary jobs earned her a massive cut in rent...even though she's not exactly paying that.

As if taunting her, the cans of paint sitting in the hallway gleam in the morning light as Lina walks past them.

"Yeah yeah," she mutters as she walks into the kitchen. "You'll get your turn soon enough."

The pathetic bag of groceries takes just minutes to put away. Lina pauses to shake her head when she realizes she prioritized s'mores fixings over anything truly meal-worthy or healthy. A carryover from spending so much time with her community-minded best friend back in New Jersey, she's taken massive pride in supporting small and local businesses in the Outer Banks by ordering amounts of takeout that would normally induce some sort of shame in her. The truth is, the emptiness of everything around her serves to remind her how much she misses her best friend and neighbor—especially how often she'd bum a meal off Caitlin or strong-arm her into coming over for dinner. Cooking for a party of one isn't exactly Lina's idea of fun.

Satisfied with her organization of the tiny grocery load, Lina takes her coffee and steps through the sliding door onto the deck that faces the ocean. She inhales deeply, eyes shut, as the late April air curls around her. By no means is it summer, but it's a hell of a lot warmer here than it is back in Jersey, and that alone is an excellent reason to be in North Carolina at the turn of late spring.

She leans against the deck railing, watching the waves and their synchronized dance. The sun is trying its best to warm the air but it's not enough for Lina to take off her sweatshirt. It might hit seventy today, if she's lucky. The water is too cold for her taste, though again it's way warmer than the ocean in New Jersey right now. So while the thought of hopping out on the SUP or even the kayak is appealing, spilling into the sixty degree water is *not*.

Suddenly antsy, Lina drums her fingers against the splintering railing. Right, another project on her to-do list: refinishing the deck. Either the list keeps growing or she wasn't fully aware of what she was getting herself into when she asked for the temporary relocation and accepted these amazing living conditions. Amazing and in need of major TLC, that is.

Whatever the case, she's here now, and there is work to be done, a bargain rental agreement to uphold while balancing her real-world job responsibilities and Army obligations.

And since she's here, that means the majority of her problems are far, far away and completely unaware (so she assumes) of the fact that Lina is equally far away. For now, there couldn't be a better solution.

CHAPTER TWO

"You're miserable."

Lina presses her thumb against her eyelid. The regret of answering the phone zips and zings like an errant pinball in her brain. She knows, though, that *not* answering would have been far worse than answering and listening to the well-intentioned, if blunt, lecture from her best friend.

"I'm not miserable. I'm…figuring things out."

From 400-plus miles away, Caitlin's scoff comes through clearly and loudly. "Is that what you're telling yourself?"

There's a murmur from the other end of the phone, quickly followed by a muffled smart-ass retort from Caitlin.

"Is that Mallory? Could you please put her on the phone?"

"It is, and no. You need some tough love right now, Ragelis, and we both know that Mallory is soft when it comes to you."

Lina can't argue that; since her abrupt departure from home, there's been a wave of hurt radiating all the way down the coast. It's turned Caitlin into someone harder than she normally is, and her girlfriend, Mallory, while icy on the edges, has become more sympathetic toward Lina. It's a flip that Lina didn't expect, and she doesn't mind it—except for moments exactly like this, when Caitlin's stubbornness takes over.

Knowing there's no escaping the probably necessary weekly lecture, Lina leans back into the sofa, props her feet on the coffee table, and settles in. "I'm listening."

Caitlin clears her throat. "Good. I've prepared some notes."

"For fuck's sake, Caitlin. This isn't as big of a deal as you're making it."

"On the contrary, my friend, it is. You literally up and left without an explanation." The hitch in her voice gives her away. "Do you have any idea how that made me feel?" Another murmur from the background and Caitlin makes a noise that crosses between a growl and a sigh. "Right. This isn't about me."

Lina smiles, picturing Caitlin and Mallory side by side at the kitchen counter where she spent many hours listening to Caitlin move through her divorce, her unexpected attraction to Mallory, the complexities of that attraction, and her determined fumblings to find a career that feels right. She misses Caitlin—and Mallory—and she won't lie about that. But Mallory's reminder is dead-on: Lina's departure from New Jersey had absolutely nothing to do with Caitlin.

It had everything to do with, well, Lina.

And possibly a lot to do with her trampled-upon heart.

"Cait, listen. This is something I needed to do for myself. I needed a change of scenery, a different pace." Lina toys with a thread that's unraveling from a throw pillow. She adds "interior design" to her mental to-do list. "I need to be totally by myself for a while."

"You are not built to be alone."

The statement comes hard and fast, leaving Lina reeling a bit. Caitlin, for as sharp-tongued as she can be with her wit, isn't normally so...harsh.

As Lina struggles to take in that bullet, she hears Caitlin mumble, "Hang on," and the background noise on the other end of the phone rises. Lina waits it out, thankful for the time to settle her emotions.

When Caitlin gets back on the phone, she's contrite—another new tone. Lina absently wonders what the hell kind of impact Mallory's having on her.

"Can we start over?"

"Of course."

Caitlin breathes deeply. "I miss you. And I want you to be happy, but I hate how far away you are. I know you, um, got very hurt, and I get that, but you didn't have to run away. I—we—could have helped you get through it. You've been there for me through so much, Lina, and I guess I'm upset that you didn't let me be there for you."

"That sounds more like my best friend."

"I know, I know. I've been informed that I was letting my emotions get the best of me. Sorry about that." Caitlin pauses. "But seriously, Ragelis. What's this shit about needing to be alone?"

Lina laughs; she knew Caitlin wouldn't let go of that. "Just trust me, it's what I need right now. I'm not saying it's forever."

"It can't be forever. You can spew whatever nonsense you want, but you and I both know that you want, and deserve, someone who loves you and respects you every bit as much as you love and respect her."

The words, sweet and honest as they are, pierce Lina's skin and fortify an army to get inside. The shield she's worked so hard to cover her entire body ably bats them off. It's fine. She's fine.

But to appease Caitlin, she says, "Maybe someday." Lina hears the words, knows they came from her, yet doesn't have it in her to believe a single letter of them. "I'm happy here, Cait. Believe me, okay?"

It's another phrase to appease, one Lina desperately wants to be true. It's not entirely a lie; it's just not the complete truth.

"Oh, you're happy? Okay, answer me this. How many nights in a row have you had quesadillas from Bad Bean?"

Caught. "I have made it my goal to support small businesses, thank you very much. Now put Mallory on the phone."

With another growl-sigh, Caitlin acquiesces and Mallory's voice, surprisingly soothing, slides into Lina's ear. "Exactly how many quesadillas are we talking about?"

"Trust me, you don't want to know."

Mallory laughs, a full, hearty sound that Lina misses. She never really liked Caitlin's ex-wife, Becca, so Mallory has been a consistent breath of fresh air. Getting along with her best friend's girlfriend is a bonus that Lina wasn't sure would ever happen.

It was simply bad timing that Lina left New Jersey a matter of weeks after Mallory moved in with Caitlin. She'd thought that having the happy couple in her face all the time would have worn her down, but the opposite had been true. If her own life hadn't blown up in such a thorough and magnificent manner, Lina imagines she would have really enjoyed being the third wheel.

As it happened, however, the woman she was painfully in love with (obsessed with? she still isn't sure) for five years had hammered the final nail in their dilapidated coffin of an affair by renewing her vows with her husband and disposing of Lina as though she had never existed.

To say that Lina had broken into a million pieces is a massively clichéd understatement, and yet, two months later, she's still struggling to pick her heart out of the pile of bodily rubble.

One of those errant brain-pinballs zaps around, making it difficult for Lina to focus on whatever Mallory's saying. She closes her eyes and takes the deepest breath she can muster. The zaps stop and Mallory's words softly filter back in.

"...maybe we could come down midsummer?"

Lina nods before remembering the distance and the fact that they're not all sitting in the same room. "That could work."

Mallory must sense that Lina's noncommittal answer is indicative of something bigger than the actual question and she lets it go. "Caitlin wants to know if you've met anyone."

"Sure," Lina says. "The older ladies who work at the grocery store. Oh, and Trip, the guy who owns a new bakery right on Beach Road. He makes really good iced coffees."

"That's not what I mean!" comes the yell from Caitlin.

"Did you put me on speaker?"

"Yeah," Mallory says, stretching the word out. "I told you I was."

Lina shakes her head, warding off the incoming pinball. "Right. You did." Did she? She must have. But Lina doesn't remember.

"I *mean*," Caitlin says, her voice loud and hopeful. "Someone attractive. A lady someone, perhaps?"

"Nope. No dice. That's not what I'm here for."

"Just keep your mind open, Lina. Okay? Can you promise me that?"

No promises. The words bypass the finely tuned armor of Lina's brain and bounce around recklessly, their tone and accent unmistakable. She grits her teeth only to realize she's been clenching her jaw and has a headache coming on.

"Sure," she says, hoping it's enough to get her best friend off her back. She'd never realized how obsessed Caitlin was with Lina finding someone. It would be sweet if it wasn't such horrible timing.

"I think," Caitlin starts, then pauses. "I think you need to find something to get your mind off Candice."

"Some*one*," Mallory adds unnecessarily.

"She knows what I mean," Caitlin says. "But seriously, Lina. Have a one-night stand! Go do something totally out of character!"

"You're on vacation—"

"This isn't vacation," Lina interrupts. "It's work. Just in a different location."

"Right," Mallory says. "Sorry. What I mean is, you're away."

"Different zip code!" Caitlin exclaims. "No one knows you!"

"Exactly," Mallory says emphatically, and Lina can picture how enthusiastically she's nodding. "Live a little."

"It's not like there's a bustling nightclub scene here," Lina says. *Nightclub? Am I that out of touch?*

The peanut gallery on the other end of the phone must be equally upset by Lina's flashback to 1975 because they've gone silent.

"Well," Caitlin finally says. "That was enlightening."

"Is that Pepper I hear? Meowing like a lunatic?"

"What?" Caitlin pauses. "I don't hear anything."

"Poor thing sounds like she's out of meat crackers. Must be feeding time." Lina pushes herself to the edge of the sofa. "You better go feed her, make sure she doesn't waste away to nothing."

"It would take decades for that cat to—*ouch.*" Mallory grunts. "Call us soon, okay?"

"Of course."

After Lina hangs up, she flops back onto the sofa and stares at the ceiling fan. *Fucking nightclub,* she thinks, and snorts. Even if there was one on this stretch of barrier islands, there's not a single chance in hell she'd walk into it.

CHAPTER THREE

It's the cloudless sky that gets Lina's hopes up. She wants to take a deep breath and inhale that seamless blue sky right into her lungs, but there's no time, and even if there was, she's forgotten how to take the kind of breaths that make her lungs feel like they could burst from fullness.

Everything is short, quick, abrupt. Her breaths, her steps, her thoughts. The jerk of her head at any unusual, unexpected noise.

The grind of motors and gear shifts layered over the cloud of other-language chatter doesn't get her attention anymore. She's grown used to the way these streets feel, the sounds they make. The dangers they hold.

But today—no danger is in sight. That crystalline sky wouldn't allow danger, she's sure of it.

Nonetheless, Lina finds herself gripping her M4 tighter as she scans the area, doing the best she can to appear casual as she makes her way toward the building across the dusty street.

No. The conscious thought breaks into the unconscious. *No weapon.*

The memory rights itself and Lina looks down to find her hands empty. *Right. Now walk.*

She obliges and starts the slow trek across the street. It's taking far longer than she thought it would, and she looks down to see she's knee-deep in what looks like honey. Honey on sandy pavement? Lina shakes her head, trying to clear her sight. No, that's definitely honey, and it's preventing her from getting across the street, where she really, *really* needs to be.

The air around her shifts, and the bustle of the street lapses into silence. Her ears ring, a high and heavy buzz that won't let up. She shakes her head again. And again. She shakes so hard she starts to feel dizzy, which is a feeling she cannot afford to be feeling right now. As she struggles to steady herself, she feels the press of a hand on her arm, fingers curling slowly but forcefully until her forearm is in a vise grip. There's a noise she can't place, a voice that sounds like the honey that has risen to her hips. Lina lifts her non-gripped arm and hits her ear, hoping both to disrupt the ringing and to allow the voice in. Instead, a whistling screech fills her head, a sound so strong and painful she is knocked down into the thick liquid, kicking fruitlessly as it inches over every centimeter of her body, and she thinks maybe the honey isn't so bad and she can—

"*No!*" With a ragged gasp, Lina sits straight up in bed. The quilt is on the floor and her sheets are knotted around her ankles. She kicks anyway, which only tightens the hold.

Sweat trickles down her bare chest, and she flops backward onto her bed, allowing herself the grace of catching her breath. Her limbs continue to tremble even as she stares, wide-eyed, at the ceiling fan, tracking its movements. *Inhale for five, hold, exhale for six.* The thought emerges from the dark rubble of her mind and Lina shuts her eyes, giving in.

She breathes, slow and steady, waiting for the shaking and sweating to stop or at least ease up. The dreams—right, nightmares—weren't this bad back in Jersey. She had a handle on them, mostly, or at least she could get a sense of when they might arrive and disturb her attempts at sleep. Since she's been in Kitty Hawk, however, everything feels…unpredictable. The nightmares, the intrusive thoughts, the sudden and uninvited flashbacks. They've moved right in and rented out rooms in Lina's brain. She's a terrible landlord, but they thrive on that, taking up as much space as they want and barging into locked rooms despite not having keys.

She hates, *hates*, that her brain has begun betraying her like this. She honestly believed she'd conquered it and taken control. She's learning at an accelerated rate that she was wrong about that.

After another round of breathing, the shaking subsides. Lina rolls over into a puddle of her sweat and grimaces. Even if she wanted to date, how unsexy would it be for a woman to wake up covered in her nightmare-fueled sweat?

"Not happening," she mumbles as she reaches for her phone. This whole nightmare bullshit thing is something she refuses to talk about with Caitlin; Lina knows the alarm bells would ring with a ferocity that Caitlin wouldn't be able to ignore, and she'd fly down to the barrier islands in a flash. There is one person who knows—fine, sort of knows—but Lina hesitates once she pulls up her therapist's contact info.

She could call. She could text. She could calmly request that her next appointment be moved up by two days. Carolyn wouldn't bat an eye. It's just that Lina can't.

No, she *won't*.

And she doesn't. Instead she puts the phone back down and gets out of bed, ignoring the fact that her hands continue to tremble slightly. She stretches her naked body in the early morning light leaking through the blinds. She can get through today, and tomorrow, and then she can maybe tell her therapist exactly how bad and how frequent the disjointed memories have become.

* * *

An hour later, Lina's driving down 158, headed toward Manteo. It's a decent drive, one that gives her time to listen to nine of her favorite songs. She takes advantage and cues up a playlist she and Mallory made a year ago. It definitely does *not* include any of Caitlin's depressing, "I'm so lonely I might die" songs.

Not five minutes into her drive, a flag hanging from a house catches her eye. Though she prefers the blue and white design, she'd know that white star on a black background anywhere. As she coasts to a stop at a red light, Lina takes a moment to stare down the flag. She can't help but wonder who's in the house and what they've experienced; maybe they crossed paths at some point (ridiculous, but you never know). Would they bond over memories or avoid each other to stop the memories? Why did they enlist and are they still happy they did?

A beep jolts Lina's attention back to the road and she continues on her way. She's happy—mostly—with her choice to enlist, but less than happy with all the baggage that's come along with it. That choice, though, the initial choice made eighteen years ago, was one she'd felt coming for a long time and one she knew she couldn't suppress.

* * *

Sixteen. That was the year Lina decided she'd had enough. She'd gone sixteen years without feeling like she fit, always sensing she was some kind of outsider within her biological family. Her own siblings—three older brothers who were doted on like princes by her parents—treated her like an outcast, and that began way before she'd acknowledged and announced her sexuality upon graduating high school.

For a period of six months or so when she was fifteen, Lina researched ways to find out if she was adopted. That had to be it. There was no other explanation (never mind that she was the spitting image of her father). When she came up empty-handed, she turned to the one relative she knew she could trust.

Aunt Susan had laughed so hard she'd had to steady herself by sitting down at her kitchen table. "You've got to be kidding me, Lina. You're kidding. Right? You must be."

"I'm not." Almost-sixteen-year-old Lina was stubborn and insistent. She'd convinced herself this was the truth of her life and needed to be validated. "Why else would they all hate me so much?"

"First of all, no one hates you." At Lina's raised eyebrows, Susan shrugged. "Okay, your parents don't love your friends and think that one girl—the one with all the heavy eyeliner and the baggy jeans that could fit three of her—is a bad influence on you, but they don't hate you."

"I try to do everything right and it's never good enough for them." Lina slumped in her chair. "I play every freaking sport a girl can play and no one comes to my games. I don't get it."

"Lina, honey. Your parents love you. They don't show it in the best of ways, but they do. I promise you that."

The promise wasn't enough—a recurring theme in Lina's life—and as she continued through high school and started to become aware of the other looming reason her traditionally minded family would ultimately not want her around, her decision to get as far away from them as possible became more concrete. She did her research and decided to enlist in the Army immediately after graduating. She'd never felt smart enough to go to college, nor was she encouraged to aim for that. Truthfully, she had very little idea of what she wanted her adult life to look like outside of knowing she had to get away from the family that never seemed to want her around.

Her enlistment came as a shock to her parents, but that was it: a shock and then nothing. Her brothers, all out of college and beginning their adult lives by then, didn't seem to care. Aunt Susan was the only one who sent her letters during basic training. Had she not done so, Lina would have been devastated. Aunt Susan was the only family member Lina felt connected to and the only one who showed any interest in her. She got bonus points for not batting an eye when Lina finally came out to her. Lina was pretty sure she'd known all along, but Susan took the announcement in stride and asked right away if Lina was seeing anyone.

Lina's parents, on the other hand, made it very clear they didn't need to see her except for on holidays, and though it was never spoken aloud, Lina knew she would always have to go alone.

Being in the Army wasn't a lifetime of roses and butterflies, but it made it a hell of a lot easier to maintain distance from the people who had repeatedly broken Lina's heart, so all in all, she found it to be an easy decision—and a worthy escape.

* * *

The hand-painted signs for the farmers market guide Lina down a pebbly path near the waterfront in Manteo. Once she makes it to the parking lot, she's grateful to see that it's not crowded. After her panicked wake-up call, the idea of being in a large crowd of people is less than thrilling.

As she hops out of her Jeep, a gentle waft of lavender hits her nose. Lina inhales deeply, relishing the scent. Aunt Susan grows several varieties of lavender, so much that Lina often tells her she should have a lavender farm, and the smell always reminds her of the only good, genuine family memories she has.

Lina follows the scent to the tents scattered through the dry, sand-streaked grass. She scans the area, looking for both possible threats and things she might like. The dichotomy of her thoughts causes a cynical laugh to slip from her lips as she approaches the first tent, which is filled with handmade soaps.

The atmosphere is light and inviting. Lina walks between tents, sampling and sniffing. She falls into easy conversation with a local farmer while she purchases watermelon and sweet potatoes. This will make Caitlin happy, she thinks, eyeing the goods she'll have to cut and cook. Instantly, she craves a quesadilla from Bad Bean.

Another farm stand at the far end of the area catches her eye with signs boasting freshly picked corn. Lina looks down at her purchases and considers doubling back to the Jeep to empty her arms before going on a corn binge. A bright trill of laughter distracts her from that rational thought, and she looks up to find the source of the beautiful sound. Standing at the farm stand is a gorgeous woman, probably in her early thirties. Thick chestnut hair falls over one of her suntanned shoulders, and she leans in to laugh again with another woman. Lina's eyes shimmy up and down the dark-haired woman's body, taking in her long legs, tiny waist, and ample chest. Forgetting all about the purchases occupying her arms, Lina moves toward the alluring sound of that laugh.

She stops short when both women turn toward her. Her brain wants to focus on that impressive chest, but something else causes her to shift her gaze to sea-green eyes that are shining with humor and happiness. Paired with those eyes—the color is nothing Lina's ever seen before—is a wide smile and a head full of short, tousled, wavy blond hair.

"Hey," the beholder of the smile and unreal eyes says. "Looks like you've got your hands full."

Her voice isn't what Lina expected; it's deeper than her own, a little raspy. Smooth and even, something that could be soothing. Lina's brain eats that thought, destroying it upon entrance.

"I want corn." The words flip-flop right out of Lina's mouth, and she feels her face heat up instantly. Seriously? Has she regressed to the point of barbarianism?

The dark-haired woman laughs and moves behind the stands. "We have plenty of that. And don't worry about carrying it. Regan can help you."

Regan of the sea-green eyes shrugs amiably. "I think Erin only keeps me around for my muscle."

Lina fumbles to find words, any words other than "I want corn" would be great, but her tongue is not cooperating with her mind. She's stunned at her own silence; this simply does not happen to her. And why the hell is it happening now?

Regan turns to Erin and banters back-and-forth with her as Erin packages up some corn, seemingly making a guess as to how much Lina wants since Lina is still mute. She takes a slow breath in and holds it before exhaling. Her senses return right along with the burn of shame.

"I'm sorry," she says, gesturing with her somewhat-free hand. "I'm normally a better, and more polite, conversationalist."

Erin grins, utterly unaffected. "Totally okay. People are often overwhelmed by our display of home-grown fruits and veggies. Right, Regan?"

"Absolutely." She holds up an errant ear of corn. "I mean, when was the last time you saw corn this flawless?"

Lina can't help but laugh. There's something so pure, so unapologetically real about these two women, and she feels herself drawn to them. Also, she'd kind of forgotten how good it feels to laugh.

"Honestly? Never. Make sure that fine specimen goes home with me, please."

"As you wish," Regan says, and slips the cob into Erin's waiting bag. "Can we get anything else for you?"

Yes. Lina looks around the various baskets and crates. "Oh my God. Yes. Plums."

"Aren't they gorgeous?" Erin floats over to the plums. "My uncle farms them further inland."

Lina's mouth waters. At least two of those plums will be gone by the time she gets back to Kitty Hawk. "I'm pretty sure plums are my favorite fruit." They were, in fact, one of the top five things Lina missed during her deployments.

"You'll have to come back next week and let us know what you think." Erin winks at her and Lina flinches internally. Is she flirting? No. That's just Southern charm. The closeness between Regan and Erin is evident; if Erin has the balls to flirt with Lina right in front of her girlfriend (a bold assumption, but Lina's senses on such things are rarely wrong), she isn't someone Lina wants to be around. Not that she can afford to be picky right now.

"I will," Lina says, surprising herself with her agreement. "I'm Lina, by the way."

"Erin," she says, pointing to herself, "and Regan"—a point to Regan, who smiles so hard dimples pop out—"but you already knew that."

Lina pays for the corn and plums, and true to Erin's word, Regan hangs on to Lina's bags and walks with her to the Jeep. Once they get to the driver's door, Regan lets out a low whistle.

"You've put work into this."

A surge of pride rushes through Lina. "I have. She's my baby." Lina affectionately pats the frame of her Jeep. "We've been together a long time."

"Lucky girl." Now Regan winks at Lina. What the fuck? Do all Southern women wink for shits and giggles, regardless of their girlfriend being thirty feet away?

"Yep," Lina says, totally unsure of what's happening here. She takes the bags from Regan and gently places them in the back. "Thanks for carrying these."

"My pleasure." Regan takes a step away and lifts her hand, waving slightly. "See you next week?"

"Depends on how good those plums are." Lina catches herself before she winks. Oh God, is it catching? Is there an airborne winking disease floating around down here?

"And the corn." Regan nods sagely. "Don't forget about the corn."

"I would never." Lina hops into the Jeep and turns the key. She waves as she backs up, then shifts and slowly pulls out of the parking lot, wondering what in the world just happened.

CHAPTER FOUR

A quick glance at the clock in the lower right corner of her laptop proves that Lina is too early. She still has six full minutes until Carolyn will sign in. That's too much time to sit and worry about how the session will go.

Lina stares at her reflection on the computer screen. She brushes her golden-brown hair out of her eyes. She'll need a cut soon. The longer pieces are hitting close to her chin, and when she scratches the back of her head, she realizes with a start that the normally nearly buzz-cut hair is almost an inch long.

"Great. I'm shaggy," she mumbles. She twists and examines the right side of her head and sure enough, the hair there is at least an inch long. With a sigh, she blinks at herself. Long, full lashes frame her light brown eyes, a color that past lovers have alternately described as "luscious" (really? Lina shudders, remembering that), "intense," and "mystical." To Lina, they just look light brown, a shade that nearly exactly matches her hair and, when she has a deep summer tan, her olive-toned Greek skin. Caitlin has on more than one occasion described her appearance as "weirdly monochromatic," which reaffirms one of the many reasons why they never dated.

A soft chime sounds, bringing Lina back to the task at hand: therapy. She takes a deep breath that doesn't fill her lungs and braces herself.

"Hey there," comes the gentle voice. Paired with it is a kind smile, steady hunter-green eyes, and the rest of her therapist's rosy-cheeked face. Carolyn's expression is the calmest thing Lina has ever known, and while she likes it, she's also unnerved by it. How can anyone be that chill?

"Hi," Lina says, wiggling a bit in her chair. She was comfortable a second ago. Unable to return to that good spot, she presses her back, hard, into the chair and crosses her arms over her chest. She waits.

Carolyn watches Lina with a small smile. Her serene expression doesn't flinch, and nothing about her moves except for the tiniest rise and fall of her chest as she breathes. She watches Lina carefully, but not intrusively, and it's that exact look that pushes Lina to open her mouth after two full minutes of silence.

"I don't have anything to talk about," Lina finally offers, knowing she's in a losing battle. Carolyn can out-wait her *and* read her mind. Or so it seems.

"I doubt that's the truth." Carolyn's voice, hundreds of miles away over the threads of wireless Internet, retains its placidity, her tone every bit as soothing as it is when Lina is seated a mere four feet from her. The only thing missing is the subtle scent of sandalwood that permeates Carolyn's office and, if Lina's being honest about her daydreams, maybe the inviting nook of Carolyn's neck. Her tiny crush on her therapist has never been problematic, just a funny little escape, and she's read about transference and all that psychobabble shit so, you know, it's fine.

Lina huffs a silent reply. Their therapeutic relationship began two years ago. She knows damn well that Carolyn will silently, peacefully, wait for her to knock off her stubborn bullshit and start talking. If she doesn't, they will sit in silence for the next fifty minutes, Lina staring out the window past her computer screen, Carolyn's eyes holding steady on her face.

"I'm doing fine," Lina says, and cringes immediately. She has just handed Carolyn the ultimate therapeutic kryptonite, and there's no turning back.

"Fine," Carolyn repeats, the slightest hint of amusement in her voice. Lina risks a glance at her and sees the slow upward tick of a smile. "Tell me what fine looks like, Lina."

Knowing there's no getting out of this, Lina shakes off one layer of armor and shares what's been going on in North Carolina. She sticks to the safe topics, like working on the house, her upcoming weekly trip to Fort Bragg, the scheduled lectures with Caitlin and Mallory. She rambles for so long that she forgets what she's saying and accidentally mentions her lack of sleep.

"You're not sleeping?"

Dammit. Lina blinks rapidly. "I am. Just not well, I guess."

"I wonder if that's because you're away from home, your safe place."

In her Jersey condo, Lina had, upon Carolyn's firm suggestion, turned one of her two spare bedrooms into what Carolyn calls a "quiet room" and what Lina refers to as her "bunker." She slipped and said that once during a therapy session and Carolyn had been less than pleased, so Lina has since been very careful to stick to something more benign, like "safe place."

Lina painted the walls a pale gray, threw down a plush rug on top of the hardwood floors, and on a whim bought a couple oversized beanbag chairs that she often lumped together into one giant beany pile. She kept the decor to the bare minimum, wanting a clean slate, and had a portable speaker to amplify the weird meditative music that spas play during massages, which Carolyn had casually sent her YouTube videos of. Begrudgingly, Lina could now admit it was a good, and helpful, space.

And Carolyn is right. Lina is missing that space now.

She nods once. "I think that's part of it." She scratches the back of her head, again agitated by the length of her hair. "Some things have been coming up."

"What kinds of things?"

"Memories. Vague memories." Lina grips her thigh. Cognitively, she knows it's safe to open up to Carolyn, but emotionally? That's where her struggle lies, and her heart tends to be a hell of a lot louder than her brain. "There have been some nightmares."

"Tell me about them."

A sharp inhale jabs Lina's lungs on its way up. "They're blurry, not what I think they should be. I'm walking. And I can't get there fast enough, I can't make my body move. But things are wrong. I have a gun and I didn't have a gun but maybe I should have, maybe that would have—" Her next inhale hurts more, is sharper, filled with bubbly spikes. Her grip on her thigh tightens and she winces. That'll bruise. "So Caitlin won't stop telling me I need to start dating."

"Lina, I think we need to stay on the—"

"No." The word is as firm as Lina can muster, considering she's not sure she's breathing anymore.

Through the screen, she watches Carolyn watch her, assess her, take in everything she can see. Lina doesn't have the energy to squirm, though she wants to. Badly.

"I'll shift with you as long as you agree that we will come back to the nightmares. Maybe not today, but someday soon."

Lina nods. "Okay. Okay. Yes."

"I'm getting the sense you think Caitlin's wrong."

For the first time all morning, Lina laughs. The release feels like a rainstorm in the middle of a heat wave. She should definitely laugh more often. "Very wrong. Been there, done that. I'm clearly not made for a healthy, long-term relationship."

"You're judging yourself pretty harshly." Carolyn pauses, tilting her head. "Though considering some of your past experiences, I can see why."

"Yeah, I know, family of origin issues." Lina scoffs.

"Partly, yes. And also…"

"My historically amazing ability to pick women who are unavailable in some extremely important way?" Lina pushes her too-long strands behind her ear, preparing for the second half of the session. "Yep. There's also that."

* * *

That evening, Lina finds herself lying prone on the living room floor, staring at the leisurely spins of the ceiling fan. She isn't sure what time it is and is less sure that it matters. When she gets tired, she'll go to bed. Until then, the floor is fine.

Some people have morning meditation. Arguably, Lina's current location couldn't be better for such a thing, considering the daily majestic sunrises over the ocean. But meditation isn't her thing; even Carolyn agrees. Lina's mind never stops. So, she lets the meditators do their whoo-sa. Other people, like Lina, have online therapy sessions.

And someday, she'll start digging into her stuff during those therapy sessions. Really, she will.

Lina bends her elbows and slides her hands under her head. The rug in her bunker—oops, *safe place*—is more comfortable than this threadbare situation. She adds yet another item to her shopping list.

Her mind drifts to her upcoming trip to Fort Bragg. She's able to do most of the work for her temporary duty assignment from the house in Kitty Hawk, but she has to go to Womack Army Medical Center once a week, sometimes every other week. It's a little over four hours away, and Lina finds that she likes the drive and slight change of scenery. She's also taken a liking to a particular Latinx doctor who works at Womack.

But Candice. Her brain throws that familiar jab and with it comes less of the anguish Lina is accustomed to. *But Candice nothing. She made her choice*, Lina reminds herself. Loud and clear, she made her choice.

"And it sure as hell wasn't me," Lina says to the ceiling fan, which spins in agreement.

CHAPTER FIVE

Driving along 158-W, Lina scrubs her hand against the back of her head. She smiles, pleased that she finally got around to getting that much-needed haircut a couple weeks ago, and her hair is back to being super short. The tiny stubs prickle her hand, and she moves to the left side of her head, running her fingers through the shorter and more manageable asymmetrical length.

She catches a glance of herself in the rearview mirror and nods. Yeah, she looks good—except for those inflated bags beneath her eyes. Last night, someone decided to have a fireworks party on the beach, just a few houses down from where Lina's staying. The bash lasted maybe fifteen minutes, but the echoes of the blasts and booms ricocheted in Lina's head long after the last colorful explosion. Her alarm went off at four a.m. and she's pretty sure she managed a grand total of two hours of sleep. If that.

Traffic is strangely heavy as she cruises down the stretch before hitting US-17S, and an equal heaviness settles in Lina's chest. Her idyllic, isolated existence in Kitty Hawk is about to come to an end. The end of May has arrived, and with it has come the beginning of Outer Banks tourist season. The fireworks party the night before was a clear sign of this, but Lina tried to write it off as one wild family enjoying a single night of excitement. The traffic headed in the opposite direction, however, tells her something different.

As if cued by the anxiety tourist season brings, the small gash on Lina's right hand begins to throb. She makes a fist, hoping the pressure on her palm will ease the pain. She's still surprised about how unbelievably stupid she was while finishing up deck repairs over the weekend. Well, stupid and clueless: She can't actually remember how she got the slice down the middle of her palm. One minute she was entirely focused on using the pry bar to remove a stubborn rusty nail, and the next, she was on her ass, staring at blood dripping from her hand. It's unlike her to make such a careless mistake, and she's tried to put it out of mind so as not to obsess over what the hell went wrong. Her slap-dash job of cleaning and bandaging it seemed to do the trick in the moment, but now she's starting to wonder if she should have gotten stitches.

The thought of medical attention involving needles flees Lina's mind as she hits a stretch of totally open road. She's still three hours away from Womack, and while the fatigue weighs on her, she knows her only choice is to cue up some energetic music and hit the gas pedal.

A new mix that Mallory made and shared with Lina does the trick. As Lina hits the last mile of restricted-access road, she's feeling a renewed surge of energy and anticipation. Of course, she can't give all the credit to the music. She knows some of that extra-excited feeling is coming from being pretty sure she's going to have another run-in with Dr. Alvarez tonight.

Lina parks, gathers her things, and makes her way toward the medical center where she'll spend the next eight or nine hours.

The thing about Luciana Alvarez is that she's exactly what Lina does *not* need right now. She hasn't mentioned the hot and heavy flirtation to Caitlin because she knows precisely what she'll say, and Lina simply isn't interested in hearing that (correct) opinion. Besides, nothing has happened outside of some stolen glances, not-so-casual touches while passing by one another, and a tantalizing amount of coded flirting. It's nothing. Just a distraction.

Lina snort-grins as she adjusts her mask and walks into the medical center. Her history of "nothing" precedes her, and she has a feeling that Luciana is about to be added to this overstuffed file folder.

Sure enough, the first person Lina sees after she's stashed her things in her locker and made her way into the lab is Luciana. She's exceptionally easy on the eyes, with long, thick, curly black hair she keeps in a tight ponytail, flawless tan skin, and eyes that run the color line between mahogany and copper. They're electric and captivating. Lina's fallen under their spell several times since she first met Luciana back at the beginning of April.

"Nice of you to join us, Sergeant."

Lina catches herself melting a bit at the melodic but firm sound of Luciana's voice. Not ready to fully puddle, she avoids eye contact and moves to her spot near the back of the lab.

"Good morning to you, too, Dr. Alvarez."

"It is a good morning."

The lack of further information to illuminate the goodness of the morning forces Lina to look up and meet Luciana's eyes. She hates that half of that beautiful face is hidden behind the required mask, but she knows high cheekbones and lips that look as soft as velvet are hiding behind the protective layer, begging to be seen.

"Is it? Did you get some new supplies? Or was it your protein smoothie that set you off on the right track this morning?"

Luciana leans against the table, keeping just enough professional space between her hips and Lina. "Yes on both accounts, but you're the best part of the morning."

"Dr. Alvarez, you flatter me."

"I know." She leans closer, pushing the boundary of acceptable space. "And it's not like you're in need of more flattery."

The words chafe against Lina's deflated ego. It amazes her how people always assume her confidence is directly connected to the fact that women find her very attractive. Sure, she gets hit on often, and yes, she could have her pick of many women—single, married, straight, gay, bisexual, nonbinary, transgender, pansexual; she's been propositioned by every female walk of life. She's sure it sounds amazing and sexy to an outsider.

Lina actually kind of hates it. None of it feels real. Her looks are superficial. Her career is just a part of her, and the uniform doesn't define her personality the way many women assume it does. Being hit on just because she's in uniform has happened more times than she can count, and her feelings toward that have morphed from being taken aback to flat-out disenchantment.

And for the record, flattery does nothing for her confidence, or her ego, or her sense of self-worth. It usually ends up making her feel even more alone.

Lina stuffs down all of her scattered self-reflection and tries to lean in to Luciana's backhanded compliment. Caitlin's right: She needs a distraction. And Dr. Luciana Alvarez has been giving all the right signals that she's ready to distract.

"You know, Dr. Alvarez…" Lina trails off, purposely speaking in a low tone that's difficult to hear over the hum of machines in the lab.

Luciana takes two steps so that she's in Lina's bubble, dangerously close at this point. "Yes, Sergeant?"

"I'd like to be the best part of your evening."

The line makes Lina want to gag. It's exactly what women like Luciana expect her to say, and sometimes she finds it's easiest to play along—especially when she's decided to give in to the temptation and see what's hiding behind that lab coat.

Luciana's eyes sparkle with interest. Just before she walks away, she says in an equally low tone, "I've no doubt that you will be."

Once Luciana has moved on to a technician requiring her assistance clear across the lab, Lina exhales slowly and shuts her eyes. Okay. She's going to do this.

At the very least, Caitlin will be happy to hear she's found herself a distraction.

* * *

Luciana's condo, just a few miles off base, is sparsely decorated, which surprises Lina. She knows Luciana will be moving on to a different hospital in a year, but the lack of personal effects seems discordant when considering her effervescent personality.

"Make yourself comfortable," Luciana calls over her shoulder, disappearing upstairs. "I'll be right back."

Unable to distract her circuitous thoughts by examining family pictures or other decorations, Lina drops onto the leather sofa in the living room and gazes out the large windows. The back of the condo butts up against a bit of forest, and with the low lighting in the room, Lina's able to stare at the trees and busy her mind with the wonders of what truly does happen when a tree falls and no one is there to hear it.

"See anything good out there?"

Lina opens her mouth, preparing a flirtatious response, and turns to the sound of Luciana's voice. Whatever she was preparing dies a quick death when her eyes send the message to her brain that, yes, this woman is standing right here, completely naked.

"Now I do," comes the delayed response. Lina reaches out her hand, then pulls Luciana onto her lap. "That's what you've been hiding under your lab coat?"

Luciana leans her head back and laughs, her heavy breasts swaying with the movement. Lina wastes no time in running her hands up and down the curves of Luciana's mouth-watering body. When her fingers glide over and pinch both of Luciana's dark pink nipples, a throaty groan escapes Luciana's mouth and she drops her head down to meet Lina's waiting mouth.

Losing herself in sex is easy for Lina, and this time is no exception. She teases and trails, scratches and strokes. She holds Luciana tightly on her lap, forcing her to maintain eye contact as she fills her and brings her to a fast, loud orgasm. She flips her easily onto her back and forces her mind to go blank as her tongue explores, flicks, and circles until a second orgasm sends Luciana into a renewed state of ecstasy. Somewhere in the middle of bringing Luciana to staggering heights for a third time, Lina lets her mind drift and realizes, with blank awareness, that she's not entirely sure that it's her hand that's rocking deep inside of Luciana. She stares at her arm, watching it move rhythmically to a tempo Lina isn't in control of, until Luciana's screams fill the room. When she withdraws from her, she turns her hand back and forth. She wiggles her fingers. Yup, that's her hand and her fingers. All there, all attached. She pushes the odd sensation from her mind.

Lina props herself on one elbow, snaking her fingers over the rounded lines of Luciana's body. She's beautiful, even sexier than Lina imagined. Her lips are every bit as velvety as Lina expected, and while she isn't the best kisser, she at least tried to mimic the movements of Lina's skilled mouth.

"You were right."

Lina tilts her head, looking down at Luciana's flushed face. "About?"

"Being the best part of my evening." A husky laugh escapes her mouth. "Probably the best part of my month." Luciana wiggles a bit and pushes herself up on her elbows. "Tell me what you want."

The question knocks Lina off-balance. "I just got what I wanted."

"Yeah but," Luciana starts, then bites her lip. "Should I touch you now?"

Any sensual mood that was still lurking in their bubble pops. Lina knew this was coming. Luciana is not the first woman of her kind, so to speak, that Lina's gotten entangled with. But still—she was hoping it wouldn't come to this.

"No, I'm good." Lina pushes herself upright and stands next to the sofa. "That was fun."

Luciana's forehead wrinkles. Lina doesn't have the energy to learn what emotion is attached to the action, so she leans down and plants a parting kiss on Luciana's lips.

"It's late. I should get going."

"Sure." Luciana stares at her. "I'd tell you to stay, but, well, you know."

Something in her voice triggers a lost thought in Lina's mind, and she turns around before she leaves the room.

"No, I don't know, Luciana. Care to fill in the blank?"

Luciana peers at Lina from over the top of the sofa cushions. "Rick. He's scheduled to come home, but not until early morning. Still, I have to shower and clean up, and, well, it wouldn't be good for you to be here when—"

Lina fights several verbal urges and instead makes her way, hastily, to the front door. "I understand. Good night, Dr. Alvarez." She closes the door as quickly as she can, cutting off any kind of protest or retort from Luciana.

In the safety of her Jeep, Lina takes a few cleansing breaths, bringing herself back to the moment and readying herself for the four-hour drive. She should have known the rumors running around the lab were true.

As she turns her key, Lina mentally moves Luciana over to the "taken" category, where she is situated right next to none other than Candice Barrows. A sardonic laugh escapes Lina. Even she can't ignore the absurd similarities between the two women.

This time, however, she promises herself that it'll go no further. After all, she already knows how that type of story ends.

CHAPTER SIX

Afghanistan, six years ago

Leaning over the table, Lina wiped at her sweaty brow. The heat that morning was unbearable. She'd assumed the lab would be cooler, or at least comfortable, but apparently there'd been some kind of electrical malfunction overnight and now everyone was scrambling to ensure all the blood and urine samples were properly stored.

"The fucking generator!"

If Lina heard that exclamation one more time, she was liable to punch someone. The generator clearly wasn't working. Yes, they were in crisis mode, but the yelling and panic were not helping.

As usual, Lina was staying to herself, trying to be invisible in the back corner of the lab. This wasn't her first deployment rodeo—she'd done her time in Syria six years earlier—but it was her first time in Afghanistan. She'd learned quickly that minding her own business and keeping her head down was the easiest way to get through the days, the endless weeks, the interminable months. It helped that she liked her work and the makeshift hospital setting. It was the people that got to her.

And this time, she was without her battle buddies. Prior to leaving, she'd repeatedly assured herself that it would be fine, that she didn't need them. Now, two lonely months in, she was ready to admit she was dead wrong. She needed them.

A series of loud, fast clicks and vibrations came from outside the lab, and every soldier's head turned to the noise. The moment was suspended in equal beats of terror and surprise. It wasn't until the first puff of cool air descended upon them that deep breaths were taken and postures slowly relaxed.

Well, some postures relaxed. Lina had to tell her muscles to chill, and even then, it was a process that would take the rest of the day.

"Crisis averted, soldiers," an unfamiliar voice called over the murmurs of the lab technicians. "Burkowitz, Donchez, and Harrington—I need you on the first round of stat samples."

Sharp "yes, ma'am" responses echoed through the lab. Lina mentally counted while she remained focused on the task on her lab table. Three soldiers accounted for, which left just her and McGinley.

"Ragelis." Lina cursed internally. She wanted to finish her damn task.

"Ma'am," she responded, looking up and standing at attention. Seeing the woman before her, she wobbled a bit before steadying herself and projecting what she hoped was a look of total professionalism and respect.

"You seem busy."

It was a dig, and Lina knew it immediately. She also knew she'd fucked up by not standing to attention when this mystery lieutenant had entered the lab, but she'd blame that on the fact that none of her idiot fellow technicians had called the room to attention. Oh, and the whole lack of electricity crisis.

"Yes, ma'am. These urine samples needed immediate relabeling. There was a problem with the date on the label, uh, machine."

Sharp blue eyes stared her down. Lina swallowed hard. Who the hell was this woman and how was her mere presence twisting Lina's insides into a ball of panic and intrigue?

"Yes, I heard about the date issue. I'm glad to see you're being so fastidious in correcting the error."

"I take pride in my work, ma'am."

"So I've heard."

Lina cocked her head slightly. The blond hair on the woman standing opposite her was neatly tied back in a smooth bun. It was a tiny bun, and Lina marveled at the fact that no stray hairs had escaped. She glanced down at the lieutenant's uniform. Barrows. Right. She'd heard about her.

Lieutenant Candice Barrows had a widely known reputation on base as being an absolute no-nonsense laboratory supervisor. Working with her was both electrifying and terrifying, or so Lina had overheard from various conversations in the mess hall. One soldier had been dismissed from the lab because his boots weren't tied tightly enough. Granted, that was exactly the kind of rumor that whipped through base and gained traction for being absurd, but other anecdotes about Barrows's zero tolerance for mistakes flew beside the embellished tales.

What she was doing *here*, however, was a mystery to Lina. She was under the impression that Barrows was stationed on a base closer to Kabul, closer to, well, the "action."

At that moment, Barrows interrupted Lina's train of thought. "Your precision and dedication to tasks have not gone unnoticed, Ragelis. I'd like to talk with you about a research project I'm spearheading. Come to my office at 1600 hours."

"But—" Lina caught herself. "I don't know where your office is. Ma'am."

An embarrassed smile slipped over Barrows's mouth before disappearing into the blank slate of the rest of her expression. "Of course. I've moved into Officer Nemeth's office. I trust you know where that is." She turned on her heel and seemingly as an afterthought, called, "At ease, soldier," as she walked away.

Lina's shoulders dropped but the knot in her stomach refused to loosen its hold.

* * *

Moments before her watch hit 1600, Lina rapped her knuckles on the closed door of what, apparently, was Lieutenant Barrows's office. She did know where it was, as Barrows had stated earlier. Officer Ben Nemeth had become a friend of Lina's, and when he was abruptly transferred several weeks prior, she'd been surprised and angry. Officer Nemeth was the kind of guy who really listened and didn't take conversations past the walls in which they occurred. Lina had treasured him during the brief time they'd spent together.

She had a strong feeling she wasn't going to feel the same way about Lieutenant Barrows.

When she heard Barrows call out "Enter," Lina opened the door and stood at attention.

"Ma'am."

"Sergeant Ragelis. Please, sit."

Lina did as she was told and sat ramrod straight in a chair facing the desk. A cursory glance around the room proved that the office had indeed changed hands. There was a plant hanging by the window. A plant. In an office in an Army base in the middle of Afghanistan.

"You may be wondering why I'm here."

Appreciating the directness, Lina nodded. "It was a surprise to see you in the lab today."

Barrows mimicked Lina's nod, though slower and more thoughtful. "There was a need here and I was able to fill it."

Lina waited, but no more information was forthcoming. She wasn't surprised; her superiors held their cards close to their chests, and she was accustomed to being in the dark about motives and changes in plans. It was yet another reason why she was trying her damndest to fly under the radar during this deployment.

"We're happy to have you here, ma'am." Was she, though? Lina wasn't sure. It sounded nice, anyway.

"I think it will be a positive change for many. Now, about the reason why I wanted to speak with you today. I've been told you're the go-to analyst for transfusions." Barrows launched into a long-winded explanation of the research she was conducting about blood typing and transfusion success in high-risk situations, mostly involving soldiers, of course. Lina followed along, occasionally distracted by the way Barrows's lips curved to the right when forming hard vowel sounds. They were very nice lips. Surprisingly nice. Maybe a little too nice for the circumstances.

"I'd like to hear your thoughts."

Lina snapped back to attention just in time to catch that prompt. *Now is not the time to be daydreaming about your superior's lips, idiot.* She straightened in her chair, an admirable feat considering her posture was already as tightly braced as a two-by-four behind drywall.

"This sounds like an interesting and important project, ma'am. I've done some research on the transfusion topics you mentioned, but I'm always eager to learn more."

"That's why I've selected you to assist me with my research." Barrows relaxed her posture the slightest bit and something that could have been a smile ghosted over her lips. "I think you're the perfect candidate, Ragelis. Take some time to think about it. We'll meet again next week."

* * *

Much later, in the dark confines of her bunk, Lina replayed the conversation in her mind. She knew she would accept the offer to assist Barrows with her research. Not only would it give her name a boost in her platoon, but it was also a topic she was genuinely interested in. Plus, any extra knowledge would only help her during the rest of her Army career, and could be applied into whatever came after the Army.

Lina rolled onto her side, hugging her pillow tightly to her chest. There was something about Barrows that felt familiar, maybe even safe. It was a ridiculous concept considering the rumors that circulated about her in addition to the clear-cut fact that Barrows was her superior. Lina should probably feel afraid, or at least intimidated. But that piece wasn't there.

She was, unfortunately, intrigued. Lieutenant Candice Barrows was the kind of attractive that didn't hit you at first. It snuck up on you, hours after you first saw her. Lina was there now, closing her eyes to see the tall, obviously strong body and those lips that were dying to smile but refused to give in.

Maybe that was it. *Yeah. I want to make her smile.*

She snorted into her pillow. Oh, the lies she told herself.

CHAPTER SEVEN

Kitty Hawk, present day

Lina has spent the drive back to Kitty Hawk doing everything in her mental power to push both Luciana and Candice out of her immediate thoughts. It's hard work, especially when one wound is superficial but fresh, and the other runs much deeper, with tangled roots that seem hesitant to scab over. At both her therapist and Caitlin's behest, Lina has been doing her best not to dig back into those scars. She assumed the distance—both geographic and emotional—would help, but some days it seems the opposite is true.

It's not that Lina *wants* to hyperfocus on all the ways Candice Barrows destroyed her over a span of five years. Absolutely not. It's just that every time she thinks she's let something scab over, a new speck of blood appears, trailing foggy memories and sharp feelings with it.

Of course, willingly putting herself in a position to be half-heartedly stabbed by another unavailable woman doesn't exactly help the overall healing process.

Having left Fort Bragg much later than she'd originally intended, Lina's surprised to see the first muted fingers of dawn reaching through the sky. As she approaches the driveway of the house on Beach Road, she watches the gentle spread of pale pink leak through the remaining nighttime clouds, sending glowing rays over the sandy road. There's something extra magical about Kitty Hawk sunrises, and Lina is already mourning the day she leaves them behind to return to New Jersey.

She's so caught up in the sky's performance that she doesn't notice the black Lexus parked in the tight driveway until she's right next to it. Caught between chastising herself and battling confusion mixed with fear, Lina's hands grip the steering wheel as she jerks her head from side to side, quickly assessing any level of threat that might be lurking in the dune grass that surrounds the driveway. It's low enough that she can eliminate that possibility. With a deep breath, Lina exits her Jeep as quietly as possible.

Most people would probably assume the car was the product of a sunrise-chaser who assumed that no one was in the house and therefore decided it was an acceptable place to park and run out onto the beach.

Lina, however, is not most people.

Tinted windows prevent her from getting a full examination of the car's interior, but she can see enough to tell herself that it's empty. She scans the front perimeter of the house, not finding anything amiss. From her vantage point, she can't see if any lights are on inside, which doesn't make her feel better or worse. She doubles back a few silent steps and checks the Lexus's license plate. North Carolina. For a moment she wonders if the homeowner has stopped by unannounced, but Ben Nemeth, her old Army buddy who arranged Lina's stay, told her the homeowner is spending time with family in Alaska, so a surprise visit doesn't seem plausible.

An absent slap to her hip reminds Lina that, no, she definitely does not have a weapon on her, and why would she? Her guns are safely locked up in the house, exactly where they should be.

She's felt safe here in Kitty Hawk, so safe that she, at times, has forgotten her guns even exist. Now, however, she's wishing she hadn't let that part of her guard down.

Deciding that it's best not to enter the house without checking the entire perimeter, Lina creeps silently up the steps that lead to the deck at the back (well, front) of the house. A board that needs replacing creaks, letting loose an ungodly rusted grating sound, and Lina freezes. All she can hear is the repeated beat of waves hitting the shore. It's lovely when it's not busy covering up the sound of possible threats.

As she crests the top step, her breath is coming unevenly and her heart is pounding in a crescendo that out-volumes the crashing surf further down the shoreline. Any self-regulation technique Carolyn has taught her eclipses Lina as she places both feet on the deck. Her body has gone into full panic-protective mode. Her nervous system has hit the point where she's internally shaking so fiercely that the exterior of her body has become stone.

Lina takes one cautious step forward, hushing the parts of her body that want to get low and crawl. *You are not in Afghanistan*, she reassures herself. *But the sand*, her tightly wound body screams back. *The fucking sand!*

Another step forward and she sees it. A body. There, lying like a corpse on the bench near the steps that lead down to the beach, an actual body. *A person*, Lina self-corrects. Her hands move with a speed not even recognized by a turtle to her hips, and again, she pats, wishing for a weapon. Her right hand slides, dejected, down her thigh and hits the cargo pocket of her fatigues. With a mind of their own, her fingers slide into the pocket and emerge with her knife.

Of course. Her knife.

Lina clenches her fist around the knife—a paltry mode of defense, considering the circumstances, but she's relieved not to be totally unarmed. She takes another uncertain step forward, wishing suddenly she'd had a reason to stay with Luciana.

No. The thought comes hard and fast, and Lina isn't sure if it's about Luciana or the other three steps she's taken toward the body—*person*—now just a foot away.

Just as a flicker of recognition starts to build within Lina, the person opens their eyes and stares dead into Lina's. *Put your hand down*, her internal voice yells as Lina raises her knife-holding hand to chest level.

"Don't even think about stabbing me, Latch. I'll have your skinny butt on the ground so fast your little brainless head will spin right off into the sand."

The nickname hits Lina right around the same time she fully recognizes the wild, springy black curls that fan out around the person's head. *Latch*. She can't remember the last time she heard that name, or this voice.

"Key," she finally says, the single syllable scratchy and filled with disbelief. "What…how…"

"Still a lady of few words, I see." With an exaggerated yawning stretch, Keeley Younes sits up, her eyes still locked with Lina's. Her pale brown eyes, ringed with a green-gold color that doesn't fall in the normal spectrum of eye colors, hold memories and secrets, an entire timeline of things Lina would both love and hate to forget. It's been years since the two women have been in the same place, and Lina is too shocked to find and ask the necessary questions.

That, and her body is stuck in fight mode. She flexes her fingers, hoping her fist relaxes enough to get that damn knife back into her pocket.

"Put the knife away, Latch. It's just me. You're safe."

Keeley's words, achingly calm against the backdrop of Lina's internal blizzard of anxiety, hit the right places, and Lina casts her eyes down, watching her fingers replace the knife in her pocket.

"Much better. How about a hug?"

A laugh-like sound shoots from Lina's mouth. Keeley is now standing up, her long, lean body having risen from her notoriously deceased-looking sleeping pose. How could Lina have forgotten that her number one battle buddy was teased mercilessly for truly looking dead while asleep? She gives her head a quick, fierce shake, hoping to reset her brain.

"Is that a no?"

"It's not a no," Lina finally says. She shakes out her body next, trying like hell to give her muscles a reprieve. "Not a no," she repeats, clenching and unclenching her fingers.

Keeley waits her out, watching with a compassionate, nonjudgmental expression. There's always been something calming about Keeley for Lina, which butts up against her outgoing, sometimes outlandish personality. She is the categorical life of the party everywhere she goes. But there's something far deeper about her personality, something few people get to see, and Lina has always felt connected to Keeley, her Key, in a way that she can't put into words.

"Okay. I'm ready for that hug." Lina opens her arms, and a grin breaks out across Keeley's face as she sprints the small space between them. She launches herself into Lina's arms, wraps her legs around her hips, and squeezes so hard Lina worries she might break a rib or two. A heavy exhale blows from deep in Lina's lungs and she squeezes back just as hard, wishing she could bottle this feeling of ultimate safety.

"I have questions," Lina says, still holding on to Keeley.

"Girl, I do too." With a final squeeze, Keeley releases Lina and hops onto the deck. She gives Lina a long look, scanning her body. "And I have answers for your questions. But more importantly, why the heckin' holy high waters are you coming home at this time of morning? And in uniform?"

Lina cocks a sideways grin. Having been raised in the depths of Alabama, Keeley came into the Army with the cleanest mouth in their platoon. It still amazes her that Keeley made it through her time, deployments and all, and maintained her inability to curse.

"Long story." A sear of pain zips up Lina's right arm, and she looks down to see that damn wound has opened yet again. Caught in surprise and not yet having shifted to her usual reactive mode, Lina stares at the blood easing its way down her fingers and dripping onto the deck.

"What happened? Did I do that?" Keeley grabs Lina's hand and peers at the wound.

"No, I had a run-in with a nail and a pry bar." Lina tries to laugh it off, but the glare Keeley levels her with destroys the laugh on its arrival.

"And you call yourself a medical professional? When did this happen? Did you clean it? Why don't you have stitches?" She looks closer. "Or did you have them and rip them out like you did with that wicked slice on your shoulder you got when we were in basic? Or the knee gash in Syria?"

Lina opens her mouth, ready to answer every question in the order they were blurted, but Keeley shuts her up by gripping her wrist and tugging her back to the stairs leading to the driveway.

"I can tell that you didn't have stitches. Honestly, Latch, what am I going to do with you? And you call yourself a medical professional," she repeats, the words coming out with a huff.

"What are you doing? I can take care of it," Lina protests meekly, knowing exactly what Keeley's intentions are.

"Escorting your dumb keister to the hospital." She yanks open the passenger door of the Lexus and extends her arm. "Your chariot, my idiot friend."

With nothing more than a grumble of acquiescence, Lina drops into the car and settles in for the short ride to OBX Hospital… Which is exactly where she should have driven herself just days before.

Keeley whistles approvingly as they walk through the sliding glass doors. "I could get used to working at a hospital that's across the street from the beach."

"You can't even see it." Lina looks behind them as they walk through the vestibule. "I mean, it's back there, across the street and behind all those houses, but still."

She jumps a bit when Keeley puts an arm around her shoulders. "Just knowing it's there is what counts. Go sign yourself in. I'll wait here." With that, Keeley makes herself comfortable in what looks like the world's most uncomfortable chair.

Lina goes through the sign-in procedures, wishing she'd taken a moment to change out of her fatigues and into street clothes. Keeley hadn't given her the chance, though, and now she's stuck sticking out when all she wants to do is blend into the background.

Then again, maybe the uniform is a bonus—just ten minutes go by before Lina and Keeley are whisked from the waiting room and delivered into an exam room. Now it's Lina's turn to settle in comfortably while Keeley paces the small area, peering closely at the range of medical accessories.

"What are you doing? Sit down."

"Just looking," Keeley says, her voice a notch above a shout. It's her tell, and Lina knows it well. Lina had been wrapped up in Keeley's insistence on going to the hospital... And in doing so, she'd forgotten how much Keeley hates hospitals.

"Key, come on." Lina changes the tone of her voice, aiming for something soothing. "You're fine. We're here because of me and my stupidity, right?"

"You really are stupid." Her voice has come down one tick on the volume button. Not enough.

"So stupid. Probably the stupidest person you know."

"Hmm, not exactly." Keeley leans against the counter and crosses her arms. Her eyes are a little wild, but her volume is steadily decreasing, which is a good sign. "Let's not forget about my darling brother."

Lina grins, remembering the stories Keeley told to distract them from the banality and alienation of basic training. Her brother Byron, just a year younger than Keeley, had a knack for getting himself into the most compromising positions Lina had ever heard of. She'd never met the kid, so she still wasn't sure if the stories were all true, but it hadn't mattered. Byron's antics were the perfect salve for, well, everything that happened during basic.

"Remember that time he got pulled over for the busted taillight and he had that stupid keychain that looked like a miniature bong?"

The wildness in Keeley's eyes shifts to excitement. Goal achieved. As Keeley launches into an exuberant retelling of that famous Byron tale, Lina relaxes into the familiar cadence of her words and imagery.

Mid-story, Keeley is cut off by a nurse entering the room. Though her face is mostly hidden by a medical mask and her body equally hidden by scrubs, Lina feels a strange pull toward her. There's something familiar about her walk, the way she holds herself as she pauses and waits for Keeley to wrap up her long-winded sentence. Amusement dances in shockingly bright sea-green eyes, and when the nurse makes eye contact with Lina, a trail of bubbles floats up through her stomach, popping and zinging.

"In conclusion, he out-stupids you, Latch. One hundred percent." Keeley nods confidently. "You are correct."

"If we're having a stupidity contest, I have some entries," the nurse says.

"I've no doubt you do!" Keeley exclaims, then points to Lina. "Can you please start with addressing how stupid my friend here, who by the way is a *medical professional*, is for not coming directly to your fine place of employment when she first received that gaping wound on her hand?"

Lina grits her teeth and glares at Keeley, who simply grins in response. The nurse, meanwhile, approaches Lina and appears to give her a once-over.

"An Army medical professional, I see." Her eyes glitter, probably with the realization that Lina should be smart but is in fact a bit of a moron. "And what kind of damage do we have here?"

With the gentlest touch Lina has ever experienced, the nurse takes her hand, removes the paper towel Keeley had found in her glove box, and unfurls Lina's fingers to reveal her wound.

"I'm guessing this isn't a corn-husking injury."

Keeley snorts in the background. Lina tenses as her brain fumbles for the connection between those words and this person who is holding her hand like it's a newborn baby.

"No...I had a run-in with a nail. And a pry bar. And maybe some old decking."

"Did you go for a tetanus shot?"

Lina winces. Her stupidity is on full blast today. She should have Keeley sell tickets and make some money from this public show of vacuity.

The nurse presses her thumb lightly on the base of Lina's palm, close to her wrist. "I'll take that as a no, and I'll be right back." She pauses at the door and turns back to look at Lina. "And when I come back, I'd like a full review of the corn." With a wink, she retreats.

Lina's brain is still scrambling to put the pieces together when she hears a low whistle come from the corner of the room.

"She's cute," Keeley says, drawing out the *u*.

Lina grumbles, willing herself not to watch the nurse's retreating form. "So ask her out."

"Hoooo boy, Latch. Have you forgotten how well I know you?" Keeley wiggles her eyebrows. "Historically, any time you've told me to date someone, it's because you've wanted to date them."

"I don't even know her." The refute sounds pathetic even to Lina's ears. But it's true. She doesn't know that woman. Like, at all. And she's so not Lina's type. Like…at all.

"She sure seems to know you. What's with all the corn talk? Some weird North Carolinian pick-up shtick?"

Just like that, the memory slides into the front of Lina's mind. The corn, and the plums. The farmers market. *Come on, Lina.* The woman's name is right there, waiting to be picked up—

"Here we go, one overdue tetanus shot coming right up. And then, a proper cleaning! It might hurt, considering the wound is still open." The nurse taps Lina's wrist. "Stitches would have been a good idea."

Regan, Lina thinks, placing those otherworldly eyes with the jumble of wavy blond hair. "I'm not normally this careless. I'm a pretty careful person," she says, watching the agile movements of Regan's hands as she administers the shot.

"And a medical professional." Even though she's wearing a mask, Lina can see the upward curve of her cheeks as Regan grins. She remembers the dimples and imagines tugging down the mask to see if they're visible. "Hey, it happens. We're all human, right?"

"Most of us," Keeley pipes up. "Lina here has some very special talents that place her just slightly outside the human realm."

Lina jerks her head up and sends Keeley a silent message to shut the hell up. In response, Keeley gives her a cheeky smile.

"Don't listen to her," Lina says. "She's operating on very little sleep and doesn't know what's coming out of her mouth."

"Excuse me, Sergeant, I'm not the one who drove back from Fort Bragg in the middle of the night and then nearly—"

Lina's sharp look effectively cuts off Keeley's spiel, which was about to go into that funny little story involving her pulling a knife on the absolute last person she'd ever want to hurt.

"Lina's also very tired," Keeley concludes, batting her eyelashes.

"Sounds like you two need some rest." Regan's tone has shifted, and Lina notices immediately.

Apparently Keeley does as well, because her response is perfectly aligned with Lina's thoughts. "Once you fix up my old friend here, yes, I'm feeling a very long nap in her guest room."

Lina watches Regan's fingers move over her palm as she deep cleans her oozing wound and applies an elaborate pattern of bandages over the stubborn cut. Yup. Lina definitely should have gotten those damn stitches days ago.

"I'd also recommend a beach nap," Regan says, her tone light once again.

"Nope." Keeley shakes her head, her untamed curls bouncing freely. "Sand. No thanks."

"Oh." Regan looks up, then glances between Lina and Keeley. "Right. I'm sorry."

"Nothing to be sorry for," Lina says, hoping her voice is as gentle as she wants it to be. The idea of upsetting or embarrassing Regan feels awful for some reason. Before she has time to work through it, Regan is patting her hand and standing up.

"You're all set." She dazzles Lina with another masked smile that reflects in her sparkling eyes. "Next time, don't wait so long, okay? I put in an order for antibiotics just in case."

"Thank you." Lina smiles cautiously. "Really, I promise I'm not this—"

"I believe you. Sometimes we get in our own way."

Lina waits for a retort from Keeley, but nothing comes. After making Lina promise to take the antibiotic and come back if the wound doesn't start healing properly, Regan leaves with a wave.

"Who is she, Latch? And don't even try to lie your way out of this. You nearly got me the first time, but that right there was more than a normal hospital visit."

"Just someone I met a while ago. It's nothing."

Keeley elbows Lina in the ribs as they begin their walk back to the car. "Didn't seem like nothing. Like I said, she's cute."

"And like I said, you can ask her out."

"And get between you two? No thank you! Been there, done that."

The two stop in their tracks at the same time. Neither says a word. As always, when they hit this point, there's nothing that can be said.

Breaking the moment and the silence, Keeley tosses the keys to Lina, who deftly catches them. "Take me somewhere for breakfast. I'm flippin' starving, and it's all your fault."

CHAPTER EIGHT

Yet another beautiful day is unfolding. It's just past seven a.m. but Lina can already feel the warmth rolling in from the sun's outstretched arms. June is pressing onto the scene, the official beginning of summer nipping at its heels. The shift in the air seems extra obvious today, Lina thinks as she bends forward and rests her elbows on the deck's railing. She's not sure she's ready for the heat and humidity that come with full-blown summer in North Carolina.

Taking a highly satisfying sip of freshly brewed iced coffee, Lina closes her eyes against the glare of the sun and musters up a deep breath. She's exhausted. She doesn't have to examine herself in a mirror to know that the bags under her eyes have probably blown up to the point where they've permanently joined forces with her cheeks. A gentle probe of the tender skin there confirms that this is not a look she's going to enjoy seeing reflected back at her.

The sliding door squeaks open behind Lina and she's proud of herself for not flinching. Concurrently, she adds a can of WD-40 to her mental Lowe's shopping list.

"Holy smokes, it's bright out here." Keeley caps her sentence off with a loud yawn before coming to stand next to Lina. "And warm. Whew."

"Local news said we're in for a heat wave this week."

"Seems a little early for that, huh?"

Lina shrugs. "I'm still learning the intricate weather patterns of coastal Carolina."

"Dork." Keeley nudges Lina. "I'm surprised you're up already."

Lina knows what's coming next, and half of her hopes Keeley has the grace and compassion to avoid the topic, but the other half sort of wants to go there. Kind of. A little bit of her, anyway.

She takes the silent approach and offers a half-shrug in response. Maybe it's the jolt from the caffeine, but Lina realizes something that she's not particularly happy with: She's changed.

Keeley smoothly interrupts that cracked lightbulb moment and, in a way that only she can manage, cautiously steers Lina right into the topic she's half-hoping to avoid. "Latch, why didn't you tell me how bad it's gotten?"

She's referring, of course, to the nightmares. The midnight bolts of panic that consume Lina, the very ones that have overtaken her attempts at sleep for the past several months. Last night was so bad that she woke Keeley up. Granted, Lina has no idea if previous nightmares included the howling, as Keeley called it, that last night's did, so who knows if she would have been waking someone up this whole time. Even when she dealt with nightmares back in Jersey, Caitlin never said anything, so she couldn't have been loud enough to be heard through walls separating joined condos. According to Keeley, the volume of Lina's nightmare would have woken up anyone sleeping within five hundred feet of her.

"I know you don't love talking about this stuff," Keeley continues. "Heck, I don't either." At Lina's sudden twist to look at her, Keeley shrugs. "I have them too. Of course I do. But that…I don't know, Latch. I've never seen that."

All Lina remembers is darkness and pressure. It wasn't like the usual dream, the one where she's standing across the street from where she thinks she needs to be. This one was claustrophobic, filling her sleeping body with sandbag weights that threatened to choke every last breath out of her. And she was sinking. The sensation started slowly, then ticked up in speed until Lina was certain she was free-falling down a very dark, airless hole in the ground.

When she woke up, Keeley was holding her tightly, her entire body wrapped around Lina's. She was so wrapped up in the continued threats from the dream that she couldn't even worry about the fact that she was naked and covered in sweat. It felt like hours went by before she fell back into a restless sleep, still locked in Keeley's hold.

"I don't know what to say." Lina's voice is low and pained. "I thought I was in the clear, you know? It's been almost four years since I was overseas. I don't know why this is happening now."

She could name it. She knows what to call it. But naming it gives it power, gives it a bigger depth of meaning, and Lina refuses.

Keeley clears her throat. Lina looks at her, recognizing the faraway look in her eyes. "Do you think it's, um, the time of year?"

The two women stare at each other, the only sound surrounding them the reliable smack of the ocean meeting the sand.

"Maybe." Lina's whisper barely rises above the cacophony from the sea. "Maybe."

A curt nod is Keeley's only reply before she straightens up and slaps Lina on the back. "Caitlin did the right thing, sending me here."

Lina shakes her head. She'd managed to pry that fact out of Keeley when they were at breakfast following the hospital visit. Leave it to Caitlin to see through Lina's weak attempts at claiming she's perfectly fine. She's still confused, though— Keeley is *not* Caitlin's favorite person. There's some weird jealousy there that Lina has never been able to fully understand. So for Caitlin to reach out to Keeley and send her this way… Well, it's certainly surprising.

"You're lucky I'm between jobs right now and have time to hang out with your sorry tuchus."

Lina laughs. "I love the way you spin the fact that you've been living off Daddy's money for years."

"Hey! I paid my dues." Keeley mock-salutes, her posture purposely sloppy, tongue sticking out the side of her mouth. "It's not my fault my dad hated me being deployed and offered to subsidize my expenses until I find the perfect job outside of the Army."

"Well, Key, your perfect job today involves several cans of paint and a good old-fashioned roller." Lina returns the back slap. "Move your tuchus. We have work to do."

* * *

Lina learns the hard way that Keeley is not meant for manual labor. After far too many failed attempts at correctly painting a damn wall, she sent Keeley out to run the Lowe's errands that had been piling up. It shocked neither of them that Lina had both the smaller bedrooms painted by the time Keeley returned. While Lina tackled edging the entryway and living room, Keeley "helped" by providing moral support and a steady supply of water.

They called it quits around five and headed for the Outer Banks Brewery. Lina put up a fight at first, stating plainly that she didn't want to be around a ton of people. Keeley convinced her to go, using the time of day, the time of year, and the limited time they have together as coercion.

Lina looks around the outdoor area of the brewery. She won't tell Keeley, but she was right. It isn't crowded, and the tables are spaced far enough apart that the breeze snakes through the area and no one is too close. Lina leans back against the picnic table, her arms crossed over her black T-shirt. She does like it here, she can admit that. There's something pure about the Outer Banks—no memories, endless possibilities. It's a combination Lina isn't familiar with, and she's finding she likes it.

"One LemonGrass Wheat Ale, which sounds disgusting for the record." Keeley hands the glass to Lina before sitting down next to her. "And a Gatoritas for me."

"I can't believe you still drink that." Lina wrinkles her nose. "I'll never forget the time you forced me to try it. I honestly thought I was going to die."

"Well you didn't, and you're stronger for it." Keeley takes a long sip, closing her eyes dramatically. She smacks her lips after swallowing.

"Calling it a Gatoritas doesn't make it classy, you know. It's still just Gatorade and tequila."

"Am I judging you for your drink?"

"Actually, yes, you said—"

Keeley breaks through Lina's correction with a flick of her wrist. "Listen, Latch. We all have our vices. Let me enjoy my Gatoritas in peace, thank you very much."

After another sip of her bright-red drink, Keeley does a little chair-dance of happiness. Lina can't help but smile and for a moment, she feels relaxed. Having Keeley around could have gone one of two ways: disaster or relief. Lina's happy it seems to be the latter, though she also wonders if the heightened panic of last night's dream has something to do with Keeley being around.

"Incoming, incoming." Keeley grabs Lina's knee. "We've got company."

Sure enough, a small group of people is filtering into the outdoor area. They're giving off a subdued vibe, but Lina scans them anyway. It's a habit she's come to terms with, one she knows she's stuck with for life. People = possible threats. It's one of the many reasons she prefers to keep to herself within the confines of her own home.

Keeley's elbow jabs into Lina's ribs.

"What the fuck was that for?" Lina exclaims, steadying the wobbling drink in her hand.

"See anyone familiar?"

Lina scans again, paying closer attention to what the people in the group look like as opposed to how they're carrying themselves. *Oh.* That wavy, almost out of control mop of blond hair is bouncing on the head of someone who's starting to become familiar, or something like it. Bright eyes, sparkling with the reflection of her grin, bounce around the space before landing on Lina. A quick nod follows, the grin slipping into a lopsided smile.

Lina nods back. She contemplates holding up her hand to prove she still has the bandages in place, but she's distracted by Regan's arm being grabbed by another woman. *Right*, she thinks, watching the two women laugh together. Erin from the farmers market is right there, dark hair piled into a messy bun atop her head.

"Oh, I get it now," Keeley says, her voice soft and teasing. "The blonde is a way to get to the brunette. I'm with you, Latch. She is *hot.*"

There's no denying that—clad in enticingly short cutoffs and a slightly cropped white T-shirt, Erin projects a wholesome, girl-next-door vibe that is extremely sexy. Her body is firm, toned, and curvy all at once, and her smile is genuine, full of life.

"Again," Lina says, putting her arm around Keeley's shoulders, "if you think either one of them is so hot, go for it."

"About that." Keeley drains half of what's left of her Gatoritas. "I have a boyfriend."

Lina raises her eyebrows. "Hot damn, Keeley Younes. It's about time you 'fessed up."

"You know me. I love to keep you guessing." Keeley pokes Lina's leg. "Or, I guess, being bisexual keeps me guessing, too." She laughs and kicks her legs out in front of her, shaking her feet. "Anyway, I really like him. Think I might keep him around for a while."

"I'm happy for you, Key. Really. You deserve someone good in your life."

Keeley exhales loudly, nodding. "Truer words have never been spoken. But hey! You do too, Latch. Big time." She jerks her head toward Erin and Regan's group. "Like maybe that ridiculously hot woman in the cutoffs?"

"Nah," Lina says, the excuse coming easily. "I'm pretty sure those two are together."

Through her meandering conversation with Keeley, Lina watches the interactions between Regan and Erin, and as the minutes tick by, she becomes more and more certain that she's right. There's no mistaking, even from a short distance, the easy back-and-forth between them. They're affectionate with each other, they laugh at the same things, and everyone seems to address them as a unit rather than individuals.

Just as well, Lina thinks as she drains her beer, then motions to Keeley that it's time to go.

They're a mere ten steps from the parking lot when Lina hears her name called. She turns toward the sound and finds Regan approaching them, her smile bright but tinged with caution.

"Y'all leaving so soon?"

Keeley nudges Lina. "This one looks older than she is. It's past her bedtime."

Lina bites back a flare of irritation. She tries to find a witty response to right the wrongs of Keeley's statements, but no words are coming into her brain as she stares at Regan's legs, which are really quite nice, if a little pale for someone who lives at the beach.

"Well, you're welcome to join us if you can stay up for another hour or so."

Despite Regan's teasing tone, Lina's embarrassment doesn't fade. She sighs inwardly as Keeley bounds off toward Regan's group of friends, leaving her alone with this woman she barely knows.

Lina peers at Regan, who's staring right at her. The caution in her expression remains, but now Lina's reading it as nervousness, which doesn't make any sense.

"You have paint on your neck," Regan says suddenly.

Lina presses her hand against the spot. "Yeah, Keeley kindly pointed that out when we got here. She couldn't bother to tell me before we left the house."

Regan stifles a laugh. "Sounds like a good friend."

"One of the best I have," Lina says, her voice unintentionally serious. She clears her throat, trying to remove some of the heaviness that's fallen over their casual conversation. "She's an ass, actually, but we've been through too much for me to get rid of her."

Something shifts in Regan's eyes, almost like a curtain slipping halfway down to the stage floor, then stopping abruptly. "Yeah. I get that."

Lina instinctually leans in, wanting to know more about whatever Regan's alluding to, but before she can say anything, the curtain in Regan's eyes flies up and the brightness returns. Regan grins and nods toward her friends, where Keeley has made herself quite comfortable.

"Come on. You can hang a little longer."

* * *

Keeley pushes her big toe into the side of Lina's thigh. Lina barely moves, her posture tight and controlled. She's leaning forward in a seated position, elbows on knees, cradling the sides of her head between her hands.

"Come on, Latch. Talk to me."

It's tempting, Lina thinks. If anyone could begin to understand at least part of what's happening in her head, it would be Keeley. But getting to the point of using words to describe the state of her brain feels impossible.

The moment they left the brewery, Lina felt herself close up. It was as though her entire body put up shutters only to slam them shut, leaving her confined within herself without a recognizable way out. It's been two hours now, or however long it took to drive home and watch *Twilight*, and she still can't bring herself up for air.

Keeley shifts on the sofa, and just as she moves closer to Lina, a thunderous boom blasts through the silence of the room.

Lina is on her feet immediately, panic surging through her body. She scans the room frantically, vaguely noticing that

Keeley has retreated so far into the sofa that she's basically disappeared into the cushions, hands pressed over her ears, eyes shut tightly.

A second blast echoes into the house. Lina feels her fingers ball into fists, and in spite of some quiet internal voice mumbling words of rationalization, she bends at her waist and screams, "NO!"

Her scream repeats entirely against her will, but it's exactly what brings Keeley back into the moment. It takes Lina a few minutes to realize Keeley has tackled her back onto the sofa and, just like the night before, is holding her in a grip that Lina would struggle to get out of even if she had her wits about her. And she definitely doesn't have a single wit about her in this moment.

"Breathe," Keeley commands, her voice somehow soft and authoritative all at once.

Lina, starting to find her way back to the present, fights against the hold. She grunts in her struggle to get free, clawing at Keeley's arms.

"Stop. Latch, stop. It's fireworks. Stop."

The words slide into Lina's mind, taking root and slowing before transmitting their meaning. Fireworks. Okay. Right. Fireworks.

Not bombs. Just fireworks.

Lina's not sure how much time passes, or how long she fights until she feels herself tire and slump. Only then does Keeley loosen her grip, but she continues to hold Lina, stroking her hair. The fireworks haven't stopped, but now that Lina has a word for them, she can tell her nervous system to calm the fuck down.

"Relax your freaking jaw. I can feel your teeth grinding against my shoulder."

Lina shakes her head and pushes her forehead against Keeley's. "I'm sorry."

"No." Keeley pulls away and waits until Lina makes eye contact with her. "Do not apologize. You are okay. I'm here, I have you. You're safe."

A strange feeling behind Lina's eyelids catches her off guard. It feels like something is burning, like her eyes are melting. It's hot and wet and confusing.

She blinks furiously. Nope. Not happening.

"Lina, you're safe." The rare sound of her actual name in Keeley's voice reroutes Lina away from the tears that threatened to spill for the first time in...an inconceivably long time.

"Okay," Lina says, her voice muffled against Keeley's shoulder. "You can let me go."

"I don't know about that quite yet. Just stay with me a little longer, okay?"

Lina wrenches her body out of Keeley's hold, which has loosened just enough. "I'm fine, Key. I'm fine. I can handle this on my own." Lina is standing now, the adrenaline surging one last time before she completely gives out. "I don't need you. I don't fucking need anyone. I'm not weak!"

Eyes wide, Keeley stares up at Lina. Another firework booms from the beach and Lina jumps. Keeley doesn't move, and when she speaks, her voice is steady.

"I know, Latch. I know you're not weak."

CHAPTER NINE

Fort Leonard Wood, Missouri, eighteen years ago

Lina took a deep breath, willing her pulse to settle. She hadn't expected to be thrown into exercise drills immediately after getting off the bus. Throwing herself into every sport available in high school was definitely paying off now, even if she was a little winded, but she figured that was more from anxiety than actual physical exertion.

While she waited to grab her luggage from the carefully arranged line, she glanced around, keeping her head low. So many people—so many strangers. It was both intimidating and refreshing. After all, this life-altering decision to enlist in the Army immediately upon graduation was what she'd wanted, what she'd been obsessing over for several years. It was a fresh start, a clean slate.

It was the very first opportunity Lina had to be herself.

Except, that is, for the little snag of having to hide her sexuality.

That was a small task; she'd been doing it for years. She also had it on good authority that while she couldn't be *out* out, she'd at least be able to find and build friendships with like-minded women. She felt confident that she'd find her bubble and within that translucent sphere be able to fully be herself.

But first: actually meeting people. Lina gritted her teeth as she followed the line of women into the barracks. Aside from some murmurs here and there, they were a quiet group. Lina had a feeling it was more about exhaustion from the day's activities than it was an indication of personalities. She'd seen some showboating earlier and had already made mental notes of who to avoid. The last thing she wanted to do was bring unnecessary attention to herself. That was not part of the grand plan.

A short blast on the drill sergeant's whistle brought the group to attention.

"Welcome to your new home," Lieutenant Snyder said. "Make yourselves comfortable. You'll report for dinner at 1700 hours." With that, she was gone, leaving the thirty female soldiers in her wake.

Lina moved quickly, establishing herself on a top bunk near the door. Her natural tendency toward organization fell into place as she unpacked and put away her belongings, keeping her ears trained on the conversations spilling out around her.

"They used to have coed barracks," a stocky Black woman said. *Private Harris.* At least, Lina was pretty sure that was her name; the day had been a whirlwind of faces and names. "But there were some 'incidents,'" Harris added with a laugh.

"Just as well," another soldier piped up. "I'm fine being as far away from men as possible."

Lina smiled. Maybe her bubble wasn't too far away.

"Please, Suarez. You'll be riding the first dick you find."

The room erupted into laughter and Suarez, who apparently didn't want to be far away from men or their appendages, slugged a short redhead on the shoulder.

"Fuck off, Lochlan." Suarez dropped her voice to add something only the redhead could hear.

Lochlan returned the punch and added a middle finger.

Having been distracted by the raucous interaction, Lina was surprised when she turned back to her bunk and found the bottom bed had been claimed.

"What's up?" The friendly tone matched the woman's wide grin. "Isn't this wild?"

Lina nodded, self-consciously smoothing her tight bun. She'd spent her entire senior year daydreaming about chopping off her hair, but once she'd made the decision to enlist, she'd shelved that daydream for post-Army life. "It's something."

"Is it cool if I take this bunk? I figured we should stick together."

Confused, Lina peered at the woman. Nope, she definitely didn't know her. Hadn't even seen her earlier, or if she had, it was through the fog of hundreds of other faces. Looking at her now, though, she felt certain she would have remembered this woman's face.

"Okay." Lina shrugged. "I'm not sure what you mean, but the bed's open so it's yours."

The woman jerked her head to the right. "I totally get it if you'd rather have Lochlan beneath you." Her eyes sparkled with mischief. Lina stared at them, captivated by the unusual ring of color surrounding pale brown irises. "I mean, I would too, but it looks like she's bunked up with Suarez. Not that Suarez cares about having such a hottie sleeping on top of her."

Lina's reply caught in her throat. There was no way, *no way*, this woman would be so blatant. Right? No. That definitely wasn't what was happening. Lina glanced around to see if anyone else was listening, but the other women were wrapped up in their own business.

"It's cool," the woman added. "I'm cool. You know, *cool*."

"Honestly I have no idea what you're talking about."

She stood up, brushing invisible lint from her fatigues. Lina was surprised to see the other woman was a solid six inches taller than she was.

"You give the vibe," the woman said simply. "Am I wrong?"

"No, no, you're—wait, I don't think—" Lina cut herself off and frantically looked around again.

"Goodness gracious, you're a tough one." With surprising strength coming from her willowy body, the woman grabbed Lina's wrist and dragged her toward the bathroom, which was deserted. "Maybe I should introduce myself. I'm Keeley Younes."

"Lina Ragelis."

"I know." Keeley grinned. "I pay attention. But more importantly, I cover all the bi's: biracial, bisexual, and"—she drummed her fingers in the air—"biped!"

Lina snorted a laugh as her paranoia ebbed. "How? How did you know?"

"About you? Please, Ragelis. You throw a vibe harder than Melissa Etheridge. Well, that and I saw you checking out Lochlan's very nice tush." Keeley tapped her finger against her chin. "I noticed that because I was also checking out her delightful derriere."

Lina made a mental note to stop checking out nice butts. "Shit. Okay. I'm with you now."

"Thank God because I was starting to worry there's not much going on in that adorable head of yours." Keeley lightly knocked her knuckles against the side of Lina's head. "Cute but stupid. I could deal with that, but I was hoping you had a brain."

Lina swatted her hand away. "You're going to be a pain in my ass."

"Absolutely!" Keeley crowed. "And you're going to love every minute of it."

* * *

Four weeks into boot camp and Lina was alternately loving and hating it. The pacing and tight schedule calmed her, but the rigor was more than she'd expected. Her muscles ached every night, and getting up at the ass crack of dawn every morning was starting to suck.

Keeley had been right. She was a pain in Lina's ass, and Lina loved it. She loved her. Their bond had come fast and hard, sparked by the mentally and physically challenging environment they met in, further cemented by being able to be open with each other. Never before had Lina connected so quickly with another person. A day didn't go by without Keeley rapping her knuckles against Lina's "stupid cute, cute and stupid" head, but no day went by without an "I love you" either.

That was new for Lina—the love thing and the expression of it. She'd learned to accept the "love" her family gave her. It had never felt genuine, and it often felt like it didn't exist. But still, she assumed they loved her because that's what families were supposed to do. Even worse, she'd learned to believe that her family's version of love was the true definition of love. With Keeley, it was different, and Lina was slowly learning a new meaning of the word. Keeley had no issue showing Lina that she did love her and that she supported her, cared about her, wanted her to be successful. She was a mother and sister wrapped into one boisterous, annoying, solid human being. It had only been four weeks, but Lina already could not imagine her life without Keeley in it.

The heavy thoughts of family weighed on Lina's shoulders as she sat hunched over her weapon, trying to remember the exact sequence for reloading the magazine. It wasn't hard, but she was psyching herself out. Her shooting was…not going well. Something about the action of pulling the trigger, knowing that someday someone could be on the receiving end of the flying bullet, messed with Lina's head. Keeley kept reminding her that "it's just part of the gig," but Lina struggled to get her head and fingers to work in synchrony.

"You've got to pull that lever back."

Lina jerked her head up at the sound of the familiar voice. Brit Lochlan walked toward her. Despite being in the same platoon, Lina had had very little interaction with Brit other than admiring her from afar. Worried about being caught staring at her ass again, Lina figured it was best to avoid her as much as possible. Besides, Brit spent most of her time with Suarez, and Lina was attached to Keeley.

Brit sat down next to Lina, close enough that their legs were touching. Lina swallowed hard against the burst of arousal that jumped to attention low in her belly. Keeley teased her mercilessly about having a crush on Brit, but this was the first time Lina had been this close to her and she realized she could no longer tell Keeley she was wrong.

"May I?" Brit gestured toward the rifle, and Lina awkwardly handed it to her. She leaned in as Brit narrated the steps she was taking, her fingers moving slowly over the parts of the gun. It was the same sequence that had been drilled into Lina's head, but it sounded different coming from Brit. Maybe it was the honey-like quality of her voice, or her proximity. Lina listened, paying more attention to Brit's long, elegant fingers than to her words.

"Now you try." Brit handed the rifle back to Lina.

With shaking hands, Lina fumbled through the steps. She felt Brit's steady gaze on her the whole time, and when Lina missed a critical step, Brit put her hand over Lina's and guided it back to the required lever.

"I think the latch is stuck," Lina said, coming up with a random excuse to help her not look so incompetent.

"The latch isn't stuck." Brit laughed as she flicked the safety. "Your brain is what's stuck, Latch."

Lina looked over at Brit and found her dark green eyes filled with amusement. She'd heard other soldiers calling Brit "Lock" and assumed it was just a shortened version of her last name. Now she wasn't sure.

"Dammit," Lina muttered, glaring at her trembling hands. "I know how to do this, I swear."

"I know you do. Mind over matter, kid. And you've got to stop the shaking," Brit said, buffering the firm words with a kind smile. "They'll think you're weak."

"I'm not weak," Lina fired back.

"Whoa, easy." Brit held up her hands, then stood. "I'm not saying you're weak. You just don't want anyone to *think* you're weak."

"I'm *not*," Lina said forcefully. She too stood, facing Brit, the rifle hanging between them like a solid boundary not to be crossed. Lina clenched her jaw. "You don't know me."

Brit seemed as surprised as Lina to hear the words. She took a step backward, then stopped, holding eye contact. "You're right. I don't." Her eyes softened. "So let me know you, Latch."

With a half-smile, Brit turned and left the room, leaving Lina wondering what the hell had just happened.

* * *

"Sweet heavens and all things beautiful!"

Lina rolled her eyes as Keeley bounded toward her. She'd been hoping for a couple minutes of silence before heading to her shooting qualifications, but Keeley had other ideas.

"You're not going to believe this, Latch. Are you ready? But really, you have to be ready. Are you?"

The nickname, bestowed upon Lina just a week and a half earlier, had not only stuck but also spread. Gone was her birth name; her platoon only addressed her as Latch now. Considering the source of the nickname, Lina wasn't upset about it, but a part of her wished it had stayed between her and Brit.

"Latch! Tell me you're ready."

"I'm trying to get ready to shoot," Lina said, playfully shoving Keeley. "So hurry up and deliver this incredible news."

Keeley stopped walking, forcing Lina to do the same.

She raised an eyebrow. "Well?"

"I kissed her."

Lina shook her head and laughed. "Her" could be any of the six or seven women Keeley had been actively crushing on for the past several weeks. "You need to be more specific, and we need to keep walking." She nudged Keeley into forward movement.

"Lock, dude. I kissed Lock."

Lina was the one to stop in her tracks this time. As jealousy snaked through her body, she trained her face to stay neutral. She had zero claim over Brit. Sure, Keeley loved to give Lina shit about her crush, but Brit had shown negative twenty signs that she reciprocated Lina's interest. It had been a slow process so far, becoming friends, but Lina was trying. After all, Brit was the one who had set the friendship in motion.

But this... Keeley kissing Brit? This felt weird.

"Good for you." Lina started walking again, hoping the motion would regulate her tangled emotions.

"That's it? You don't want details?" Keeley practically bounced as she walked. "It was *hot*."

"I believe you." Lina ran her fingers over the cold metal of her rifle. "Can we talk about this later? I have to shoot."

"Yeah yeah yeah, we totally can, and we will." Keeley continued bouncing. "She's totally gay, by the way. Did I call it or what?"

Despite trying with all her might to tune out Keeley and get into the head game of shooting, those words landed firmly in Lina's head. She'd been wondering, of course. Hoping, too. Knowing threw a little wrench in the process of growing a friendship. Lina bit her lip.

The woman of the hour, Brit, breezed past them, a deadly serious look on her face. "Keep moving, Key. Those targets don't wait on anyone." For someone who was just a couple inches over five feet, she sure moved quickly. She was twenty feet ahead before Lina formulated a response.

"*So hot*," Keeley whispered.

"Did she just call you Key?" Lina blurted.

"Oh, yeah. Get it? Lock and Key." Keeley did a little hip-swagger-filled dance before righting herself back to military posture. "Actually Suarez started it, but whatever. Best couple name ever, am I right?"

"*So cute*," Lina mocked. It pained her to admit that Lock and Key sounded a hell of a lot better than Latch and Lock. She shook her head. *Shut the fuck up and focus.* Now was not the time to debate couple names for couples that didn't exist.

"Hey, Latch!" Brit's voice rose above Lina's jumbled thoughts. She'd stopped and waited for them to catch up.

"What's up?" Lina aimed for casual, hoping it hit and didn't betray her angsty-crush feelings.

"Watch those hands." Brit flicked her gaze down to Lina's offending extremities. "Remember what we talked about."

A hot zip of anger steadied Lina's shaking fingers. *Don't look weak.* "Yeah. I will."

Brit nodded. "I'll be watching."

Oh fuck, please don't, Lina thought, but all she could do was nod.

A muffled sound that was the unmistakable noise of Keeley trying to smother a burst of giggles sounded from beside Lina. She rolled her head to the side and found her friend, her battle buddy whom she loved more than life itself, grinning like a cat who'd snagged a bird.

"You're next," Keeley mouthed, then darted off before Lina could punch her.

But of course, she was right. Lina was next.

CHAPTER TEN

Kitty Hawk, present day

"I still hate sand," Keeley grumbles, kicking midstride at a pile of sand that has tumbled off the dunes. "I don't understand how you like being down here, surrounded by all this *sand*. Doesn't it make you itch, just looking at it?"

Lina, too out of breath to respond, offers something like a grunt, but it doesn't impact Keeley's monologue about sand. Just as well, since Lina has zero breath to spare on words.

It took a full week and a half of Keeley's visit to convince Lina to go for a run. Now, a mile in, Lina remembers precisely why she spent nine days lying to Keeley, saying she's been running while Keeley sleeps in.

For the first time in her life, Lina is out of shape. And there is no way she can hide that from Keeley, who would be sprinting down Beach Road if Lina wasn't holding her back to a slower pace.

"Call me crazy, but didn't you run circles around me during basic?"

"Yes," Lina huffs. "I did." She exhales forcefully, drinking in the sweet elixir of a fresh lungful of humid air. "And I will. Again. Just not. Right now."

Keeley laughs loudly, swatting Lina on the butt before picking up her pace and zooming down the road. Lina drops her stride down to a pace she can manage, keeping her eyes on Keeley's flying form.

Being physically fit is something Lina has always prided herself on. Plus, she simply functions better when she's in a constant state of activity. Pushing herself at the gym or during a run forces her to switch gears in her brain, pushing the darker thoughts to the back and allowing the pure focus of stamina and strength to sit front and center. She felt herself slipping a couple weeks before she came to North Carolina and promised herself she'd get it together once she arrived and settled in. Considering it's been about two and a half months, she can now admit that she hasn't gotten anything together. Quite the opposite, really. Things keep falling apart, herself included.

The thoughts slap against themselves in her mind as her feet pound against the pavement. Keeley will be leaving soon, meaning Lina will once again be alone. Back in April, she thought that was what she wanted, what she needed. Having Keeley around has shaken something loose in her packed-away memories, and Lina's not sure if she'd be better off if Keeley stayed to help her unpack, or if her exit will force the mental suitcases back onto their dusty shelves where they'll sit unattended until something else triggers their tumble.

Either way, it's the *alone* piece that's causing Lina distress. Maybe she doesn't want to be alone after all.

Lina slows to a stop, not much of a change from her snail pace of a run, a few feet from where Keeley stands with her hands pressed against her hips.

"You've been lying to me," she says, her tone matter-of-fact.

"Caught." Lina gives what she hopes is a distractingly beautiful smile. "I'm sure you'll forgive me."

Keeley shakes her head, jerking her thumb over her shoulder. "Maybe. But don't think I'm not leaving a fitness regimen for

you when I leave. We need to get you back into tip-top shape."
Keeley pokes Lina's stomach, which has the kindness to still
be relatively firm. "Against my better judgment, I'm going to
suggest that we walk back via the beach."

"But the sand?"

"I'll deal." The exerted flush on Keeley's cheeks fades a bit.
"Facing your fears and all that, right?"

"I'm with you," Lina says, squeezing Keeley's shoulder.
"Besides, the sand never did anything bad to you."

Something that can only be described as a guffaw flies from
Keeley's mouth, and Lina guides them up the steps that carry
them over the dunes to the beach. They pause to remove their
shoes and socks, then make their way down to the shoreline.

"I can admit it's beautiful," Keeley says after a couple minutes
of blissful silence. "But I will never like sand."

"Again," Lina says, "what did sand ever do to you?"

"Latch. Do you mean to tell me that pea brain of yours
doesn't remember Syria?"

Lina half-expects the word itself to shoot jagged ribbons
of memories through her body, but she's surprised to realize it
doesn't. Syria wasn't all that bad, truthfully. She was twenty-four
at the time, and it was her first deployment. Young, naive, and
raring to go. Besides, she had both Keeley and Brit with her,
which made everything easier.

"Of course I remember Syria. Mountains, blue skies, rocky
terrain, some sand here and there."

"Here and there? Are you frickin' kidding me?" Keeley
shakes her head dramatically, her midnight curls springing in
her ponytail, spraying droplets of sweat onto Lina's arm. "You
don't remember the patrol incident."

Lina sorts through her Syria memories, getting stuck on
Brit, Brit, and Brit again. Her time in Syria is forever linked
with Brit. She tries to put Brit to the side, the flames of her
vibrant red hair spread out against Lina's pillow, to find whatever
mystery memory Keeley is stuck—

It clicks, and Lina stops in her tracks, laughing uncontrollably
at the image that has resurfaced in her mind.

"Well, I see you've remembered."

"I can't believe I forgot," Lina says, gasping for air between laughs. "That moment was priceless. Your face! Oh my God, Key. Such a good memory."

"For you, maybe." Keeley cracks her annoyed composure and grins. "You're not the one who fell for Snyder's bullcrap story about the scorpions and screamed like a two-year-old when she threw something."

"The look on your face right before you fell off the back of the truck, and then you popping up with a face full of dirty sand." Lina shakes her head. "I'm so happy you reminded me."

"I'm thrilled I can entertain you. I was coughing up sand for an entire week."

"What I want to know," Lina says as they continue walking, "is why in the hell you thought Snyder would be holding an actual scorpion in her hand?"

"I didn't! Or, I don't know, maybe I did. I was too busy worrying about whether or not Sanders was watching me."

Lina laughs again. She hasn't felt this light in weeks, maybe months, and she doesn't want the feeling to escape. "I totally forgot about your Sanders fling."

Keeley shrugs. "He was hot, and you had your whole thing going on. I needed someone to hang out with."

"More like bang out with."

"Did you…Did you actually just say that?"

Lina cringes. "Yeah, I did, and I'd like to retract it, but it works." She slows her walk, forcing Keeley to do the same. "That whole thing I had going on," she repeats, then bites her bottom lip. Her light feeling is slipping away. "That feels like forever ago."

"It kind of is," Keeley says, her voice soft, barely audible above the waves.

Not sure where this conversation is headed, Lina wraps her arm around Keeley's waist and feels Keeley slide her arm around her shoulders. They haven't ventured into this territory too often, but now seems as good a time as any.

"I'm sorry I kinda disappeared on you in Syria. I got pretty consumed with Brit, I guess."

"Yeah, you did, and it sucked. But I forgave you a long time ago. I saw how hooked on her you were."

"I was," Lina agrees. "Brit was…She was a lot to me then." The words don't suffice, and Lina tries to find a better way to express the impact that relationship had on her. Before she can, Keeley interrupts her thoughts.

"It's weird when you call her Brit. No, not weird. Funny, I guess."

"Why? That's her name."

"Uh, yeah, I know that." Keeley shrugs, scanning the ocean. "She's just Lock to me."

Lina tightens her grip around Keeley's waist. "She's a lot of things to me."

"Just say it, Latch. It's me you're talking to."

Lina loved her. Really and truly loved her. And that's the entire problem—one of the biggest fractures in her concept of love.

Keeley had been right back during basic: Lina was next, but it took years for it to happen. All the time leading up to Lina and Brit's clandestine relationship overseas was spent building a friendship that was both challenging and deeply connected. The bond between Keeley and Lina was one of pure love and support, whereas the bond that developed between Lina and Brit was built on their differences and curiosity about each other, smattered with a wild combination of love and lust. Lina, unfortunately, was the bearer of love, while Brit was consumed with nothing but lust. Being overseas poured gasoline on their slow-to-ignite sparks, and Lina had soon found herself consumed by all things Brit. They'd only slept together a handful of times, but every moment of their coming together was seared into Lina's brain. She refused to release the memories, entertaining them every so often and falling into the trap of wondering *what if.*

It was a big question. Too big for Lina, most days.

"I don't know," she says now, kicking at the sand as they walk. "I think a part of me will always wonder."

"I get that." Keeley squeezes Lina to her before releasing her. "Just like I always wonder about Sanders."

Lina snorts. "You do not. You know exactly how that relationship would have panned out. You'd be a stay-at-home mom, serving dinner every night at five thirty sharp, only for him to leave to see one of his many mistresses after you went to bed, exhausted from having entertained your six children all day."

"Okay, maybe, but you have to admit—he was so hot. And"—Keeley gestures toward her pelvis—"very well-endowed, I might add."

"File that under Things I Never Needed to Know."

"Lina," Keeley says suddenly.

The use of her real name startles Lina. "Yeah?"

"Do you ever think Lock has something to do with—with, you know."

Lina peers at her friend, her battle buddy who so rarely holds back in conversation. "With what, Key?"

"Your...stuff." She casts her eyes at Lina. "Your PTSD."

The letters jab Lina directly in the heart, then slice down toward her gut. She looks down at her torso, fully expecting to see blood spurting from the wound. She stares, trying to figure out why she's not bleeding out. It sure feels like she is.

"I'm sorry—"

"I don't—"

They stop walking and stare at each other. Lina feels the warmth from Keeley's caring gaze. She could talk. She could. She could let some of this out, these traps and landmines that alternately sink and float within her.

"I don't have that." The words spit from Lina's mouth, her denial fueling their launch.

"I think maybe you do."

Lina shakes her head and begins walking again. That brief moment of possibility, of waning openness, is shuttered behind her thick walls. "Let's go home. To the house. You know what I mean." She shakes her head again, searching for a calmer feeling than what's currently fogging through her body.

"Okay." Keeley's voice is soft again, and she picks up her pace to match Lina's, an easy feat considering her height and longer legs. "So," she says, her voice now amused. "I'm feeling a Gatoritas. Wanna see if your hottie is at the brewery again tonight?"

"Nope."

"C'mon, Latch. My time here is slipping away! We've gotta go out and live a little, and we at least have to find a way to get you into her cutoffs."

Lina relaxes a bit, realizing Keeley's talking about Erin. "When did you get so crass?"

Keeley barks out a laugh before smacking Lina on the arm. "Again, Latch. *Syria.* Everything in my life circles back to Syria. You know that."

With the house in sight, its calming facade welcoming them as they trek across the sand, Lina lets her muscles lose some of their tension. She does know that. With the addition of Afghanistan, it's also true for her.

It's just that sometimes, she'd really like to forget.

CHAPTER ELEVEN

"Screws, screws, screws," Lina mutters, the word becoming an incantation as she strides through the hardware store. She meant to get the damn screws when she was at Lowe's yesterday but got distracted by ceiling fans. Three newly installed fans later, she's still missing the screws and has had to run out to a local hardware store a couple blocks from the house. She couldn't risk being sidelined by something else sparkly and new at Lowe's.

Aisle six. Right. Screws. Lina meanders down the aisle, scanning the neatly organized sections. It's a small store, the kind that feels like a grandfather's garage, and Lina likes the comforting vibe. She likes to imagine her own grandfathers being handy and having workshops in their garages, but one died before she was born, and the other called a handyman for every household trouble. Her father isn't much with a hammer and nails either. Lina's skill with home improvement tasks comes from her middle school industrial arts teacher, Mr. Jacoby, who instilled in her the belief that anything could be fixed with a little skill and a lot of know-how.

She silently thanks Mr. Jacoby every day lately. Without his patience and encouragement, she wouldn't have developed the skills that enabled her to escape to Kitty Hawk and work on the vacation home. Thirteen-year-old Lina had no idea that a little skill and a lot of know-how would one day help her run away from her problems.

Lina laughs to herself, then quickly looks around to make sure no one heard her. It would be so easy if she could run away from her problems. Physically, sure, she nailed that. But mentally? Emotionally? It feels like the dagger drags deeper every day.

"Okay, screws. Come to me."

She slides her fingers along the rows of screws, searching for the right size. She should have written it down.

"Do the screws talk back?" The whisper comes from her right side, and Lina forces herself not to jump. It helps that she recognizes the voice now, but she's still knocked off-balance by the sudden appearance of another person.

"If you ask them nicely, yes." Lina pushes a smile onto her face before turning to Regan. She's not prepared for the internal lightning that zips from her stomach up through her chest, and she takes a perplexed step back as their eyes meet.

There's only one way to say it: Regan looks absolutely adorable. It's not a word Lina would ever think to use to describe a woman, but it's the only word that fits this moment, and this particular woman. Regan's tousled hair is stuffed under a backward baseball hat, little blond pieces sticking out around her ears. Clad in flip-flops, khaki shorts that sit perfectly on her hips, and a bright blue T-shirt with *Lady Beavers* scrawled in white above a screen-printed basketball, Regan grins at Lina. The unguarded smile knocks her back another step.

"Lady Beavers?" she sputters, feeling a laugh surging.

"Oh God, yeah," Regan says, laughing. "My high school team. Classy, right? If you're thinking we were teased mercilessly by other teams, you are correct."

"You played?"

Regan spins around, displaying the back of her shirt. *Murphy* is written across her broad shoulders, the number 21 below it. She turns back to face Lina, the grin still in place. "Small forward, top scorer my senior year."

"Power forward, top scorer my junior and senior years." This smile is genuine, and Lina relishes the feel of it.

Regan raises an eyebrow. "You're not competitive at all, huh?"

"I was also the top scorer in field hockey, but just in my junior year. I got lazy when I was a senior." Lazy and crushing hard on a sophomore player, which distracted her during games.

"Okay," Regan says, drawing the word out as she taps her pointer finger against her chin. "Is there anything you don't excel at?"

The lightning zings again, but Lina shoves it down, reminding herself that not only is Regan unavailable, she's also not Lina's type. She's got that androgynous, tomboy-butch image—the very same image Lina has cultivated for herself. That would be weird, two butch women together. Right? Lina thinks for a moment. Yeah, yeah, totally weird. Or maybe not weird for other people, but for sure weird for her. Right. So weird.

When Regan reaches past Lina and their arms brush, the friction definitely does not feel weird. *Weird*, Lina quickly reminds herself. *Weird and unavailable.*

Regan looks at the package of screws she plucked off the shelf, then glances up at Lina. "Well? I'm waiting. What aren't you good at?"

"Lots of things," Lina says seriously. "Would you like me to write you a detailed list?"

"Actually, yes. I would like that. I'd also like your top five greatest talents on the reverse side of the paper."

Are we flirting? What in the hell? Lina bites her lower lip. She does not miss the way Regan's luminous eyes flicker down at the movement, seeming to watch Lina's teeth until they release her lip. Only then does Regan meet her eyes again, and there's no ignoring the way the colors have shifted. They're a deep turquoise, shining with something Lina isn't prepared for. Or expecting.

Unavailable, she yells internally.

Regan clears her throat. Lina assumes she's realized the line she's crossing, even if it's just with a look in her eyes, and some mild-mannered, verbal almost-maybe-flirting that could just be casual conversation but *oh my God*, Lina has forgotten how to exist as a normal human being who chats for the sake of chatting because two women who previously met have run into each other in a hardware store. In the screw aisle. Naturally.

Lina does jump, just a little, when Regan abruptly takes her hand and pulls it close to her, inspecting it.

"This healed well," she says, gently prodding the skin of Lina's palm.

"Yeah." Lina resists the unexpected urge to capture Regan's fingers in her hand. "But you were right. I should have gotten stitches when it happened. Maybe you could have stitched me up." *Abort, abort!* Lina fumbles, trying to reroute the flirtation that's slipping out of her without invitation. "Um. Because you work there." *Smooth, idiot.*

"I do work there. And I would have been happy to stitch you right back up." Regan releases Lina's hand. "I'm there a lot."

"Not right now," Lina points out. *Way to go, Captain Obvious.* Lina briefly considers showing Regan her cool party trick of stuffing her entire fist in her mouth, just to make herself shut the hell up.

The grin reappears, and Regan's eyes shift to a lighter hue. "Very astute, Lina. I have the day off." She hesitates, stuffing her hand in her pocket. "And you? Also have the day off?"

"Not really. I'm working remotely right now, but I do most of my assignments later. At night," she adds. "I use the days to work on the house."

"Building or remodeling?"

"Remodeling, but more like fixing up. A bunch of odds and ends that needed taking care of, mostly. It keeps me busy."

Regan nods, her eyes never leaving Lina's. Normally the eye contact would make Lina want to retreat, but there's something about Regan that puts her at ease. That alone is enough to freak Lina out—never mind the fact that she thinks she might be attracted to this woman who is definitely not her type *and* seems to have a girlfriend.

Lina fights a laugh. It's so typical of her life, it hurts a little.

"What's so funny?" Regan asks.

Okay, apparently Lina didn't hide that laugh so well. "Nothing. Just my head."

"Your…head is funny?"

Lina wishes for a trapdoor to appear below her. Being sucked down into an escape hatch sounds awesome right now. "No, my head isn't funny. The thought in my head was funny, but it wouldn't be if I said it out loud." Lina shuts her eyes. "I must sound like a complete basket case."

"No, you don't." The answer comes fast and firm. Lina opens her eyes and peers at Regan. "You just seem like you have a lot going on," she adds.

"I guess I do," Lina says quietly.

"Well," Regan says, jiggling the box of screws in her hand, her shoulders hunching a bit. "I know we don't really know each other, but I've been told I'm a good listener, so if you ever want to talk…" She trails off, lifting her shoulder in a half-shrug. "If you need stitches, you know where to find me."

Her right hand exits her pocket and waves, then she turns and walks down the aisle, leaving Lina in a state of confusion and curiosity.

* * *

Later that night, Lina's making her way through two days' worth of tasks from work. She's exhausted, both from the physical labor she exerted during the day and from the emotional hangover from Keeley returning home. It's been a day, one solitary stretch of twenty-four hours, since she left, and Lina is feeling the loss acutely. She barely slept last night, too afraid of lapsing into a nightmare that Keeley couldn't rescue her from. Part of her wonders if the nightmares will ease up now that the flesh and blood reminder of things better forgotten is gone, but the ferocity of her last nightmare lingers, its aftermath a silent threat against taking the chance of sleep.

Lina's going to crash, and she knows it. But first, she wants to get through this last bit of a research proposal she needs to look over. If she can wrap this up, she won't have to log on tomorrow other than to check her email, leaving her free and clear to refinish the floors in one of the bedrooms.

As if summoned by her thoughts, a soft ding sounds from her laptop. Lina rubs her eyes, making her way through the next-to-last paragraph of the proposal before clicking on her email tab. She scans the message that came in an hour ago before opening the brand new one. As she reads it, a wave of nerves unsettles her stomach.

So much for working remotely. She's been temporarily reassigned to the lab at Outer Banks Hospital, effective immediately, her first shift beginning in forty-eight hours. She breathes a small sigh of relief. No trips to Fort Bragg for a while, which means an easy escape from Luciana Alvarez. Plus, she'll be working nights, which is a bonus. There's something else, something that seems positive but has a nervous edge to it, but Lina can't quite put her finger on it.

"Oh," she says, the word echoing into the silence of the kitchen where Lina has set up her makeshift office. The image of Regan pops into her mind.

Unavailable. Not her type.

And the third strike hits. Lina swore off workplace entanglements after the Barrows shit hit the fan, and she's already broken her own rule with Luciana.

She has already learned that nothing good can ever come of a workplace romance, no matter if it's an affair, a committed relationship, or a one-time fuck. Lina will not shit where she eats. Nope. Not happening.

Not anymore, anyway.

CHAPTER TWELVE

Fort Bliss, Texas, five years ago

Ending up in Texas was not part of Lina's plan. Back in Afghanistan, when she'd agreed to join up with Lieutenant Barrows's research, she'd imagined a nice hospital in New Jersey, somewhere close enough to home that she could spend every night in her own bed. No one had mentioned the possibility of spending ten months in the hairy, steamy armpit of Texas.

But there she was, standing outside William Beaumont Army Medical Center, sweating her ass off in the Texas heat. She almost preferred dusty Afghanistan heat to this thick veil of unrelenting humidity.

"Good morning, Sergeant Ragelis. Nice to see you bright and early."

"Good morning, ma'am. It's a lovely day." Lina looked over at Barrows, who had come up beside her.

"Lovely? It's hot as hell."

Lina stifled a laugh. She'd been working closely with Barrows for close to a month and was still thrown off by the personality that lived beneath the uniform and title. It was slow going, getting to know her, but Lina didn't mind. It wasn't like she had anything better to do for the next nine months. Barrows was all she had here in El Paso, and Lina wasn't in the market for new friends.

As they walked inside, the sun caught something on Barrows's swinging hand, causing a glare to momentarily blind Lina. She rubbed her eyes, then looked for the offending item. What she saw nearly stopped her in her tracks.

A wedding ring, something that absolutely had not been present in Afghanistan nor any day in the previous month, circled Barrows's finger. Lina was too shocked to say anything, not that she could exactly question her lieutenant. Had she eloped overnight? What the fuck was going on?

Lina knew the rules, and she wasn't interested in getting herself into a sticky, doomed situation… And yet, she couldn't help the fact that she was dangerously attracted to Candice Barrows. She repeatedly told herself that Barrows wasn't interested, nor would she be under different circumstances. The woman was definitely straight, definitely not interested in Lina.

And yet.

As the days passed and Barrows's boundaries loosened by the tiniest unraveling threads, Lina felt something rising between them. Glances were getting longer. Accidental touches were happening more frequently. Space separating them in the lab was getting smaller. But the biggest change was the way Barrows spoke to Lina. Her guard was coming down, slowly and steadily. Her tone had changed from all-business to something friendly, even warm at times. She laughed more often, even joked around. Just last week, Barrows had sat down next to Lina at a table, and her leg brushed against Lina's, then returned and stayed, pressed tightly. Twenty minutes later, when Barrows had finally unglued her thigh from Lina's and moved to another area of the lab, Lina was left squirming in her seat, trying like hell not to get up and run after her.

Lina cleared her throat as they entered the lab. As usual, they were alone. That had been the case for the majority of their stint in Fort Bliss. Lina still didn't know how Barrows had managed to commandeer a space just for them. But she wasn't complaining.

"Lieutenant," Lina said slowly. She'd realized within the first week in Texas that Candice didn't mind her dropping the "ma'am" when they were alone, but Lina still wasn't comfortable moving past "Lieutenant."

"Yes?"

"I can't help but notice something's different about you."

Barrows cocked her head to the side, studying Lina. "I'm not sure what you're referring to."

Lina pointed to Barrows's left hand, and as she did, she watched that hand ball into a fist.

"Oh, that," Barrows said breezily. "I'd misplaced it."

End of conversation, apparently. Barrows walked briskly to the computer and began tapping away. Lina watched her for a moment, then focused her attention on sorting a new batch of samples that had arrived overnight. They went about their morning tasks in silence until Lina couldn't take it anymore.

"Are you recently married?"

Barrows stopped mid-keystroke. "No. No, I've been married for twenty years."

Lina swallowed the various questions that were trying to jump out of her mouth. Twenty years? She realized with a start that she had no idea how old Barrows was. And why the hell didn't she wear that ring overseas? Also, why did Lina even care?

"It's not what you're thinking, Lina."

The words barely made it through the perpetual hum of the lab, but Lina caught them. It wasn't the first time Barrows had used her first name, but it still caught her off guard. She liked it too much, frankly, and she wanted to hear it again.

"How do you know what I'm thinking?" Words Lina never would have aimed at Lieutenant Barrows in Afghanistan now came easily. She had learned to let Barrows open the door that signified the shift in their communication. Considering she was Lina's superior, it was a necessary give and take.

Barrows turned from the lab table and faced Lina. Her normally sharp blue eyes were stormy, clouded with an emotion Lina couldn't identify.

"Have dinner with me tonight."

Lina, too shocked to use words, merely nodded. Barrows moved away from the computer, on to whatever task she deemed necessary at that moment. Lina went through the motions of her day, well aware of the shift in energy between them. By the time their workday ended, Lina was a mess of sweat and arousal, lust and confusion. She had no idea what dinner would bring, and while Barrows seemed to think she knew what Lina was thinking, Lina had absolutely no idea what was happening in Barrows's head.

* * *

Their military issued apartments were a floor apart and identical. The stark interiors were taking some time to get used to, but Lina noticed a different, warmer energy in Candice's apartment that definitely wasn't present in her own. Lina leaned against the kitchen counter, watching Candice move fluidly around the space, stirring and dicing.

Candice. It was the first indication that something major was changing. When Lina had walked into the apartment, Barrows had looked her dead in the eye and said, "If you're so much as thinking of calling me ma'am, Lieutenant, or Barrows tonight, turn around and leave right now."

Lina had settled on not calling her anything.

Instead, she listened to the soft jazz playing in the background. She hadn't pegged Candice for a jazz fan, but they hadn't gotten around to discussing their tastes in music yet. Their lab talk was mostly based around friendships, perfunctory information about family (excluding marriages, apparently), and their experiences in the Army. Boring topics. Unrevealing topics. Safe topics.

"Dinner will be ready in a couple minutes." Candice wound the dish towel around her wrist as she looked at Lina. "Thanks for eating with me."

"Anytime," Lina said. "This place is kind of lonely."

"That it is."

Lina saw the opening and took it, her curiosity getting the best of her. "You must miss your husband."

"Lina."

The weariness in Candice's voice halted Lina's planned interrogation. Instead, she waited.

"I told you, it's not what you think."

"Then tell me what it is," Lina said, keeping her voice calm and level.

"It's a marriage." Candice sighed heavily, dropping the dish towel onto the counter. "That's it. Two rings and a piece of paper."

That statement said more about Candice than anything else ever would. Years later, Lina would acknowledge this was the moment she should have turned and walked away. Instead, thirty-one-year-old Lina, consumed by a fierce attraction to someone she could not, should not, have, saw only the holes in that statement, the very holes that led to her opening, her one chance.

"Maybe you need something more than that." She didn't mean for her voice to be husky, laced with desire. It just sort of happened.

"Maybe I do." Candice met Lina's eyes then took a step toward her.

Lina pushed off the counter and met Candice in the middle of the room. She waited, again stalled by the rules that surrounded everything about them in that moment. This was wrong on so many levels; if Lina had taken the time to realize how wrong it was, she would have recognized that moment as her second sign to walk out of the apartment.

But thirty-one-year-old Lina, doused in the flames of forbidden attraction and having identified her grand opening, thought bending the rules *just this once* surely wouldn't be too much of a problem—especially if no one found out, and she had no intention of sharing this with anyone.

"Make me feel something." Barely lighter than an exhale, Candice's words floated to Lina, sounding nothing but sexy in that moment and the context surrounding it.

They were close enough to kiss by then. All rational thought departed from Lina's brain, taking with it the majority of her common sense and rule-following nature. But still, she waited for Candice to lean in a fraction of an inch. She waited for Candice's lips to brush against hers, tentatively and sweetly. She waited for the feel of Candice's hand on her hip.

And then, Lina dove into her opening.

She grabbed Candice, crashing their lips together and eliciting a low moan. The sensation of finally kissing this woman who had been the source of many daydreams was overwhelming and utterly satisfying. Lina bit Candice's lower lip before drawing it into her mouth and sucking gently. As the intensity of their kissing rose to a powerful height, Candice began clawing her nails down Lina's back.

"Take me to bed," she whispered, her words ragged against her heaving breath. "Now."

Wasting no time, Lina picked Candice up and walked her backward through the small apartment, thankful for the matching layouts.

As they fell onto the bed, Candice laughed, pulling Lina's face down to hers. "I knew you were strong, but damn."

"That's nothing," Lina said, dropping to her elbows, relishing the feeling of her leg slipping between Candice's thighs. "I've got all sorts of talents you don't know about."

"Show me," Candice whispered.

Encouraged and aroused beyond belief, Lina wasted no time in stripping Candice and showing her a couple talents she'd stashed away for this very moment. Judging by the sounds and bodily reactions, Lina felt confident that Candice was both surprised and impressed.

It wasn't until she had Candice on all fours and was bringing her closer to her fourth orgasm that Lina looked down and realized she was still fully clothed. She pushed it from her mind, concentrating on the talent she was currently showcasing. There was more time in the evening. They were just getting started.

As it turned out, Lina was wrong about that. Candice collapsed onto the bed after that last talent overtook her. She

CHAPTER THIRTEEN

Kitty Hawk, present day

Lina stretches her legs out, admiring the way her naturally olive-toned skin has finally started darkening. The "finally" is her fault, seeing as she's spent the majority of the warm, sunny, early summer days distracting herself inside the house with improvement tasks. Today is the first day she's letting herself relax, and she's not sure what to do with herself. Relaxation isn't something that's ever come naturally to her.

But it's Sunday, and while she can't partake in Sunday Funday—or, she could, but she'd be doing it by herself which loses some of the fun aspect—she can at least enjoy a lazy day on the deck.

She pokes at her right quad, examining the muscle. The embarrassment of running with Keeley hasn't faded, but it has reignited Lina's desire to stay in shape. She's nowhere near where she prefers to be, but her early morning runs are getting easier as she inches toward longer distances.

The unmistakable sound of a Taylor Swift song bursts into the air. Lina grins and reaches for her phone.

was nearly asleep when Lina, having almost given
touched, finally moved to get up.

"Wait," Candice said, her voice thick with sle
excitement shot through Lina. "I'll walk you to th

The excitement fizzled, taking Lina's heart d
rungs. *It's the first time*, she thought. *She's never d
It's fine. There's always next time. Wait. Will there b
Following Candice, who had wrapped herself ir
walked awkwardly to the door, quite uncomforta
rush of thoughts and her own level of untended ar

At the door, Candice put her hand on Lina's sh
felt the weight of the statement before Candice
her mouth. She knew with sudden acuteness that
not be a next time.

"I can't promise you anything." Candice v
free arm around her torso, building a gentle but
between them. "You know how…You know how tl
us. But I don't want to regret this, Lina."

"I understand." And she did. No one could kn
never happen again. Check, and extremely disappoi

"I hope you do."

Not wanting to unpack that statement, Lina
from under Candice's light touch and slipped ou
making her way upstairs where she could, not for tl
and certainly not for the last, tend to her own arous

"Hey, Mal."

"Hey, hang on, I hit the wrong button." A moment later, Lina's phone beeps. She accepts the change and waits for Mallory's face to light up her screen.

"Shit, you're tan!"

Lina tilts her head from side to side, modeling her new tan. "Thanks, I just got it."

A snort comes through the speaker. "She's not kidding. She's probably been sitting outside for a whopping two minutes, and already she's tanner than you or I will ever be."

"Hello to you too, best friend."

Caitlin's smiling face appears next to Mallory's. "Hey, little buddy. Glad to see you're properly enjoying your vacation."

"Yet again, it's not a vacation. I'm—"

"Yeah, yeah, we know, you're working." Caitlin squints. "Looks like you finished the deck!"

"I did." Lina flips the phone so she can give them a quick tour of her deck-refinishing talents. "It was a bitch, but it's done."

"Good, so that means you're almost done? And you'll be home soon?"

Lina hears the undertone in Caitlin's voice. She looks to Mallory, who lifts her shoulders in a quick shrug.

"No, we talked about this, Caitlin. I'm here for a full year. I won't be home until April."

Caitlin huffs and looks away from the phone. "Fine. Okay. But for the record, I don't like this."

"Babe, it's her job."

"I know, *babe*, but she *asked* to go away."

"Yes, *darling*, because she needed a break."

As Caitlin opens her mouth to fire a return shot at Mallory, Lina clears her throat to interrupt the couple's squabbling. "What's happening at home? Anything exciting?"

"Nope. Absolutely nothing. Same old boring town, same old boring people. Which is exactly why I miss you so much." Caitlin bats her eyelashes at Lina. "Life here is simply not the same without you."

"I could have told you that. But you're clearly surviving."

"Not thriving." Caitlin sighs heavily, leaning closer to the phone. "What's happening there? Have you met anyone who's almost as awesome as I am?"

An image of Regan, standing in the hardware store with that backward baseball hat, floats through Lina's mind. "Not really. The people here are pretty nice, but I keep to myself—unless someone randomly shows up at my door, that is. Or, more accurately, my deck."

A beat of silence sits between the three women. Lina waits, curious how Caitlin will react.

"Yeah…So…About that." Caitlin half-smiles. "Is she still there? With you?"

"No, Keeley went home a week ago." Lina counts backward. "A little over a week, I guess. And I could never quite get her to tell me how you orchestrated her unannounced arrival."

Mallory leans back, pushing the phone closer to Caitlin, who has the good sense to look ashamed.

"Lina, I could tell you weren't okay. You forget how well I know you. Everything about you was telling me that something was wrong, and you wouldn't talk to me about it, so, I don't know, I know you and Keeley have this…" Caitlin pauses, gesturing uncertainly. "Bond. You have a bond with her, and she knows you in ways that I don't—"

"In ways that you *can't*," Lina corrects.

"Right. In ways that I can't, because you two have experienced things that I know nothing about." Caitlin smiles proudly. "How'd I do?"

"B+. Go on."

"B+? Seriously? Fuck you." She holds up her middle finger for extra emphasis. "Anyway. I figured since I couldn't be there, the least I could do was see if Keeley could. And she could, so she did. And…"

Lina nods slowly. "And it was really great to have her here." Mostly, since Lina still isn't sure if the nightmares have intensified because of being near Keeley. "Also? I'm okay."

"Lina…"

"I am. Okay?"

Caitlin grunts and wrinkles her nose. "I don't exactly believe you, but fine. Wait. Fine on one condition."

"I'm listening."

"Give me a release so I can talk to your therapist?"

Lina laughs loudly, startling a seagull from its perch on the railing of the deck. "That may be the craziest thing you've ever asked me to do. And the answer is no."

"Worth a shot," she mumbles, passing the phone to Mallory. "I have to pee. Talk to my gorgeous girlfriend for a minute."

"She worries about you," Mallory says a moment later.

"I know. But the more she worries, the worse I feel. So if you can get her to stop worrying so much, that would be wonderful."

Mallory shrugs. "Doubtful, but I'll try. Seriously, though. You haven't met anyone? No one at all?"

Luciana Alvarez's face flashes in Lina's mind, and she grabs the half-truth. "I may have spent some time with a woman."

"Whoa, wait, what?" Caitlin zooms back onto the screen. "A woman?"

Mallory looks at Caitlin in surprise. "That was fast. Did you wash your hands?"

"No. I heard Lina say 'woman' and I came running." Caitlin waves Mallory away, clearly uninterested in the horrified look on Mallory's face. "I want to hear about the woman! Did you meet her at the *nightclub*?"

It's Lina's turn to offer Caitlin her middle finger and she happily does. Barring the nightclub jab, she's pleased to have a diversion from the topic of her mental health. Lina launches into the full story of her short-lived fling with Dr. Alvarez. She spares the details that her best friend and her girlfriend simply do not need to know, but spins a pretty dazzling story, if she must say so herself.

"Wait a minute," Caitlin says once Lina's finished. "She's married?"

"Apparently."

"No." Caitlin shakes her head, her ponytail swinging wildly. "This reeks of Barrows, Lina. I don't like it."

"That's fine, because it's over. I don't know when I'll be at Fort Bragg next. I got reassigned to the hospital here in OBX."

"I bet that's a better commute," Mallory says from wherever she's gone off-screen.

"Much better. Less stressful environment, too." The first week of working night shift was pleasantly calm. OBX Hospital has a totally different feel than Womack, and she's found the slower pace agrees with her. Lina likes the hospital and the few people she's interacted with.

"Great. Have you made any friends?" Caitlin asks.

"Not yet." Again, Regan flashes in Lina's mind. "But maybe soon."

Caitlin tilts her head and inspects Lina from 437 miles away. "So you did meet someone."

Lina's surprised to realize she doesn't want to lie. Besides, Regan is just a potential friend. There's no harm, no risk, in telling the truth about meeting her.

"Two people, actually. At a farmers market a while ago. One of them happens to be a nurse at OBX Hospital."

"I like this." Caitlin nods sagely. "I'm getting good vibes about this."

"From what?" Mallory pipes up. "She's hardly told you anything. Don't be weird, babe."

"There's literally nothing to be weird about," Lina interjects. "They're a couple and they're very nice people."

"Oh." Caitlin's voice drips with disappointment.

Lina sighs heavily, running her hand through her hair. "Why are you so obsessed with me finding a girlfriend?"

"And I'm out." Mallory waves to the phone and darts out of the room.

Caitlin looks back at the door her girlfriend has just shut behind her. "I'm not obsessed. I just don't like that you're alone."

"You do realize that's completely out of your control. Right? Caitlin, this is *my* life. Not yours."

"I know, I know. I do, I swear. I just…Lina, I know how amazing you are. I know how much you have to give. And I'm so fucking tired of seeing you give yourself, give your *everything*, to women who do not deserve a single thing from you." Caitlin flushes. "Oops."

"Yeah, oops. How long have you been holding that in?"

"Um, a while. Years, maybe. But that's beside the point. I know I can't summon the perfect woman for you, but I can make you promise me that you won't sleep with Lucy again."

"Luciana."

"Yeah, her. Done deal. Okay?"

"Done deal," Lina repeats.

* * *

The smell of hospitals is something that Lina has loved since she was a child. That and the cleanliness, the order, the shift in pace from unit to unit—it all fascinates and invigorates her. The Army was always planned to be a stepping-stone for a career in medicine, but eighteen years later, she's still enlisted and still not sure which medical path to take.

For now, being a lab technician works. She likes the structure and routine in labs. Most of the labs Lina's worked in have been relatively quiet, which appeals to her. The hands-on work combined with nerdy research satisfies her desire to learn and discover new things.

What she could do without, however, is the amount of urine she's been testing since she started working at OBX Hospital. It's her second week and the pee supply is endless.

"Where did this even come from?" she mumbles as she labels yet another container of urine.

"Didn't they teach you the answer to that in science class?"

Lina jumps, slamming her knee against the metal cabinet she was leaning over. "Fuck!" The urine, apparently not safely secured in its specimen bottle, has started a slow spill over the sterilized table.

"Oh shit, I'm so sorry." Regan reaches past Lina and grabs the bottle, righting it before any more precious yellow liquid can slip and slide away. "It's just a little bit. I think we're okay."

Lina eyes Regan. "You have to stop sneaking up on me." She's surprised to hear the firmness of her words and worries too late about how they'll land.

"I do. You're right." Regan takes a step backward. "I saw you come in here a while ago and just wanted to say hi, and maybe ask you what the hell you're doing here. I mean, obviously I can see that you're working, but when did that start?" Regan grins behind her mask, her cheeks lifting and eyes sparkling. "I didn't mean to startle you."

"I know," Lina says, keeping her voice even. "I, uh, startle easily. It's not your fault. But if you could stop doing that, that would be great."

"I can. I'm sorry. Again."

Lina sighs behind her mask. This isn't how she wanted her next conversation with Regan to go. She's not sure how she wanted it to go but this—this is definitely not it.

"I'll be more gentle with you."

Those words pierce Lina directly in the heart, and she vacillates between wanting to run away and wanting to scream. It's not the words themselves, but the unspoken theme resting beneath them.

She thinks I'm weak.

Lina clenches her fists, digging her fingertips into the softness of her palms until she feels the slow burn of pain. Her brain clouds, failing her attempts to locate a worthy response, a way to set the goddamn record straight with this woman who absolutely does not know anything about Lina but now has the audacity to have the fucking idea that she's—

"Hey." Regan's voice is soft, questioning. "Are you okay?"

"I'm fine," Lina retorts, sharpness stabbing the edges of the words. "I need to get back to work." She spins around, faced with the splash of piss on her pristine lab table.

Her focus shifts immediately to the need to clean, to sanitize, to begin again. She's so involved in her mental task list that she doesn't notice Regan's departure, or the way she stops and turns at the door of the lab, her eyes locked on Lina, nothing but wonder shining in her eyes.

CHAPTER FOURTEEN

"Okay. You're okay. You're—you're safe. You're okay."

The incantation, having been on repeat for well over an hour now, isn't working its intended magic. The tumble of feelings in her gut and chest continues its animated fistfight. Lina's fairly certain she's worn a path in the gorgeous new flooring from her frantic pacing. She stops in the kitchen, glancing behind her. The floors are intact, even boasting a bit of a shine. Good. Great.

Inhaling slowly, letting the air flow deep into her belly, Lina pauses at the counter while she holds her breath and gazes out at the ocean. As she counts and exhales, she watches the water. The waves are low and slow this morning, carving a soft fringe against the shore. This is one of the biggest allures of the barrier islands—when the ocean relinquishes its power and turns into Lake Atlantic. For as beautiful and calm as it is, there aren't many people out taking advantage of it. Lina sees one lone kayaker paddling, stopping every so often to gaze further out. She stands on her toes and looks closely. There: a silver arc and a playful splash, followed two, three, four times.

"Oh," she breathes, captivated by the sight of dolphins playing just twenty feet from shore. Moments later, she feels the watery burn pooling in the corners of her eyes and swipes furiously.

Really? Crying because of dolphins? Lina presses the heels of her hands into her eyes until the threat subsides. *Unbelievable.* With a sigh, she pushes off from the counter and goes to sit on the deck.

Weekends never used to be this hard. Maybe it was the exhaustion from the weekly trips to Fort Bragg, or the initial enormous list of house tasks, but prior to being reassigned at OBX Hospital, weekends were simply part of the routine. They didn't stick out like a throbbing, sore thumb the way this particular weekend is. Lina contemplates calling in, seeing if extra hands are needed, but the thought of being elbow-deep in urine again makes her quickly reconsider her options.

She casts her eyes to the side of the deck, and the flickering lightbulb in her head goes full blast. There sits the bright green and white paddleboard, its oar nearly waving her over.

Less than fifteen minutes later, Lina is wading out into the ocean, which has warmed up significantly since her arrival two and a half months ago. It's still not as warm as she's been told it gets, but considering the way the sun is already boiling the air and it's only nine a.m., refreshingly temperate works.

She hops onto the board once she's certain she's far enough out, then slowly raises from her knees into a standing position. A little adjustment of her feet and she's off, pushing the paddle into the lazy surf, moving forward with no destination in mind. Tapping into the words of her therapist, she tries to sync her breathing with her paddling.

Even in her state of anxiety, Lina can't deny the beauty of her surroundings. The ocean, determined to live up to its nickname, is glassy and placid, interrupting its serene reflection for only the smallest of ripples. Lina watches the disturbance her oar and board provide, wishing she could glide without impact. She squints into the distance, seeking the horizon. At this time of day, the blue of the sky collides with the blue of the water, giving the image of endless azure. And up above, the sun shines without interruption from the few and scattered cotton ball puffs of clouds.

Taking another deep breath, this one salted and misted, Lina feels some of her muscles begin to relax. It's better than nothing, she thinks, then continues paddling down the coast.

An hour later, the serenity from her paddling trip has disappeared. Though her hair is still damp and her skin is still salty, the feeling that settled in her bones as she slid along the surface of the ocean has departed, probably back to the surf where it prefers to be. Lina could go back out on the water—it's not like she has any pressing social plans—but what's she going to do? Sit on her paddleboard all day? Sleep out there? Float off toward the horizon and disappear?

It's the final thought that shakes her. It's mild, sure, but Lina knows its quiet power. She presses her hands into her knees as she stands, then strides into the house with purpose. Her phone is where she left it, right there on the kitchen table. Only a brief hesitation pauses her action before she picks it up and texts her therapist. The response comes only moments later.

And it's not what Lina was subconsciously hoping for.

Do you feel like you need to go to the hospital? I trust your judgment, Lina.

Lina swipes her thumb over the surface of her phone, hating the new feeling that's growing inside her.

No, she types. *It was a fleeting thought. No plan, no intention. Just a thought.*

She chews her bottom lip, waiting. Part of her wants to ask for a session right then and there, but another part of her knows it's not what she needs.

I trust you. We'll talk more about this the next time we meet.

A few seconds go by before another message pops up.

Get out of the house, Lina. You've got to stop imprisoning yourself.

Lina snorts then stares at the words, piecing them apart and putting them back together. It's uncanny how well Carolyn seems to understand the trips and triggers in Lina's mind, as well as how she prefers to keep herself contained so as to not allow any disruptions to her finely tuned protective system.

But even Lina can admit when she's wrong and her therapist is right. She should get out of the house. Maybe she even wants to. She glances at the counter and eyes the empty fruit bowl. Her mouth waters.

"Okay," she says aloud. "Let's do this."

* * *

The dusty lot in front of the farmers market is far more crowded with cars than the last time Lina was here. She curses summer weekends under her breath as she parks her Jeep and slides out. Being around a lot of people wasn't part of the plan, but if she wants the best plums in the state, then so it is.

As she makes her way through the crowd, heading directly for the only stand she wants to visit, she thinks back on an earlier time in her life when people—crowds—didn't bother her. That time did exist, she reminds herself. And more than that, it *can* exist again. She doesn't have to live in this constant state of protection; she doesn't need to keep her guard firm and steely all day, every day. It's exhausting, and more than that, Lina is no longer certain what purpose all her self-protection is serving. A flicker of wonder, lodged somewhere deep within a handful of other muted desires, has started burning brighter, making Lina think she might be missing out on something because she's too busy keeping herself protected.

She's ten feet from the farm stand when she hears a sharp gasp come from her right. She whips her head toward the sound, her internal soldiers assembling to face whatever threat is revealing itself. A burst of laughter comes next, and Lina's vision fumbles to connect with her hearing. She can see a group of people laughing, and one woman is still holding her hand to her chest. The gasper, probably. Lina scans to be sure it's a false alarm and, after thanking and shushing her alarm senses, moves along.

She knows her life would be easier if she didn't react to every single sudden *everything* around her. It's just that she hasn't quite figured out how to do that.

Finally, the path clears to the farm stand with the incredible plums and equally delectable corn. Lina scans again, this time searching for a particular head of blond hair, but is interrupted by the gleeful greeting from Erin.

"Hey! You're back!"

Lina can't help but smile at her enthusiasm. "Yeah, sorry it's taken me a while."

"Oh, no worries. I'm sure you've been busy. Regan told me you started working with her at the hospital! That's so cool!"

Mentally taken aback, Lina makes sure to keep her cool on the outside. They don't work together—Lina still hasn't figured out what the hell Regan was doing in the lab, let alone how she knew to find Lina there, or if Regan was even looking for her, *or or or, if if if*—but maybe working in the same building constitutes the phrasing.

"It's temporary," Lina explains, running her fingers over a round watermelon. "I usually work from home and commute to Fort Bragg."

Erin wrinkles her nose, clearly confused.

"It's hard to explain." Lina smiles again, shrugging.

"You're in the Army," Erin states matter-of-factly. She nods. "That's right, Regan told me that when you showed up at the hospital that first time, you were in full uniform. Pretty hot."

Caught off guard, Lina takes an actual step back. Who thinks that's hot? Erin? Regan? Both of them? What the hell kind of weird couple shit are they into? Lina bites her cheek, fighting the laugh that's bubbling up. Are they going to ask her for a threesome? Christ. These North Carolina lesbians are wild.

Lina pauses, thinking. Would she turn down that request? She honestly can't say that she would.

She tries to tune back in to whatever Erin's chattering away about. Something about her older brother and her cousin. And steaks. What the hell did Lina miss?

"Anyway! Enough about my weird family." Erin grins and leans forward, giving any passerby an easy glimpse at her ample cleavage. Weirdly, Lina realizes she has no interest in eyeing it up. *Just as well*, she thinks. *She is not available. And neither is Regan. Not that it would matter if she were because she is* not *my type.*

"What can I get for ya?"

"Definitely some plums." Lina looks over the array of fruit assembled before her. "Whoa. Those peaches look incredible."

"They are, I assure you that. I'll grab some for ya." Erin gently packs up the fruit. "Anything else catch your eye?"

It's an admirable selling technique, Lina can admit that much. She grins and shakes her head, then wonders how Regan feels about her girlfriend being so flirtatious with her fruits.

"No, I think that's good for now."

"You'll have to come back in a few weeks. It's almost nectarine season!"

"I will definitely be back for that."

Erin hands over the bagged fruit and Lina passes her some money.

"Hey, where's your friend?" Erin asks, looking around.

"She went home, back to her boyfriend." At the mention of Keeley, Lina feels the sharp pang of her absence. She presses her fist against her stomach to subdue the sensation.

"We were wondering if maybe you two were dating." Erin's tone is entirely casual, though her words take Lina by surprise. "Okay, I was wondering." Erin laughs. "But then Regan told me about you coming to the hospital for your hand and how you two were just friends."

"Longtime friends," Lina says, not taking time to wonder why she's giving information to this relative stranger. "We went through basic training together."

"Ooh, right, I get it. Now you're stuck with each other for life."

Lina raises her eyebrows. "Yeah. We are. How..." Lina shakes her head. "You do get it."

"My brother and my cousin," Erin says, tilting her head to the side.

Fragments of Erin's words from earlier fight for attention in Lina's head. Right. Lina in uniform, the Army, Erin's brother and her cousin.

"They have their people too," Erin continues. "Well, had. My brother lost his battle buddy a couple years ago."

She doesn't need to say anything more. Lina knows that tone intimately, and she can visualize the words unspoken.

"I'm so sorry," she says.

Erin nods. "Thank you. It was hard." She forces a smile. "It's still hard for him. Hey," she says, a real smile beginning to light up her face. "We're having a cookout tonight. Super casual. You should come!"

"Oh," Lina says quickly. "That's—I mean, I don't want to impose."

"Oh my gosh, you wouldn't be imposing. It's just my family and some of my brother's friends. And Regan, of course."

Of course. Lina weighs her options, realizing she has nothing to weigh this option against. Too, she's struggling to find a valid, or even logical, excuse. She sees Carolyn's text in her mind and runs through what she knows about Erin, and now knows about her brother. It seems safe. Low-threat. Even some people with similar backgrounds.

"Okay," Lina hears herself say. "If you're sure."

"Totally sure." Erin swipes another brown bag and scrawls a Sharpie over it. "Here you go! We're in Kill Devil, sound-side, so get ready for killer sunset views."

Lina stares at the address in her hand and feels herself nod. "Thank you."

"My pleasure." Erin winks, then moves to another customer. "See ya later!"

CHAPTER FIFTEEN

Discarded outfits have created haphazard piles of clothing that have completely overtaken the floor of Lina's room. She stands in a bare space in the middle of the bedroom, looking around in wonder. She had no idea she'd even brought this much clothing with her, and naturally, not a single piece is right for tonight.

She kicks at a pair of khaki shorts, a pair she swore she looked good in. Not tonight. She looks downright hideous in them, like she's wearing a FedEx costume. She kicks them again for good measure, and the shorts sail across the room, hitting the wall before slumping to defeat against the baseboard.

Lina picks up her phone and for approximately the seventeenth time in twenty minutes checks the weather. Same story. Once the sun sets, the temperature will drop an incredible two degrees down to 80. Thankfully the humidity isn't too bad, but it's still too warm for Lina to be comfortable in a T-shirt and jeans, which is her go-to outfit of choice.

A moment of inspiration hits, and Lina lunges across the room. She rifles through the pants pile and unearths a pair of jeans that have natural rips at the knees. Built-in air conditioning. Perfect.

She pulls on the jeans and glances in the mirror. So far, so good. Now for a shirt because it would be in bad form to show up in just a sports bra. She forgoes her standard black T-shirt, opting for a worn-in white V-neck instead. Nothing fancy, nothing that says she's trying too hard. She's dying to put on her boots but realizes that would look a little weird, considering the event. Instead, Lina puts on her navy Vans. Again, maybe weird, but she refuses to wear flip-flops. You never know when you'll need to run.

A quick glance in the mirror confirms she's managed to put together an outfit that does not look atrocious, and one she's comfortable in. Lina high fives herself then cringes.

"You need a life," she mumbles, sliding her phone into her back pocket. "And friends you can high five."

* * *

The weight of her choice to: A, go out; B, go somewhere new and unknown; and C, be around people she doesn't know doesn't fully hit Lina until she's a block away from the address Erin wrote on the paper bag. She grips the steering wheel, wondering what the hell she thinks she's doing. This is out of character, way out of her comfort zone, and she feels it deep in her bones.

A Subaru crawls past Lina's Jeep, which she hastily pulled over to the side of the narrow road. She watches the car, curious if it's headed to her destination. Nope. The car turns left where Lina will be turning right. She exhales. One less person to contend with.

A mental pep talk gets Lina driving again, and she slowly coasts down the road, admiring the bay just twenty feet in front of her. When she turns right into the driveway, she's met with a handful of cars, not enough to send her blood pressure rocketing skyward, but enough to give her a nervous, wiggly feeling. After she parks, she counts the cars and estimates the number of people that could be in the backyard. It's a navigable number, Lina tells herself, and she eases out of her Jeep.

She follows the welcoming sounds of voices, thwacks of cornhole bags hitting boards, and sizzles of meat on a grill around the back of the house, which butts up right against the bay. Erin wasn't kidding about the views. Lina stops in her tracks once she hits the perimeter of the yard, mesmerized by the sparkling water and old, leaning trees that create a picture frame for the eventual sunset.

"Hey! You made it!"

Erin's voice greets Lina, pulling her from her blissful admiration of the water. Lina smiles and waves as Erin jogs over to her.

"Any trouble finding us?" Erin adjusts her high bun and brushes her hands against her cutoffs.

"Nope, it was easy to find. Not a long drive from my place, either."

"Perfect!" Erin's grin is contagious, and Lina feels her own smile widening. "Hey, come with me. I want you to meet my brother."

Lina spots him before she and Erin make it across the yard. There's something about the way he carries himself that Lina finds instantly familiar and safe, something she's not used to but understands all the same.

"Adam, this is Lina. She's working at the hospital with Regan."

Adam extends his hand, a genuine smile warming his handsome features. There's no mistaking the fact that he and Erin are siblings. "Nice to meet you. Erin tells me we have some things in common."

Lina breathes a sigh of relief. She was half-expecting Adam to introduce himself by listing his Army credentials.

"Seems that we do, especially the part where we don't love talking about what we have in common."

Adam laughs and nods. "You called that correctly. It's nice to know it but not have to talk about it, you know?"

"Exactly." Lina's peaceful feeling remains, and she falls into natural conversation with Adam, one that touches on their similar experiences but stays superficial enough for both their comfort levels. Lina feels like she's talking with Keeley but without the overhang of combined experiences that bonded them for life. It's comfortable and easy, talking to Adam.

"Murph was in Syria around the same time," Adam says after Lina tells him a story about her first deployment. "Kinda crazy to think you might have crossed paths."

"Who's Murph?"

"Oh, right, sorry." Adam shakes his head. "I didn't know how much Erin told you. Murph—Murphy O'Donnell—is our cousin. He's still enlisted." Adam takes a sip of his beer. "Gets a little confusing when he and Regan are both here."

Lina tilts her head to the side. Regan. She hasn't seen her yet.

"Why's that?"

"The name thing." Adam looks at Lina, who shrugs. "Regan's last name? Murphy. They have to be on separate teams when we play volleyball, but it still gets confusing every time someone yells 'Murphy.'"

The image of Regan standing in the hardware store flashes in Lina's mind. Lady Beavers, number 21. Lina grins, then looks around the yard, trying to look casual in her searching.

"She should be here soon," Adam says.

"Oh, I wasn't—" Lina cuts herself off and stuffs her hands in her pockets. *Seriously*? She can't let Erin's brother think that she's looking for his sister's girlfriend. Talk about not making a good first impression. "I was just looking to see who else was here," she says quickly, regretting it instantly, since she clearly knows no one other than Adam and Erin.

"Just our parents and some of my friends. Come on, I'll introduce you." Adam motions for Lina to follow him, and because she has no reason not to, she does.

Adam's friends are nice, but after ten minutes of conversation she doesn't have much to add to, she starts feeling uncomfortable. She subtly checks her watch, wondering if she's been there long enough to be able to make an excuse and leave without looking like an ungrateful asshole. As if on cue, Erin strides over and pulls Lina to the cornhole boards.

"I need your skill," Erin says as they approach the boards. "My mom has a lethal toss, and we need to take her down. And don't tell me you don't have skill—we can all see those gorgeous biceps you're trying to hide under your shirt."

Lina doesn't have time to argue or fake an excuse. She ends up on the side with Erin's mom, who is every bit as warm and sweet as her daughter. She's also exceptionally good at cornhole, and she and her partner, one of Adam's friends, are soon smoothly annihilating Erin and Lina with very little noticeable effort.

The game doesn't last long; Erin and Lina are able to score two whole points, and walk away from the scene of the crime with their heads down in shame.

"You weren't kidding about your mom's tossing skills," Lina says, twisting open a bottle of water.

Erin shakes her head, her eyes wide in disbelief. "Two points. Two points!"

"Two points what?"

Lina's breath catches in her throat. She knows she has no right to be irked with Regan for sneaking up on her at a location where Lina is definitely the interloper. But seriously, she needs to get some bells to put on her ankle or something. The thought causes Lina to smile slightly, but her smile slips when she turns around and comes face-to-face with Regan, who clearly can't hide her surprise.

"My mother," Erin huffs, oblivious to the silent waves of shock flowing from her girlfriend toward Lina. "She absolutely murdered us at cornhole. Unbelievable." She looks briefly at Regan. "I have to get stuff out for dinner now that you're finally here." She spins on her heel and stomps toward the house.

"Hi," Lina says after another moment of silence.

"Well, hi yourself," Regan says uncertainly. "I, wow. Okay." She shakes her head. "I was not expecting to see you here, of all places."

Lina's stomach ties itself into a firm knot. "I can go. I should go," she amends.

"No—"

"Yeah, I should. I'm sorry. This is your place, your girlfriend. I'll go."

"No, Lina, I don't want—wait. What did you just say?" Regan's eyes widen and then she squints at Lina. "What?"

"Your girlfriend insisted that I come," Lina says slowly.

"Who?"

"Erin."

"What?" Regan stares at Lina before bursting into laughter. "Wait. No. Oh my God." She laughs harder, bending at the waist. "Oh God that's awful. No. Wow, no." She straightens up and looks Lina straight in the eye. "Erin is not my girlfriend. Not now, not ever."

Lina takes a step back, struggling to rearrange her thoughts. "Are you sure?"

"God, yes, very sure. She's my best friend, Lina. We've known each other"—Regan shrugs, looking skyward—"forever. We grew up together." She pauses, looking like she wants to say more, then shrugs again. "And she's only interested in men."

"I—okay," Lina says. Her brain is deploying some really weird messages she doesn't want to listen to, and she fights the urge to shake her head hard to dislodge them. "Sorry."

"You've got nothing to apologize for." Regan's eyes have regained their sparkling beauty. "Not a thing."

They stare at each other, the sounds and actions of the people around them carrying on as though nothing has shifted between Regan and Lina. Lina presses her tongue against the back of her front teeth. She feels the shift. But she doesn't know what it is and isn't sure she wants to explore it.

Eventually Regan nods slowly, biting the side of her bottom lip. "This explains some things," she says so quietly Lina nearly doesn't hear her.

"Like what?"

Regan snaps her head up and meets Lina's eyes. "Did I say that out loud?"

Lina can't help but to grin. There's something about Regan, much like Adam, that eases her senses. But unlike Adam, Regan has a different kind of impact on Lina, one Lina is still fumbling to understand.

"You did. But I can pretend I didn't hear it."

"No." Regan straightens up. She looks toward the house where activity has suddenly increased. "They're setting up dinner. Let's go eat. But you're mine for the sunset, okay?"

The knot in Lina's stomach untangles itself and lets loose a slow-moving spread of warmth. She can only nod in response and follow Regan toward the food.

Later, their stomachs full, Regan and Lina sit on chairs by the water's edge, waiting for the sunset. Lina's thankful for her jeans as she watches Regan slap at the mosquitoes who are having a feast on her legs.

"My dad always said I taste good," Regan grumbles as she whacks another bloodsucker, "and that's why the bugs come after me."

"I must taste horrible." Lina stretches her legs out in front of her. She gives her bare arms a once-over, happy to find they're bug-free.

Regan snort-laughs, an oddly endearing sound. "I doubt that."

Lina stares at Regan until she meets her eyes. When she finally does, Regan sends her that lopsided grin before turning back to the water.

"I never get tired of this view," she says, her voice quiet and full of reverence.

Lina follows Regan's stare and nods, seeing exactly what she means. The bay stretches out before them, allowing only glimpses of land on the other side. The water is mostly calm aside from small waves that meet the shore with mellow claps. In the distance, a few sailboats amble over the placid surface of the water. The sky, holding just a few clouds, is beginning to unveil its cotton candy colors as the sun slowly descends.

"Did you grow up around here?" Lina asks, not wanting to break the reverie but suddenly impatient to know more about Regan.

"Yeah, about twenty miles inland." Regan toes the sandy grass with her bare foot. "I spent a lot of time here growing up since my parents were friends with Erin's parents. But then they got divorced and that stopped. I still came over whenever I could, though. I've always felt closer to Erin's family than my own."

Lina nods. She knows the feeling well, but her empathetic words trip over themselves before smacking into one of her many internal barriers. "It must be tough, having divorced parents."

Regan laughs, but it's a mirthless sound. "That's putting it lightly. It's not so bad now, but when I was a kid…It was not pleasant. It's kinda awful, watching your parents behave like children, you know?"

"I bet."

"Ah, a noncommittal answer. Your parents are still married?"

Lina lets loose her own empty laugh. "They are. But we don't have much of a relationship." She feels Regan's eyes on her but refuses to give more.

"That must be tough," she says. "Do you have siblings?"

"Yup, I'm the youngest. My brothers are the pride and joy of my parents. I just sort of…existed."

"Is that why you went into the Army?"

Lina turns sharply and meets Regan's eyes. She's momentarily captivated by the concentrated way Regan's looking at her but can't bring herself to enjoy it or even wonder about it. "Yeah. I mean, basically, yes."

"I'm guessing there are other reasons, too, but you're not ready to open up to me yet."

Lina breaks their stare and looks down at her hands.

"Lina, it's okay." Regan reaches over and rests her hand on Lina's forearm for a whisper of a second. "Just know that whenever you want to tell me more, I'm ready to listen."

They lapse into silence and turn their attention back to the sun as it makes its way toward the horizon. Lina counts to thirty-seven before she breaks down and asks Regan the question that's been swaying in the back of her mind.

"What did you mean, that night at the brewery?"

Regan looks over at Lina. "I'm gonna need a more specific question."

"When I said Keeley and I have been through too much for me to get rid of her, and you said you understood that."

"Oh," Regan says quietly. "That."

Lina watches her, waiting for an answer. Regan stares out at the bay, her body still except for her eyes, which dart back and forth. Finally, she sighs and leans her head back against the chair and stares at the darkening sky.

"I don't think it's the same as what you and Keeley have," she begins. "So please don't think I'm drawing a comparison."

"Okay."

"I was friends with someone for a long time. High school through college, and beyond." Regan crosses her arms over her chest. "Her name was Erika. She had a rough life. Honestly, it was like one thing after another went wrong for her. And I was always there to, I don't know, fix things. Or help, at least." She shakes her head. "I gave too much of myself to her, and I put myself aside for way too long."

"Were you, like, with her?"

"No, never. But I was her person, you know? She relied on me for everything." Regan's normally bright expression dims. Lina wants the brightness back, but part of her is relieved that Regan has some skeletons, too. "It took me way too long to untangle myself from her, and it wasn't pretty. Plus, she was important to me. So ending that friendship sucked. But I got through it. I like to think she did, too."

Lina rests her cheek against the back of the chair as she studies Regan. "You don't talk to her anymore?"

"I can't," Regan says, and the pain is evident in her voice. "The only boundary I could draw was a permanent line in the sand. My natural urge is to protect the people I love, but I had to learn the hard way that I should only do that if the feeling is reciprocated. And the hard way was letting go of someone who had no desire to protect me or even support me through anything."

She turns her head and meets Lina's eyes. "It's different with you and Keeley. I can tell."

Lina nods, unable to take her eyes off of Regan. "It's definitely reciprocated."

"My friendship with Erin kinda saved me." Regan smiles. "She doesn't need me the way that Erika did, and that's taught me a lot, thankfully."

Lina's throat constricts. "It's hard, needing people."

"Yeah. It is. But it's also good to need people. In healthy ways, I mean. And when you need someone who also needs you, in that really cool, healthy way, it's amazing." Regan shrugs. "Or at least that's what I've heard." She stares at Lina. "I hope to find out for myself someday."

The words, innocent but loaded, pelt Lina like surprise summer rain. She tells herself to relax, reminds herself that she's safe. She leans her head against the back of the chair and watches the dazzling theater of the sunset. She's hyper-aware of Regan's presence next to her, a silent but strong nearness, but when she stops and thinks about it later, all she remembers feeling is calm.

CHAPTER SIXTEEN

"Another fireworks injury."

"*Another*? Christ. It's not even July yet!"

"You know how it is around here, Stef. Once the summer crowd comes on-island, all bets are off."

"And fingers are off, too."

The nurse makes a retching sound, causing the other nurse, Stef apparently, to laugh.

"This one looks salvageable. Come on, I'll show you the X-rays."

Lina watches the nurses scurry down the hallway, heads bent close together. She has two hours left of her shift, and the lab had started to feel like it was closing in on her, so she decided to go for a walk and try to get lost—something she likes to do whenever she's working in a new place. OBX Hospital is one of the smaller hospitals she's worked at, so getting lost has been harder than Lina anticipated. She's wound up somewhere near the ER, maybe the back side of it. There's a spot with reasonably comfortable chairs, and Lina takes a moment to sit and relax before finding her way back to the lab to wrap up her shift.

She scratches at a spot on her dark blue scrubs, wondering what sort of fluid she's managed to get on herself today. Looks like toothpaste, but how it landed on her thigh is a mystery.

"Lina. Hey."

From ten or so feet away, Regan's voice is soft and Lina smiles. She knows her quirks are challenging, some more than others, but the fact that Regan remembered and cared enough not to sneak up on her and catch her off guard means a lot. Maybe she won't need those ankle bells after all.

Lina waves. "Hey yourself."

"Look at you, hanging out in my territory." Regan grins and perches on the arm of one of the chairs. "Did they run you out of the lab?"

"Nah, I ran myself out. I needed a break."

"I get it. That lab can seem pretty small sometimes."

Again Lina wonders if Regan can somehow read her mind, or is just weirdly attuned to her.

"That's why I like the ER," Regan continues. "I'm always moving from space to space. There's not enough time for me to feel stuck somewhere."

"That's what I like about the Army. Well, except for the fact that deployments are the ultimate in feeling stuck."

"How many times have you been deployed?"

"Three. Once to Syria, twice to Afghanistan." Lina simultaneously feels the urge to kick herself and slap herself on the back for beginning to open up.

Regan watches her carefully, nothing but curiosity and sympathy in her eyes. Neither emotion thrills Lina, but she's used to seeing them in other people when she starts talking about deployment.

"The Army doesn't define me," Lina says abruptly, then tilts her head, confused by the unprompted arrival of her words. "Sorry. I'm not sure where that came from."

"No need to apologize. I may not get it because I'm not in it, but I've seen what Adam's been through. Erin's brother," Regan adds as a reminder. "As much as I can see from the outside, anyway. He's not exactly an open book, either." Her shoe taps Lina's shin.

"Comes with the territory." Lina tries for a dazzling grin, hoping she's somewhere near the mark. "But—" She cuts herself off, distracted by the rumble of her internal walls.

"But what?" From anyone else, Caitlin included, even her damn therapist included, those words would cause Lina to shut down. *No one* can push her to talk, and she flees when someone tries to. But there's something about Regan's voice, something about her calming energy, and for once, Lina doesn't feel threatened.

Which is, of course, precisely why she meets Regan's eyes and freezes.

There's only one other person in the history of Lina's life who's had this kind of effect on her. And somehow, that feeling ended up being all in Lina's head—*only* in her head.

She can't go there again. She won't.

* * *

Fort Bliss, Texas, five years ago

Six months into the TDY from hell, and the heat hadn't let up. Lina was almost getting used to the feeling of being coated in sweat every time she so much as stuck her hand out a window. Okay, that was an exaggeration, but the heat rash on her upper thighs was very real and extremely annoying.

"Here." Candice tossed her a fresh container of Aquaphor. "This should help."

Lina caught the container and toyed with the lid. "Are you planning on helping me apply this? I could use some medical expertise over here."

Candice rolled her eyes and turned back to her laptop. "Last time I checked, you have plenty of medical experience. Certainly enough to be able to apply some salve to your legs." While Lina applied the salve, Candice glanced over her shoulder. "You could try the oatmeal bath idea."

"Uh, no thanks. The idea of having oatmeal in places where oatmeal most definitely does not belong is not appealing."

"Lina. Wear a bathing suit. Or your underwear."

"This should work fine," she said, closing the container and leaning back on the sofa. Lina closed her eyes and began to doze off, lulled by the sounds of Candice working on her laptop.

She wasn't sure how they'd gotten here, to this odd point of near-domestic-bliss that was buffered by constant sneaking around, lying, and hiding. Lina had anticipated and told herself that their initial hook-up would be the lone ranger in their history together, but Candice had had other ideas. Once a week had increased to two, sometimes three times a week. Lina, too filled with being consistently wanted and needed for the first time in her adult life, didn't spend too much time thinking about the lack of reciprocation. She loved Candice's body, and she loved having sex with her—even if it was one-sided. They didn't discuss that part of the equation, and Lina chalked it up to the whole "married to a guy" thing. She assumed Candice probably rationalized the affair (because it was, on so many levels, an affair) through her lack of participation in bedroom activities.

It was an odd night when they didn't get together for dinner. Fortunately, because they were on assignment together, it was perfectly acceptable for them to be seen out at restaurants. Lina was getting awfully good at pretending nothing was going on—so good, in fact, that she nearly had herself convinced that nothing *was* going on.

And then Candice would let her hand linger on Lina's arm for a second too long in the middle of the workday. Then, Lina would feel the jolt of sensual recall and fall right back into the pattern.

It could be worse, she thought as she opened her eyes and squinted at Candice, who was still attached to her laptop, even though it was way beyond working hours. At the very least, their affair was providing Lina with a sense of belonging and attachment, two things she'd struggled to attain throughout her life. Beyond all rational reasoning, Lina felt safe with Candice. She found herself telling her things she couldn't tell anyone else. Too, she tended to forget that Candice was married; how could she be, when they were developing such a strong bond? Maybe the whole husband thing was a farce, a way to shield the Army's prying eyes from Candice's true desire. Lina closed her eyes again, hoping the thought spiral would wear itself out.

"Hey," Candice said, nudging Lina's legs. "Have some tea."

Lina pushed herself up and rubbed her eyes. "Did I fall asleep?"

"Of course you did, just like you do every night." Her tone was teasing and sweet, music to Lina's ears. This version of Candice was by far her favorite. She just didn't see it very often.

"Are your legs feeling any better?"

Lina shrugged and sipped her tea. Candice swore by a whole list of health benefits that the tea supposedly provided, but Lina remained unconvinced. It tasted good, at least, so she drank it to humor Candice. "A little. Do they look better?"

Lina watched Candice's eyes scan the tops of her thighs. She'd rolled her gym shorts up and tucked them into the sides of her underwear—an irresistibly sexy look, no doubt—to let the bubbly rash get some air.

A sharp intake of Lina's breath coincided with Candice's thumb lightly brushing over the skin just below the rash. Mesmerized by the touch, Lina watched as Candice drew her thumb under the rash, sliding it tentatively over the skin of Lina's inner thigh, pausing at the spot where her shorts were jammed up into her underwear.

Lina mentally face-palmed herself as Candice giggled.

"This is a very nice look," she said, tapping her finger against the jumbled shorts.

"Yeah, well." Lina straightened up and turned so her feet were on the carpet. "I have a bit of a situation here, you know."

"Yes, I can see that." Candice patted Lina's knee. "Did you talk to Keeley today?"

Whatever spell may have been brewing was definitely busted by the change of topic. Lina was getting used to Candice's intimate boundaries, and while she didn't love them, she respected them because, well, it was an affair.

Besides, Candice had become the one person Lina could talk to about Army stuff without feeling judged or questioned. That may have been the real cement between them; the attraction and desire were just add-ons.

"Yeah, right before I came up here. She's definitely out."

"Wow," Candice said, shaking her head. "How do you feel about that?"

"It's fine. It's what she needs to do, I guess." Lina stretched her arms over the back of the sofa. "Or more specifically, it's what her dad wants her to do."

"The power of parents. Well, she's young. She has plenty of open doors outside of the Army."

"Yeah." Lina brought her hands back to her lap and picked at the skin around her thumb. "It was weird not having her in Afghanistan, but I kinda thought we might have another deployment together. Now that definitely won't happen. I honestly feel abandoned." Lina winced. "I can't believe I said that."

"I know how close you are." Candice squeezed Lina's shoulder. "She's not going anywhere, Lina. She'll always be your number one."

"Just not when and where I'll need her the most."

"Not physically, no. But in your heart, always."

Lina dipped her head with a nod. She knew better than to replace Keeley, her battle buddy, with Candice, the married woman she was having an affair with, but her emotions were engaging with a different plan, one Lina certainly did not approve of.

* * *

Kitty Hawk, present day

"Lina? Hey. Hello? Are you okay?"

The frantic sound of Regan's voice, a tone Lina assumed didn't exist in her vocal repertoire, pulls Lina from her frozen daze.

"Yeah," she says, then clears her throat and stands. "I have to go." She tries like hell to ignore the swinging sensation in her brain.

"Whoa, wait a minute. Lina. Wait, please."

Lina stands with her back to Regan. She can't meet her eyes. This isn't the time, the place, the moment. No. She cannot do this.

Will not do this.

Not again.

"I have to go," she repeats, but doesn't move.

Regan stands and comes around to face Lina, but Lina refuses to meet her eyes, keeping them locked on a doorway down the hall.

"What just happened?"

"You don't want to do this."

The two women stand, rooted in different shades of confusion. Lina feels like a statue weighed down by tons of concrete. Her limbs are useless, empty vessels incapable of movement.

"Don't want to do what?" Regan finally asks. "Don't want to know what just happened to you, how and why you shut down and completely spaced out? Yeah, actually, Lina, I do want to—I mean, I want to know what happened. That's what I want to do." She shakes her head, her blond hair bouncing and full of life, a cold contrast to the motionless, unsettled air between them. "You really confuse me, you know."

"And that's why you should stay away from me." With a single step to the side, Lina clears her exit path and all but marches down the hallway, leaving Regan in her wake.

CHAPTER SEVENTEEN

A low rumble cuts through the idyllic scenery. Lina shifts her glance to the right, scanning the horizon. Nothing. The ocean pushes and pulls its blank surface, the motion rocking in contrast to the stiff, unmoving air. It's hot, but hot isn't the word that Lina's searching for. This air, this environment, it's so much more than *hot*.

The rumble sounds again, echoed by a louder sizzle. It's a sound Lina's memory will never permit her to forget. The sizzle increases, rises, amplifies to an eardrum-blasting screech. Lina bends at the waist, pushing her palms against her ears. She has to make the sound stop.

No. She rights herself, and her posture goes rigid. She can't make the sound stop. She has to get to the sound.

She stares straight ahead and the ocean is gone. No, it's not gone—it's just not water anymore. Lina blinks rapidly, thinking the sand has blurred her vision, and if she can clear her eyes without touching them because her hands are full—*wait, why are my hands full?*—then she'll be able to see the water again and everything will be okay.

A cautious step forward brings the screeching sound closer, and the new tar ocean comes into sight. Thick, unctuous black waves are capped over the street—*where the fuck did the street come from?*—and they hang with threat, with determination. They're going to fall.

As Lina takes a second step forward, she feels the unmistakable sensation of a claw gripping her forearm. Spiny fingers dig through her uniform, sinking into her flesh. She wiggles her arm. She knows it's pointless, but she has to at least try. She has to get across the street, under those waves. She has to get there first.

With a forceful yank, Lina frees her arm, and she stops in her tracks, staring at the spot where she'd been gripped so tightly. The hiss of searing flesh makes its way to her cotton ball-stuffed ears, and she watches in awe as a silky plume of smoke rises from beneath her uniform. This is wrong. She's not supposed to free herself from that grip. She's not supposed to be on fire.

Not now. Right. She has to get across the street, and now she can. Lina drops the bulky weight from her left arm and breaks into a run. She's faster than Olympic sprinters now. She cuts through the oppressive air like a blade. She runs. Sprints. Flies. She's moving so fast that she can't think. Every move is automatic. Her legs sync with her arms and her lungs seem to have expanded. She's faster than the speed of light, and yet she is going nowhere.

Midstride, Lina looks down at her feet and can't see them. She stops pumping her arms and stares at the ground. She lifts her leg and nothing happens. Panic begins webbing through her body. She was *just* moving, and so fast. Where did all this honey come from? And why is it so thick that she can't even see her feet?

A frantic glance behind her confirms her suspicions. She has not moved. She is exactly where she was when she freed herself from that burning vise grip, and she is exactly where she was when she dropped that bulk to be able to run, and—

There. Lina follows the command, her stomach twisting as she cranes her neck. It's not possible. That's not how this—this isn't—*no.*

But she's there. Crumpled on the ground. Dead.

And all Lina can do is stare.

* * *

Lina leans forward and taps her screen. "You alive over there?"

Carolyn cracks a rare smile. "Stop avoiding."

"I'm not avoiding. I'm checking on you."

"Oh, no, you're definitely avoiding." Carolyn continues to smile, but Lina can see the concern weaving through the rest of her features. "I think you should tell me more about the nightmares."

With a sigh, Lina pushes back from the kitchen table and crosses her arms. She didn't mean to so readily tell Carolyn about the nightmares, but she'd had no choice. She was ten minutes late to her virtual appointment because she'd woken up from the latest one and couldn't stop shaking.

Even now, twelve minutes into her delayed session, her hands continue to tremor. Lina debates sitting on them but knows there's no point. Carolyn is well aware of the current state Lina's in.

"They kicked up when Keeley was here. More frequent, anyway. The actual context of them…" Lina trails off. "They were blurry, I guess. Hard to distinguish what was happening."

"And now?"

"Now they're clear again. And I don't like it."

"I imagine not. Tell me about the one you had this morning."

Lina huffs. It's her fault. At least she thinks it is. When she got home from work last night, she was keyed up, thinking about Regan and why she kept acting so weird, so utterly unlike herself, around her. She barely slept, and after pushing herself through an early morning workout, Lina had given in and taken a nap. She knows better. Naps are a danger zone for her, guaranteed nightmare territory.

"This one," she starts, then pauses. She really doesn't want to do this. But the way Carolyn is looking at her through the computer screen gives Lina the push she needs. "This one was different. It, um, kind of brought a memory into the present. I don't know if that makes sense."

"It does. Keep going. I'm listening."

Lina laughs, a half-hearted noise. "It might be easier if you weren't."

"Well, that's basically my job, so..." Carolyn smiles again. For some reason, that soothes Lina enough to go on.

"The landscape. I thought I was here, in Kitty Hawk. It was the beach, or at least it looked like the beach. And then all of a sudden, it was definitely not the beach, but it was still sandy. The ocean went black, like tar, and it was solid. Hovering. Waiting to crash down." Lina fights off a shudder, shakes out her trembling hands instead. "It's the same thing every time. I have to get across the street. I have to get there before it happens."

"Did you get there this time?"

"No. I thought I was going to. I thought I was running—it felt like I was running. But I didn't go anywhere, and when I turned around, she was there. On the ground." Lina buries her face in her hands. "I had her. I had her, and I dropped her because I thought I had to get across the street because—the noise, it was there and it was so, so loud, and my arm was on fire from someone holding me back, and I just—I failed her. Again."

Silence falls between them. Lina's used to this from Carolyn and takes advantage of the pause, taking some measured breaths before the next prompt comes her way.

"Lina. Look at me."

She looks up and meets Carolyn's kind green eyes.

"You did not fail anyone."

"No. I did. I should have known. I should have seen it coming."

"You couldn't have known. Everything that happened that day was out of your control."

"No, you don't understand. I should have—I should have made her stay." Lina's voice cracks on the last word and she immediately clears her throat.

"Let it out." The command is gentle and wrapped in a warmth unfamiliar to Lina. She shakes her head furiously then presses her fists against her eyes until the urge passes.

"Someday, Lina, you're going to have to cry."

"Absolutely not," she says, rubbing her eyes before looking up. "They'd be wasted tears." Words her mother said over and over again, an incomprehensible way of ensuring that her daughter was tough. It's a line Lina would like to forget, but it's tattooed in her memory.

"That's a point you and I will always disagree on."

Lina manages a smile. "Are you going to be okay with that?"

"I think I'll manage." Carolyn shifts in her chair. "I'd like to stay with the dreams if you're okay with that."

"I don't think so. I think that's all I can do for today." Lina clears her throat. "But we can come back to them another time, because I don't think they're going anywhere anytime soon."

"They might if we continue to process them."

Lina shakes her head. "I can't do more today. I'm tired of feeling so damaged."

"Lina, you're not damaged. You're struggling. There's a big difference."

"I know, but I *feel* damaged. I feel like I'm not good for other people." *Oops.* She forces another smile, hoping Carolyn won't latch onto that accidental admission.

"You feel like you're not good for other people? Like who?"

Dammit. "No one in particular. Just in general." Lina feels her cheeks heating up. The image of Regan's face appears in her mind. "I'm having a hard time, uh, making friends." There. That's safe.

"So you've met new people?"

"Yeah. A couple. Well, no, not a couple—they're not together. But literally two people. I work with one of them. Regan." Lina mentally high fives herself for saying the name out loud. She waits for Carolyn to jump in, but gets one of those lapses of purposeful silence instead. Lina rolls her eyes. "Okay. Fine. Regan—she confuses me. I like the way I feel around her. It feels different. But I'm not good for her." Lina rubs her jaw, remembering the previous evening at work. "She's so nice. So, like, pure. And I'm this terrible dark cloud, storming over her world of sunshine."

"While I like your use of imagery, I have to wonder if your assessment of the situation is...accurate."

"Meaning?"

Carolyn tilts her head slightly. "You're not as dark and dismal as you think you are, Lina. It's one hell of a defense mechanism you've built up for yourself to keep others away, but it's got to tumble down eventually."

Lina rolls her eyes again. Why she tells her damn therapist anything at all is beyond her. She hates it when Carolyn is right.

"You're drawn to her," Carolyn continues. "Maybe you need her sunshine in your life."

"What, to, like, illuminate all my dark and dusty corners? And show me that I can have light in my life?" Lina scoffs.

Carolyn laughs. "That's exactly it, Lina. That's exactly what you need."

CHAPTER EIGHTEEN

One of the wheels on the cart Lina's pushing down the hospital hallway is wobbling. No matter the speed Lina pushes, the entire cart shakes and squeaks, making a scene that causes every passerby's head to turn. She's been sending every scornful look a bright smile in return, but she's about to use all her strength to thrust the cart through the front doors and hope it catches a good wind so it sails directly across the street and into the ocean.

Her cart-tossing fantasy comes to a literal screeching halt when she spies Regan walking toward her. Carolyn's voice echoes in Lina's head, the word "sunshine" wrapping itself around Regan. She is like walking sunshine, warmth and happiness flowing from her at all times.

The look on Regan's face, however, is not full of glowing happiness. It's completely blank, with just the tiniest flicker of recognition when she makes eye contact with Lina.

"Excuse me and my extremely noisy friend here," Lina says as she pulls up next to Regan. She pats the side of the cart. "We're not making any friends on our trip."

Regan seems to hesitate. Lina silently berates herself, again, for being so cold and abrupt the previous night. Regan doesn't deserve that from her. No one does, but especially not Regan.

"I can help you with that," Regan says after a moment. She drops down and kneels on the floor. A moment later she pops back up, wiping her hands on her scrubs. "Try it now."

Lina gives the cart a cautious push forward and grins when it's smooth, nearly silent sailing. "You're a mechanical genius. Thank you."

"My pleasure." A little shimmer of sunshine peers out. "How are you today?"

Lina cringes. The shimmer disappears, waving on its way out, leaving Lina bathed in Regan's calculated coolness. "Pretty good. How are you?"

"Good, good. Busy day."

"Right. Busy." Lina stares at Regan, waiting and hoping for the familiar warmth to radiate from her, but she's all New Jersey January. "Okay," Lina says slowly. "Can we start over?"

"How so?"

"I don't like this." Lina gestures to the space between them. "Things feel weird. Uncomfortable. Like you don't want to be talking to me right now."

"That's not—" Regan sighs and shifts her weight. "I do want to talk to you. Lina, that's kind of the problem. I want to talk to you, I want to know you, but you seem hell-bent on pushing me away."

"I don't want to push you away," Lina says, her voice low.

"I'm pretty sure the last thing you said to me was that I should stay away from you." Regan quirks her eyebrow as her bright, blue-green eyes stare at Lina.

"Well, I'm an asshole sometimes."

Regan laughs, the sound creating a fissure in the ice between them. "Just sometimes?"

"Yes. Really just sometimes, I swear."

"I can deal with sometimes." Regan pauses and puts her hands on her hips. It's a cute look on her, Lina decides. Sunshine with an edge. "But I gotta tell you, you came really close to pushing me away for good last night, and it takes a lot to make that happen."

"I'm pretty talented at pushing people away," Lina admits. She bites her bottom lip before continuing, "And I have a lot going on. In here." She taps the side of her head.

"Can you let me in there?"

Regan's voice is like the feeling of that first blast of warmth after a cloud cover moves away. Lina falls into it, grabs hold of it. Her dark corners begin to glow.

"I don't know," she answers honestly.

"Can you try?"

Lina nods. She runs her fingers through her hair and watches Regan's eyes track her movement. "I can try."

"Good. Have dinner with me tomorrow night."

A surprised laugh bursts from Lina. "I'm usually the one who does the asking."

Regan leans in closer, not close enough that they're touching, but removing enough space to let Lina imagine the sensation of them touching. "And how's that been working for you, Lina?"

"Apparently not very well."

Regan grins. "So? Tomorrow?"

Lina watches her, half-amazed, half-scared out of her mind. Who *is* this woman? "Yes," she manages.

"Fantastic. I'll text you tomorrow with details." With that, Regan turns and begins to walk away.

"Wait!" Lina calls after her. Regan turns around, eyebrows arched. "You don't have my number."

"Adam gave it to me," she says, shrugging. "He said he thought I might need it."

Right—at the cookout, Lina gave Adam her number. She narrows her eyes at Regan.

"Then why haven't you used it yet?"

Regan shakes her head. "Lina, Lina, Lina. Would that really have gone over well with you? Me texting you out of nowhere?"

"Okay, no. Probably not."

"Exactly." Regan waves. "Talk to you tomorrow."

Lina watches her walk away, riding out the mash-up of conflicting feelings that are inflating inside her. Then, with the abrupt realization that she just agreed to go out on a *date*, the feelings pile up and morph into a jittery excitement that's bordering on anxiety. Lina presses her hand against her stomach. It's going to be a long twenty-four hours.

* * *

"So it's a date, but she's not picking you up?"

"Right. We're meeting at the restaurant. She texted me an address and a time. That's it."

On the other end of the phone, Mallory laughs. "My God, Lina, I think you've met your match."

"What? No. Why would you say that?"

"That is *such* a thing you would do!"

Lina brakes as she heads toward a red light. "I'm sorry, I think you've confused us. Didn't you do something like that to Caitlin?"

"Oh, shit. Yeah, I did." She laughs again. "Okay, so you're going out on a date with me. This just got interesting."

"Can you never say that again?"

"Yeah, I regret saying it. But on a side note, I'm proud of you."

Lina taps her steering wheel, watching a parade of young parents wrangle their squirmy, sandy kids into the driveway of a sprawling bright pink house. "Proud? Why?"

"Because you're going way out of your comfort zone. And I know it's probably scaring the hell out of you, but you're doing it anyway."

"Yes on both accounts." Lina hangs a quick left into the parking lot. "I'm not sure what I'm doing, Mal."

"You're having dinner with a woman who wants to get to know you. Leave it at that."

Lina nods. She turns the ignition and sits in her Jeep. "It's been a really, really long time since I did something normal like this. What if I've forgotten how to, just, do this?"

"You haven't forgotten. Besides, you know Regan. You're not walking into this blind."

"Okay. You're right." Lina hops out of the Jeep and begins walking toward the oceanfront restaurant. "I'm here."

"Have fun, Lina. I mean it. Just have fun."

"I'll try. And hey, don't forget—you can't tell Caitlin about this."

Mallory drops her voice. "I won't, but you're going to have to tell her soon."

"Yeah, yeah, I know. I will. I'll talk to you later."

"Maybe you'll be too busy to talk to me later," Mallory says in a sing-song voice.

"Goodbye." Lina hangs up before Mallory can continue to taunt her and walks into the restaurant. She gives her name, and the hostess walks her out back to the deck over the beach.

Lina spots Regan as soon as she walks out outside. She's practically glowing in the early evening sunshine. Her tousled hair is partially tamed. She's wearing a pale blue V-neck that sets off the radiance of her eyes. Lina's struck by how pretty she is; she's seen her how many times, but only *now* does she let herself really *see* Regan. And she is beautiful.

"You made it." Regan looks up when Lina arrives at the table. Her smile is bright, so big that her cheeks arch toward her eyes and her dimples pop.

"It helps that you gave me the right address."

Regan throws back her head and laughs. "What, did you want a more formal invitation to join me for a sunset dinner?"

Lina gestures toward the ocean. "Does it still count as a sunset date if we're not going to see the sunset?"

"Oh, absolutely. But I guess we could call it a golden hour date instead." Regan taps her watch. "We've got about fifteen more minutes of this glorious light."

Lina looks out over the beach and the ocean. The golden light from the low-hanging sun dapples the scene in a photographer's dream luminosity. She still prefers the rose-gold glow of sunrise, but this, the late afternoon golden hour, is a very close second.

When Lina turns her attention back to Regan, she realizes she's being watched.

"What?" Lina asks. "What's that smirky grin about?"

"You called it a date."

"It's a date. Right? This is a date."

"I guess that depends, Lina. Do you want it to be a date?"

"Well, considering I called it a date..." Lina shrugs. "I'd say that answers your question."

"Good," Regan says, her eyes shimmering in the late-day light. "Because it is so a date."

Their spell is broken, naturally, by the waitress coming by for their drink orders. Lina sticks to water, not wanting alcohol to interfere with her current level of happiness. Regan follows her lead and orders a sweet tea.

"I'd ask you to tell me about yourself," Regan begins. "But I feel like that might make you shut down."

Lina leans back in her chair and watches Regan carefully. "I don't want you to worry about me shutting down."

"I kind of have to, don't I? I mean, it keeps happening."

The vulnerability flowing from Regan raises a new sensation within Lina. She sits silently, letting some of her internal doors creak open.

"There are things I struggle with," Lina says as she wraps the paper from her straw around her fingers. "I've never had a close relationship with my family. I don't have a great track record for relationships. And then, there's the Army."

Regan has her elbows on the edge of the table and she's watching Lina with an intentness that calls up a feeling of closeness. "Go on," she says quietly.

"About which part?"

"Whichever you want."

Lina shifts her gaze back out to the ocean. She wants to go on. She'd like nothing more than to go on and on and on, but she doesn't know where to begin.

"You don't let people in easily, do you?" Regan's voice draws her attention back from the sea.

"No. Every time I have, I've gotten burned. It's easier to keep the shield up."

Regan nods. "Maybe you've been letting the wrong people in."

"I don't think anyone who knows me would argue that."

"Lina," Regan says. Her voice is steady and calm, and her eyes are locked on Lina's. "I can't promise you much. But I can promise you that I'm not a wrong person. You can let me in."

Lina swallows against the sudden ball of emotion that's lodged itself in her throat. There's something about Regan's voice, the way she's looking at Lina—it's like she can feel the deadbolts being blown off the boarded-up doors in her heart.

"You look really beautiful tonight." The words slip out, bringing with them the slow return of Lina's confidence.

Regan laughs, but it's a nervous, self-conscious laugh. "I can't remember the last time someone called me beautiful."

"You are, Regan. You're beautiful."

Their eyes meet. Warmth spreads in the short distance between them. Lina feels herself being pulled closer to Regan and doesn't fight it.

"Thank you." Regan's smile is different now—Lina doesn't have the words to describe it, only the magnetic feelings that come with basking in it. "You look pretty amazing yourself."

"But not beautiful?" Lina pairs the words with a crooked grin.

"Oh, you're beautiful," Regan says confidently. "But you're so much more than that. Sexy. Swaggery. Handsome. Gorgeous. Shall I go on?"

Regan's words filter through Lina's cluttered mind, some sticking and others falling through the cracks. A small panic slices through the otherwise perfect moment. It must show on Lina's face because Regan changes her tone immediately.

"Too much? I'm sorry. I shouldn't have—"

"No," Lina interrupts as quickly as she can, not wanting this evening to slide off the rails. "I just—I have to go slow, Regan." As soon as the words are out, doubt crashes through Lina's system. She flicks her eyes around the outdoor space, searching for the easiest and quickest exit. Just in case. Right. Just in case.

"Hey." Again, Regan's voice draws Lina out of her dark fumbling and back to the present moment. "Stay with me."

Stay with me. Lina presses her fingers against her temples. Such a simple phrase. It doesn't need to be loaded with memories. And yet it is. Painfully so.

Lina inhales deeply before looking back at Regan, who's still as a statue, watching her. "I'm sorry."

"No," Regan says. She folds her hands on the table. "I think I'm the one who should be sorry." She exhales loudly, a quiet "fuck" whispering on her breath. "I keep screwing this up somehow."

"Regan, you don't. Please don't think that. I told you, it's me. I'm—" Lina hears Carolyn in her head yet again. She's got to stop calling herself damaged. "This is new for me. And maybe a little hard for me."

"I get that. But do you even want to do this?" Regan lifts her shoulders slightly. "Because I can't really tell."

Lina nods, trusting the movement more than her words.

"You're sure?"

She nods again.

"Do you have words to back that up?"

"I do. Give me time for that. Okay?"

Regan studies Lina, her eyes shifting over the miniscule features of Lina's expression. Seemingly satisfied, she nods. "Okay. But I have one really important question that needs to be answered right now."

On cue, Lina's stomach growls and Regan cracks a smile. "I guess you don't need words to answer that question either."

"Maybe some questions are better left unanswered," Lina says with a smile as she reaches for the menu.

Long after their dinners are finished and just before the wait staff begin shooting pointed looks in their direction, Lina and Regan walk across the nearly empty parking lot. Their bodies making long shadows beneath the dull lights, the two women pause their conversation long enough to share a look that goes far beyond the surface of their chatter. Lina stalls, hesitating before she leans in, because of a rogue idea that jumps into her brain: What if Regan doesn't want to kiss her? Maybe Lina has been reading her wrong—a strong possibility, given her utter failure at normal, date-like interactions.

While Lina loses herself in an exhausting internal battle, Regan takes a step closer, planting herself firmly in Lina's bubble. She's surprised to realize the rising urge is one that beckons Regan closer instead of one that pushes her away. While she mulls *that* over, she misses the moment where Regan takes yet another step toward her.

With the gentleness and caution of a stranger approaching a skittish kitten, Regan reaches into Lina's space, her hands landing on the tops of Lina's shoulders. Lina stills, shifting her focus from Regan's face to the sandy parking lot. Regan slowly strokes her hands inward until they slide up the sides of Lina's neck and land with practiced care under her jaw. Her thumbs tilt toward each other until they meet at the center of Lina's chin, then brush up to rest against the bottom of her lips. Lina closes her eyes, certain that she will next feel Regan's lips against hers. Instead, she feels her head moved to the side by less than an inch as the silky softness of Regan's lips presses firmly against her cheek, close enough to her lips that Lina feels her heart stutter.

The moment is over before Lina can react, before she can summon her muscles to grab Regan and pull her in for a real, lingering, mouth to mouth kiss. She blinks her eyes open, saddened by the image of Regan slowly stepping away, but backward, her eyes lingering on Lina.

"Goodnight, Lina," she says, her voice carrying gently over the hushed parking lot. Her face is glowing, lit by both the parking lot lights and her radiant smile. "I can't wait to see you again."

CHAPTER NINETEEN

Afghanistan, three years ago

"I still can't believe this." Lina shook her head, emphasizing her disbelief. "I mean, I get that you're standing right in front of me, but it doesn't seem possible."

"Get used to it, Latch." A T-shirt hit her in the face. "I'm here and I'm not going anywhere. I thought you'd be happy I pulled some strings to make you my roomie."

"I am. Definitely. But I can be happy and stunned at the same time."

Brit Lochlan stood with her hands on her hips and appraised Lina from head to toe. Her appearance hadn't changed since Lina had last seen her nearly nine years ago. Vibrant red hair was pulled back tightly into a bun and dark green eyes continued to scan Lina as though searching for a missing piece, a clue to unlocking Lina's shock at seeing Brit—Lock—in her room.

Lina didn't understand why Brit wasn't having the same reaction. Other than the fact that she must have known ahead of time that they'd both be at that particular base in Afghanistan, hence the string-pulling for bunk assignment (which, for the record, Lina had no desire to discover how and why those strings had been pulled—some of Brit's activities were better left unknown), there remained the fact that the last time they'd seen each other was a week after coming home from the deployment to Syria. After a string of barely talking, Brit all but disappeared, leaving Lina wondering if their short-lived relationship overseas existed only in her memories. Not only the relationship, but also Brit. No one heard from her. No one seemed to know where she was or what she was doing, but Lina eventually heard she had gone overseas again.

It's not that Lina hadn't tried to contact Brit. She had— more times than she was comfortable admitting. Brit's responses were sporadic at best, silent at worst. Lina had never gotten the answers she was seeking about their brief romantic interlude, and for her sanity's sake, she had stopped trying. Part of her had hoped that when she stopped contacting Brit, Brit would reach out. She hadn't. It was that ultimate silence that gave Lina all the answers she'd needed. Until Brit walked into her room at the base in Afghanistan, of course, and the questions started whispering once again.

Lina stared down her bunkmate, doing her own searching for something to unlock the mysteries neatly tied within Brit's heart and mind. True to character, Brit was giving nothing away. But she did grin suddenly and sent another T-shirt flying toward Lina's head.

"You look good, Latch. I'm loving the haircut. Let's make the best of this shit situation, okay?"

Lina silently cursed her heart for flipping at that tiny compliment, which probably meant nothing, but it was enough to start Lina's mind-gears grinding away.

* * *

A month into deployment, and Lina had the hang of it once again. Afghanistan was familiar territory; just three years had passed since the last time she'd been there. She reminded herself of that daily when she was cursing the dusty air during her morning runs. It was ridiculous, hoping for a good soaking rain to clear the air and make breathing a little easier, but Lina looked for clouds every single morning. It was embarrassing how many times she whispered to herself, "You're in the desert, idiot."

Brit made a point to never join Lina for her workouts. She'd been keeping her distance in general, only letting her guard down when they were safely confined in their room together, but never enough to give Lina the green light to ask her burning questions. They skipped and skidded around their past, and yet a tension, not new but also not entirely familiar, sizzled between them. Lina was sure Brit felt it too but couldn't bring herself to ask.

It wasn't until Brit returned from a week-long mission to a notoriously dangerous part of the country that Lina noticed the changes in Brit. She was used to her stoic, fierce but calm presence, and while Brit had retained some of that, her edges were spiked with a new frenetic energy. Following that mission, which Brit refused to talk about when she came back, Lina started seeing another new side of Brit, one that was careless, unpredictable. Those two qualities were cause for concern in any person, but in a soldier, one who was deployed overseas in a combative environment: Lina was extremely concerned.

Two weeks went by following that mission before Lina saw her opening. They were in their room, cleaning up and organizing. Lina watched as Brit intently focused on correctly pairing up and folding her socks, then took a breath and dove in.

"You good, Lock?" A brilliant opening. Lina cringed.

"Yup." The folding continued.

"You sure? You seem different lately."

Brit snorted. "That's rich, coming from you."

Lina took a literal step back. Brit's tone was caustic, the words helping to widen the cracks between them. "What? What's that supposed to mean?"

"You," Brit said, looking up from her socks, "are a goddamn closed book. That's not the Lina I remember."

Lina swallowed her fiery retort, knowing it wouldn't help the situation. "I am not." It was a lie and they both knew it, but Lina couldn't explain why her pages had been glued shut. Candice Barrows was a secret that could never be told, and Lina was only beginning to see the effects of that.

"Fine. We'll go with that." Brit dropped her socks and leaned back on her bed. "Go on. Tell me what's so different about me."

After a hesitation, Lina shrugged. "You've been off since you came back."

"Yeah, well. Shit changes you."

Lina watched Brit's eyes cloud over and then take on a steely glare. She seemed to be looking straight through Lina, like Lina didn't exist. A shiver ran through Lina's body and left her chilled as she watched Brit take slow, jagged breaths. Then, suddenly, it was as though the veil lifted and life resurfaced in her deep green eyes.

"Don't stress it, Latch. I'm fine." Brit collected her socks and put them away, then turned and left the room. Lina stared at the door and sighed heavily.

"You tried," she muttered, all along knowing she could have tried harder.

* * *

Later that night, Lina was staring at the ceiling, playing back too many memories of Candice. The only time she unglued her pages was when she was alone, preferably in the dark. It wasn't just that she couldn't talk about it—it was also that she was utterly humiliated over the fact that once she and Candice had returned to New Jersey following their TDY in Texas, Candice had promptly informed Lina that they wouldn't be seeing each other anymore.

Not a week later, Lina had seen Candice kissing a rather good-looking man outside of a bar frequented by military personnel. Caitlin had been with Lina, thankfully, and after she'd gasped loud enough for the entire parking lot to hear, Caitlin had grabbed her arm and dragged her away.

And that was how Lina had the pleasure of finding out: A, Candice's husband was a real person; and B, she was definitely still married to him.

Lina gripped her pillow and fought the urge to scream. She had no one to blame but herself, and she hadn't gotten past how foolish she had been, on so many levels, by getting involved with a superior who was married to a man. The problem was that Lina couldn't forget, couldn't let go of all the ways in which it felt like Candice *got* her. It was cruel to have felt so seen, so understood—and be unable to even be near the person who made those feelings real.

Just as a wave of emotion was threatening to spill over, the door creaked open, and Lina watched as Brit tiptoed into the room. She didn't want to know where she'd been or who she'd been with. Their stunted conversation from earlier had bothered Lina all night, and she'd decided to try not to care about Brit. At least not as much. Not acknowledging her coming in was step one in the process.

Lina closed her eyes and listened to Brit go through the motions of getting ready for bed. It was reassuring, the soft sounds paired with slow and steady breathing, and it was a salve in helping Lina not feel so alone in the world.

She waited for the unmistakable creak of Brit's bed. When it didn't come in the usual sequence of sounds, Lina opened her eyes and came face-to-face with Brit's abdomen.

"What the fuck are you doing?" she asked, propping herself up on her elbow. "Watching me sleep?"

"No," Brit said softly. "I was thinking."

Slowly, it dawned on Lina that Brit's abdomen wasn't covered by her T-shirt. She stood next to Lina's bed, clad only in her underwear and a sports bra, red hair loose and tumbling over her shoulders. Lina sat up completely, legs dangling over the side of her bed, and Brit walked between her legs and put her cool hands on Lina's shoulders.

Not a thing had changed about Brit's body in nine years, and Lina drank her in as though she was parched. Her curves were paired with firm muscles, and every inch of her exposed, creamy skin beckoned Lina's touch.

"We ca—" Lina started.

"Shh," Brit whispered, stroking Lina's lips with her finger. "I need you, Lina."

The kiss came before Lina could say or ask anything in return. Brit's lips were strong and purposeful, moving with urgency and passion. Lina fell into the kiss and grabbed Brit, holding her tightly. The familiarity of kissing her mixed with the excitement of feeling wanted, even needed. Lina pulled Brit into the bed, and they silently made their way through the next couple of hours in the way they had done so many years before.

As Brit slipped out of the bed to head back to her own, Lina grabbed her hand. "Wait. I'm not playing this game again, Brit. We're talking about this tomorrow."

"Sure, whatever you want." Brit pressed another kiss on Lina's lips before floating across the room. Lina watched her go, an all-too familiar scene, then fell back into bed and stared at the ceiling for hours before sleep came.

* * *

Lina hated to admit it, but it was pretty much Syria all over again. She and Brit walked straight back into their old pattern of occasionally sleeping together, the only difference being that they didn't have to sneak around as much since their beds were about six feet apart. While they did sometimes have conversations about what they were doing, Brit remained as noncommittal as she had been nine years earlier, going only as far as to say, "I missed you and I missed this." It was enough for Lina—most days.

As the months passed, their connection seemed to solidify, and more often than not, Brit was climbing into Lina's bed. The sexual release was something they both needed, a reprieve from the chaotic world they were living in, a way to find warmth and normalcy. Some days, Lina kidded herself into thinking it was more than just sex. But each time she allowed that thought to enter her mind, Brit would do something that destroyed it, like disappearing for hours with another female soldier Lina knew she'd previously hooked up with. And then she'd come back saying something that confused Lina's thoughts and her own action, like, "You're the only person I trust."

One particularly good day, Brit made Lina give her a hug that lasted exactly three minutes before they left for breakfast. Lina held her tightly, stroking the back of her neck. She liked that Brit was four or so inches shorter than she was; the way her body tucked into Lina's felt comforting.

"Sometimes I think you're it for me." The words were muffled since Brit's mouth was smashed against Lina's shoulder, but she heard them, and she felt them as they spun through her heart, causing waves of emotion.

"You mean that?" It was all Lina could say. She wasn't sure Brit had even meant to say the words.

"Wouldn't say it if I didn't mean it." She pulled away and looked at Lina. "Don't be weird about it."

"Me? Weird? Never."

Brit snorted and opened the door, effectively ending the closeness and the conversation. "What's on your agenda today?"

Lina stuffed the conversation into her pocket and promised herself she'd bring it out later. That was not the kind of statement a person made and then walked away from. "The usual. Blood, blood, and more blood."

"No urine? Bummer."

"You never know. I could get lucky."

Lina noticed the faint blush on Brit's pale cheeks and gave herself a mental high five. She liked seeing the effects she had on Brit, and as Brit tended to hold her cards so close to her chest that even she couldn't see them, it was a rare and delightful moment when Lina caught a blush or secretive smile.

The mess hall wasn't super crowded, and as they made their way to the serving line, Lina looked around for the group of people she usually sat with. Brit's three-minute hug didn't seem like much of a delay in the moment, but Army time was strict, and there was a good chance—

Lina froze, causing Brit to walk directly into her back.

"What the hell, Latch?" Brit grumbled. She sidestepped and walked past Lina.

No. No way. Impossible. The words scattered through Lina's mind, fighting to be the most appropriate descriptor. Meanwhile, Lina's body had turned to mush encased in steel.

"Ragelis."

In that moment, Lina hated her name more than anything else in the world, even the ever-present and always annoying humid layer of dust that coated her lungs every time she went for her morning run.

Get it together. NOW. The internal command worked, and Lina straightened up and looked straight into piercing blue eyes.

"Ma'am," she said, nodding slightly at Lieutenant Candice Barrows.

CHAPTER TWENTY

Kitty Hawk, present day

As another boom sounds faintly from somewhere far down the beach toward Corolla, Lina grumbles to herself. It's not even dark—there is absolutely no logical reason to be setting off fireworks at this time, even if it happens to be July 4th. It's almost like people like the sound more than the sparkly sight, which makes zero sense to Lina, who could do without fireworks in general. In fact, she wouldn't mind if they disappeared altogether, never to return.

Standing on the deck, looking out over the ocean, Lina thinks about how much research it would take to draw up a thorough and educated report on the environmental dangers of fireworks. Surely there's information out there. But does she have the patience and stamina to find it, sort it, and draw it up into something effective? Yeah, no. Definitely not.

Dusk is beginning to fall, and Lina reluctantly turns to go inside. She'd love nothing more than to sit outside all night—the humidity has taken a midweek vacation, leaving the

North Carolina coastal air fresh, warm, and full of promise. Unfortunately, the sun decided to run off with the humidity, so the day has been cloudy and filled with periodic bursts of rain. By the looks of the overcast veil sagging over the ocean, it's not long before more rain will fall.

That, too, pleases Lina. Rain isn't conducive to fireworks, so maybe she'll get a break tonight after all.

"Wishful thinking," she says aloud to the quiet kitchen. Besides, if the rain is too bad tonight, the annoying blasts will just be postponed until tomorrow. 'Tis the season, after all, holiday or no holiday. People love beach fireworks.

After reheating and enjoying yet another quesadilla from Bad Bean, Lina stretches out on the sofa, searching for something mindless to watch. She never got into true crime the way Caitlin is, despite many attempts by said best friend to lure Lina to the dark side. Lina's idea of mindless entertainment runs more along the lines of *Seinfeld* reruns, or super old episodes of *DeGrassi*, which is a funny little interest of hers that she's never shared with anyone.

She settles on yet another cooking competition show, allowing herself the unadulterated joy of salivating over dishes she doesn't have the desire to create.

Somewhere in the middle of Carol's unfortunate burning of her crème brûlée, Lina's thoughts drift back to Regan. They haven't seen each other since their date, which feels both good and bad. It's only been two days, but Lina's surprised to find that she…misses her. Or at least misses her smile and her sunshine glow. Yeah, that's it—she misses Regan's presence, not Regan herself.

"You're an idiot," she mumbles, turning onto her side and cradling her head in the crook of her elbow.

She misses Regan. She wants to be near Regan, wants to learn more about her, wants to know what it feels like to kiss Regan. That thought strikes particularly deep and brings with it a fizzy sensation in her gut. Lina thought maybe, just maybe, their date would end with a kiss. She'd been open to it, and thought she did a satisfactory job of demonstrating that with both her words and her body language. Either she hadn't, or Regan had just had a different idea.

Lina scans through her knowledge of Regan. There's a lot of blank pages, something she wants to ameliorate. The cast of ghostly characters in her head, the fading images of lust and love past, take up too much room. Not for the first time, Lina wishes for a way to empty her memories of the failure and disaster of her previous entanglements. She's a little worried there's just not enough space for Regan.

She *wants* room for Regan. She also really wants to go back to that parking lot and kiss her, give their date a proper ending.

Safe but alone on her sofa, Lina's eyes flutter shut to the sound of rain pelting the windows and thoughts of seeing Regan again, wondering what that might bring.

It's not a nightmare that wakes Lina but a volatile gunpowder explosion that shakes the house. Lina is jolted from her accidental nap and, heart already racing, rolls right off the sofa and lands on the floor with a smack of her hip to hardwood.

For a moment, she's disoriented, uncertain of where the blast came from and what caused it. Something primal tells her to run, while something calm and rational tells her to stay put, that she's safe here. As the dualities battle it out, another rumble clangs through the air, again shaking the stilts that sit below the house. Lina sits up and brings her knees to her chest as she scans the room for signs of danger.

Fireworks, the rational voice says. Lina hears it. She knows it's true. She taps her phone for confirmation—yup, it's still July 4th, closing in on ten p.m. Either the rain has let up or the noise-making revelers down on the beach just don't care.

During the reprieve from blasts, Lina takes a few calming breaths and shakes out her body, starting with her hands. She wiggles through the movements until she gains her balance and stands. The silence from outside is eerie, and she knows it's not permanent. Her eyes flick over to the TV, and she grabs the remote, turning up the volume. Right. That will drown out the fireworks.

She paces the room, not daring to look out the doors toward the beach. A part of her brain thinks that seeing the sparkly lights will help put two and two together, thus dulling her reaction to the noise. Lina can't be bothered with rational thought at this moment and instead continues her pacing, eyes fixed on the floor.

A string of muted pops sounds off. Lina inhales as deeply as her lungs will allow. She can get through this. She understands that it's just fireworks, and people have the right to celebrate, even if it's too loud and triggering for others. Land of the free and all that.

"Fireworks. Fireworks," she mutters, repeating the word with each step across the room. She makes it through another round of explosions but can feel her body beginning to rebel.

It begins with her hands. The shaking from several minutes ago pales in comparison to the tremors that roll through her ligaments. She stares at them, awed by the determined rhythmic speed. Her hands distract her from realizing that her shoulders have turned to steel, the muscles impenetrable in their clenching. By the time Lina realizes that she's stopped pacing, the rigidity has spread toward the floor and she's frozen, all communication to her lower body muscular system shut down.

The resounding crash that comes next is the one that puts her over the edge. It's beyond loud, too close for comfort, and is precluded by a whining screech that glides past the barrier of the home's walls to zap directly into Lina's veins.

She gasps for air. Both sounds—the screeching and the blast—echo in her bloodstream, her heartbeat, her brain. She can't escape the noise. She slams her eyes shut, hoping for a reset when she reopens them, but everything is the same, only louder.

Dropping to the floor, Lina crawls back to the spot where her phone sits. She grabs for it, yelling with frustration as it slips and slides through her trembling fingers. She finally drops it to the floor and hovers over the screen, pushing one number at a time in order to unlock the phone.

The phone blinks back at her, waiting for a command. Lina, on all fours, drips sweat onto the screen. She chews on her bottom lip. Then she opens her contacts and hits Caitlin's name.

Six rings later, no answer. Lina jams her finger onto the screen and hangs up, cognizant enough to realize that leaving a voice mail in her current state would be a horrible thing to listen to. She tries Mallory next but already knows that no answer from one basically guarantees no answer from the other, and she's correct.

Bending her knees so that she's in an anxious version of child's pose, Lina comes closer to her phone as she scrolls up, back to the Cs. She looks at Carolyn's name then scrolls back to the Ks. It's a rare occasion that Keeley doesn't answer when Lina calls, and tonight happens to be such an occasion.

Frustrated on top of brimming with anxiety and fear, Lina lets loose a growl that sounds more animal than human. By habit, her pointer finger scrolls to the Bs.

A violent tremor rips through Lina's body at the sight of that particular name. Her finger hangs millimeters from the call button. She could hit it.

Another ferocious crash peals through the air and Lina loses her breath completely. She presses her fists into her eyes. There's a moment where she wonders, briefly, if she should just give in. Finally. It feels like there's a sandbag crushing her lungs, and if she simply doesn't make an effort to breathe, she could end all of this: the pain, the struggle, the uncertainty, the ever-increasing anxiety.

With a rush, air plows into her lungs and Lina chokes out a gasp. She can feel her emotions slipping wildly out of control, and without giving herself time to talk herself out of her next move, she fumbles with her phone and finally hits call.

One ring. Two rings. Three—

"Hey you," Regan says.

Lina opens her mouth and closes it immediately. She works her jaw back and forth, swallows. She tries to clear her throat, but nothing happens.

"Lina?"

Speak, she commands herself. She opens her mouth again.

"I can't do this," she croaks, her voice scratchy and flimsy.

There's silence on the other end of the phone. "You're telling me this now? Like this?"

"No," Lina says hurriedly. She clears her throat. "Not that. I can't do *this*—the noise. The sounds. It's so loud, Regan. I can't do it."

"Oh," she says, and her voice is hushed with relief and understanding. "Text me your address. I'm coming over."

"You don't have to—"

"I know. I want to. I'm hanging up. Send it to me now."

With shaking fingers, Lina manages to tap out a text that contains her address. She compels her body to shift so that she's sitting upright on the floor, knees pressed tightly into her chest. Now all she can do is wait.

When Regan arrives, Lina isn't sure how much time has passed. She's pulled from her silent waiting by the sound of a car crunching over the gravelly sand of the driveway, followed by the quick slam of a car door. She jumps to her feet. Too late, she realizes that was a poor decision. Her brain swims, the room tilting with the rush of blood and suppressed adrenaline. Lina ignores the shifting floor beneath her feet as she half-walks, half-jogs to meet Regan at the door.

She attempts a steadying breath before opening the door, but the air gets stuck in all the wrong places, forcing her to cough into her elbow as she swings open the door. Through her wheezing and tearing eyes, Regan appears, silhouetted by the moonlight.

"Hi," Regan says. Her voice is filled with cloudy softness. "Can I come in?"

Lina nods, clearing her throat repeatedly. She shuts the door behind Regan and tries to explain her flushed face and coughing fit. "The air went up the wrong tube." Another cough escapes. "Or something like that."

Regan nods knowingly. "My dad has a lifelong habit of drinking water too fast and then erupting into a dramatic choking fit. He claims the water goes down the wrong tube, but he's really just impatient when he's thirsty."

For some reason, Lina finds this hilarious. She knocks out laughs between her coughs. Her body fills with a new sensation, the panicked adrenaline giving way to a mounting hysteria. She cannot stop laughing.

Regan looks at her with confused concern. "Um. It wasn't that funny."

Bolstered by the change in feeling, Lina cracks a wide grin and tries her damndest to stop laughing. "It was, though. It really was. Anyway! Are you hungry? Thirsty?" She doubles over in laughter once more. "Maybe—oh my God, I'm so sorry— maybe I shouldn't offer you something to drink."

Lina becomes distantly aware of the fireworks beginning again but learns she can block out their chaos by focusing on this delicious spell of laughter. And so, she continues laughing, unaware of the context behind Regan's expression.

"I think I missed something," Regan says slowly.

"No!" Lina grips her sides, trying to quell her newest hysterical spell. "Drinking. Like father, like daughter, right? You could—you know." She dissolves into giggles. "Choke."

"Maybe we should sit down." Regan reaches out and touches Lina's arm.

"Why sit when there's so much we can do?" The manic laughter finally subsiding, Lina spreads her arms wide and looks around the living room. "Wanna help me paint? There's one bedroom left on my list."

Regan doesn't move her hand from Lina's arm. She searches Lina's eyes, then seems to settle on something. "I'd love to help you paint," she begins, "but it's so much better to paint with daylight."

"You're right." Lina nods enthusiastically. "Maybe in the morning?"

"If that's what you want, then sure."

"Awesome." Lina pauses. "How handy are you? We could try putting together a bookshelf." She turns and jogs into the nearest bedroom, emerging a moment later with a box. "I don't think it'll be too hard, but it's always easier with two people. Well, some people. My best friend, Caitlin—she always makes things like this harder. But I bet you're handier than she is. Can you grab my tool bag? It's in the corner of the kitchen."

Lina positions the box in the middle of the living room, pushing the coffee table out of the way. Her actions don't interrupt her rambling. "There's a box cutter in the front pocket. That's the easiest tool to use to slice tape like this." She twitches at the sound of another reverberating firework. "We're probably going to need a Phillips head. You know what those look like, right? Can you grab one? I think I have two in that bag."

Confused by the lack of a tape-slicing apparatus in her hand, Lina looks over her shoulder to find Regan standing a few feet behind her. She doesn't have the tool bag in her hand, and she's not making any movements to get it.

"What are you doing?" Lina asks, a note of frustration creeping into her voice. She's not asking for much. She just wants her damn bag of tools. With a sigh, she stands up, ready to get it for herself.

"Lina, wait—"

The next round of fireworks comes with zero warning. They're the kind that shriek and scream as they fly through the air, and in the background, their evil siblings boom and blast with a frantic, caustic energy. The collision of noises knocks Lina off-balance, and she whips her head around, searching for a safe place to land.

Lina feels bile rising in her throat as she stumbles blindly to the edge of the sofa. The booms echo and intensify. She can't tell if that's in her head or in the air, but either way, it is finally too much.

She finds herself sitting on the floor once again, her back pressed into the sofa. She draws her legs as close to her chest as possible and hugs them even tighter with her arms. She resists the urge to press her hands against her ears but wishes she could make the noise stop. Her breathing trips and stumbles over her racing heart, the two working together in a discordant duet.

The reverberations in her head finally start to slow and dull with each step Regan takes toward her. Lina tries to look up to meet Regan's eyes, but her head is too heavy, and she rests her chin against the tops of her knees.

"I'm going to sit with you. Is that okay?" Regan kneels next to Lina and smooths the hair off her forehead. The touch is enough to send Lina rocketing toward the edge of her inability to cry. She closes her eyes to ward off the urge, unable to do more than give a slight nod in response to Regan's question.

"I'm glad you called," Regan continues. "I should have known tonight...I don't know, I—" Regan rocks back and sits on the floor in front of Lina, legs spread so that her thighs are against Lina's feet. She leans forward and puts her hands on Lina's shoulders. She's as close as Lina can allow her to be, and Lina pushes past her discomfort to marvel at how Regan seems to intrinsically know how to handle her. "I wish you'd called earlier."

"It wasn't bad earlier." Lina swallows against the grainy feeling in her throat. "It was raining, and I fell asleep." With each word, Lina feels herself coming back to center. Or something that feels like center, anyway.

Though they haven't stopped, the fireworks seem much quieter than they did twenty minutes ago. Lina stares at Regan, trying to figure out how she controls the volume of the outside world.

Regan twists to look at the TV. "Are you learning how to make a gourmet dinner for me?"

Lina tries to smile. "Maybe." She feels her muscles start to loosen their grip. She slouches and shifts so that her legs are spread out in front of her, layered over Regan's. She's still tense, but the human touch helps to soften her limbs.

Regan watches Lina for a couple seconds, then maneuvers her body so that her legs are on top. She scoots in closer and wraps her legs around Lina's waist as her arms encircle Lina's torso. Their chests connect and Regan rests her head on Lina's shoulder.

Different feelings start to thrum through Lina's body, but they're no match for the fear-fueled anxiety that lingers. She rests her head against Regan's, trying to sync their breathing.

Though her breaths remain jagged, Lina can tell her heart rate is slowing.

"You're shaky," Regan says. Her fingers draw lazy circles on Lina's back.

"I'm okay." The response comes fast. Lina hears it and knows it's not true, but she refuses to take it back or amend it.

"You sure about that?" Regan pulls back to look at Lina. "I mean, you sound better than you did when you called, and better than you were five minutes ago, but it seems like you're still—not quite yourself," she finishes after a hesitation.

"I'm sure." *Say it and it'll be true.* Lina nods. She's good, great. Tip-top shape. "Since you're here, wanna watch a movie?"

A look of confusion darts over Regan's features. "Sure," she says, starting to pull backward.

"Wait." Lina grips her arms and pulls her back so that she's close. Lina knows there's only one real way to prove to Regan that she is, in fact, perfectly okay.

Lina reaches up and runs her fingers through Regan's hair. A murmur of pleasure escapes Regan's lips, spurring Lina on. When her hand reaches the back of Regan's head, she leans forward as she pulls Regan's head toward her. Their lips meet and Lina feels breathless once again.

Every move of Regan's lips and tongue pulls Lina deeper in and further away from the quiet cacophony in her brain. *This*, she thinks. *This is the answer.* She kisses the outside fireworks away, using all her power to focus on the indoor fireworks sparking from this kiss.

She feels Regan's hands on her jaw, much like they were a few nights ago. Encouraged, Lina kisses harder, nipping at Regan's lips. She grips Regan's sides, holding her as close as possible. Her thumbs slide over and press eagerly into the space below Regan's breasts. She pours every ounce of energy and desire into that kiss.

It's Regan who pulls away, eyes wide and lips parted. "Holy shit," she whispers.

Lina nods. Her words are gone. There's only one thing on her mind now, and saying it out loud would ruin the moment.

Lina stands, pulling Regan up with her. The shakes are gone, but they've been replaced by a jittery sensation that feels like withdrawal from a drug. The energy that's surging through Lina's body is something she's unfamiliar with, but when she meets Regan's shining ocean eyes once again, she knows exactly what to do with this feeling.

CHAPTER TWENTY-ONE

Regan gasps as Lina grabs her, hard, and pulls her in for another kiss. Mid-kiss, Lina opens her eyes to make sure it's really Regan that she's kissing. It's not that she thought she was someone else. She just needs to be sure.

"Wait," Regan says, pulling back. Her eyes are both shiny and dark. "Didn't you want to watch a movie?"

Lina grins as she wraps her arms around Regan's waist and tugs her close again. "Is that what you want to do?"

Regan shrugs, but there's a playful smile tugging at her lips. "I could watch a movie. Or I could keep kissing you."

"Good answer." Lina goes in fast and hard to resume their kissing. She needs to be okay right now, and she *needs* to show Regan that she's okay.

Not breaking their kiss, Lina walks Regan backward until her back is against the hallway wall. A surprised gasp floats past Regan's lips and, encouraged by the sound, Lina grips Regan's hips and pulls them out from the wall so that her back is arched slightly.

Regan's lips and tongue move faster in response to the change in her position. Lina groans into the kiss. She slides her hands under Regan's shirt and skims them over the smooth planes of her stomach. As her fingertips meet the edge of Regan's bra, something quiet clicks in Lina's racing brain and she suddenly pulls away.

The image of Regan, lips parted and wet, eyes radiating desire, nearly convinces Lina to skip her question and dive back in.

"Is this okay?" she whispers, not wanting to break the moment, but unwilling to keep going without consent.

"Very," comes the reply. Then Regan puts a hand on Lina's shoulder. "But are you sure you want to do this right now?"

"Very," Lina echoes, crushing her body against Regan's. She absently registers the way Regan's hand slides off her shoulder and cascades down her body, landing on her hip. A delicate siren rings in Lina's head, and she arches her body in response, angling it in such a way that Regan is forced to move her hand away. A moment later, both of Regan's hands are on Lina's face, cradling it as they kiss. The siren ebbs and fades into a barely audible beep.

Lina's hands find their way back to the edge of Regan's bra, and this time, they don't stop there. She pushes the sports bra up and feels warm breasts fall into her hands. Having broken the kiss a moment ago, Regan bites Lina's neck as Lina flicks her thumb over her nipple. She pauses, then smiles. As she rolls Regan's nipple between her thumb and pointer finger, Lina tugs gently on the small metal bar running through the center of her nipple. The sound that emerges from Regan is primal and uncensored. Lina inhales sharply, wanting to draw out that sound over and over again.

When she feels Regan reaching for her once again, Lina pulls her body back just far enough to send what she hopes is a clear signal. She catches the end of Regan's sigh and distracts her by unbuttoning her shorts. With a tug, the shorts fall to the floor. Lina pushes Regan's shirt up and takes her pierced nipple into her mouth. As expected, the guttural groans resume and Lina wastes no time in yanking down Regan's underwear, letting them pool on top of her discarded shorts.

She hears Regan say her name, but her voice sounds far away, too far to be real. Lina takes a half-step back, feeling unsteady, and rights herself immediately with her left hand pressed against the wall she has Regan pushed up against. Her right hand drifts with purpose to Regan's bare thigh. She registers the feel of flushed skin dotted with sweat. Lina pulls her mouth from Regan's nipple and looks down, blinking. She can barely see the floor beneath her. A shot of panic spirals through her, mimicking the fireworks that are still thundering outside.

Again, she thinks she hears Regan say her name. In response, Lina shifts her weight, bringing her knee between Regan's legs, spreading them apart just enough to comfortably slide her hand between Regan's thighs. The wet heat brings Lina back long enough to get her bearings, and with her shoulder pressed against Regan's, anchoring her to the wall, Lina thrusts her fingers inside Regan.

Seconds, minutes pass. All Lina knows is the motion of her hand and fingers. She knows she's fucking her hard, but Regan's body is open to her, taking every thrust and twist of Lina's fingers. The visceral sensations of human connection flood Lina's body, bringing with them viscous clouds that dim her vision. Each moment gets darker and louder, looser and bolder.

When Regan cries out, Lina feels nothing more than the shaking of her own legs. She blinks rapidly, holding her left hand in front of her face. It's all a blur, a static, shadowy blur.

* * *

Lina rolls over and a sharp pain stabs her ribs. She gasps, pressing her hand against the sore spot. Then she opens her eyes, confused. Looking down at her body, she sees the clothing she's pretty certain she was wearing the previous night. A quick survey of the room tells her yes, she is in what she's called "her" bedroom for the past couple of months. But the clothing? She can't make sense of that. If she's in Kitty Hawk, she's not with the Army, and the only time she sleeps in any type of clothing is when she's with the Army.

She should be naked right now.

When Lina sits up, she presses her feet (bare, somehow) against the floor with all her strength. Her limbs feel untethered. Combined with the weird clothing situation, Lina's feeling less grounded than she has since the day she left New Jersey.

She waits until she's certain she can stand before slowly inching off the bed. She wiggles her toes, watching them as they curl and flex against the floor. A few cursory bends of her knees renew her confidence, but she walks slowly when she exits the bedroom, not wanting to overwhelm her raw nervous system.

Raking a hand through her hair, Lina walks into the kitchen. Something—well, many things, but some basic thing in general—feels off. She replays the previous night in her head as she goes through the motions of making an iced coffee. Hopefully the caffeine will help restore her internal order.

One final ice cube plunks into her cup, and though she's itching to get outside and fill her lungs with fresh, salty beach air, something compels Lina to turn around. She stares into the living room, trying to make sense of what she's seeing. There, curled up and hugging a pillow to her chest, is Regan.

Lina takes a step toward the sofa and immediately steps back, jolted. Regan blinks at her before sitting up and rubbing her eyes.

"You're awake," Lina says, unable to hide the uncertain surprise in her voice. "I mean, you're here."

"Of course I'm here. I couldn't leave you like that last night."

Lina hears the words but can't make sense of them. She stalls by taking a sip of her iced coffee. The caffeine—sweet, glorious caffeine—jumpstarts Lina's hazy brain. That's right. She called Regan last night. Regan came over. Lina's eyes flicker to the unopened box on the floor. That damn shelf she's been putting off building. Had they decided to build it together? But got distracted? If so, what distracted them? And what was Regan talking about?

"Like how?" Lina has so many questions, but that's the first one that tumbles from her mouth.

Regan eyes her, a mixture of sadness and confusion etched into her features. "You…don't remember?" At Lina's shaking head, Regan blows out a sigh. "Do you remember *anything* about last night?"

"Fireworks," Lina says. "And I remember calling you."

"And then?"

Lina knows there's more, she absolutely knows it. But there's a towering steel wall standing between her memories and her conscious thoughts. She suddenly feels like she's missing something very important. "I'm sorry." Her voice breaks and she clears her throat. "Did something happen?"

Regan stares at Lina. She stares and Lina stares back, and each passing second brings a new terrible sensation into Lina's gut. Finally, Regan pushes off the sofa and crosses the room. "Yes, something happened, and I'm going to need some of that"—she nods at Lina's cup—"to discuss it."

She brushes past Lina and goes out onto the deck. Lina senses the urgency of the moment and quickly makes Regan an iced coffee, hoping she gets the ratios right since they haven't reached the "this is how I like my coffee" stage of getting to know each other. When she emerges onto the deck, she watches Regan for a moment.

With her elbows on the deck railing, Regan is leaned over with her right foot crossed over the back of her left ankle, clothing rumpled from sleeping on the sofa. Her hair isn't as lively as Lina's used to seeing it, and she fights the urge to run her hands through and muss it up.

Instead, she sits at the table and sets down both drinks. "Here's your coffee."

Regan spins around and studies Lina before sitting down next to her and taking a long sip of her drink. "Thank you."

"Did you not sleep well?"

Regan laughs, but the sound is empty. "No, Lina, I didn't sleep well. I'm guessing you did?"

"I don't really know," she says, and it's the truth. Lina has the odd feeling that she temporarily fell into a black hole.

"Yeah," Regan says on an exhale. "I'm starting to understand that's the problem here."

"I'm sorry—"

"Okay, stop apologizing. Please." Regan shakes her head and puts her glass down. "You really don't remember anything that happened last night? After I came over, I mean."

Lina stares out at the ocean, looking for answers. "No. I don't."

"Do you…Do you want me to tell you?"

The hesitation in Regan's voice hits Lina square in the chest, and she feels her heart stutter. "Please."

Regan nods, seeming to have reached a conclusion. "Okay. Well. You called me, and I came over. You were…Lina, you were so not yourself. I know I don't know you as well as, like, your best friend, but I've been around you enough to know that the way you were acting when I got here…I knew something was wrong." Regan watches Lina, who nods, encouraging her to continue. "It was like I was watching you do everything in your power to act normal, and then you couldn't anymore. When we were sitting on the floor, I felt like I had you back." Regan blushes. "That sounds weird."

"No," Lina says in a low voice. "I know what you mean."

"Okay. Good. We should have stayed right there. Or I wish I'd made you sit down and watch a damn movie, but when you kissed me, the *way* you kissed me—I knew where it was headed."

Lina pushes against her stomach, wishing the colony of bees residing there would die a fast death. She vaguely remembers kissing Regan. She can almost see it as though she's watching it happen from outside herself. The thought shakes her.

"Do you want me to keep going?"

"Yes. I do."

Regan bites her lower lip. "You wouldn't let me touch you," is all she says, and it's all Lina needs to hear.

It's not that the memories illustrating the previous night come back. It's not as though Lina suddenly knows precisely what she did, why she did it, and how good it felt. Instead, a thick wave of embarrassment topped with whitecaps of sadness fills her from the head down. She's heard enough to know exactly what happened.

"Anyway," Regan continues, not giving Lina much of a chance to interject. "You just sort of left after that. Maybe during? I'm not sure. But definitely after. You were—you were just gone, Lina. You were talking and you sounded like yourself, but you weren't really there at all. It scared the hell out of me." She laughs nervously. "So I convinced you to go to bed. Once your head hit the pillow, you were asleep. I, um, stayed with you for a while. I was nervous. Worried," she adds quickly. "So once I figured you were totally asleep, I went and crashed on the sofa." Regan shifts her gaze past Lina, not meeting her eyes. "I didn't think you'd want to wake up next to me after all that, and I didn't want it to be weird, but I couldn't stand the idea of leaving you alone, so I stayed close enough to be there in case you needed me."

The final rambling phrase pierces Lina, but the sinking knowledge of what happened weighs heavier and overpowers her emotions. She leans forward, elbows on her knees, and hangs her head in her hands. Regan continues to gaze at the beach, and they sit like that for some time, letting the world around them do the talking.

"I know what happened," Lina finally says, lifting her head. "To me, I mean. I know what happened to me."

Regan tilts her head as she appraises Lina. "Did you black out? I didn't think you were drinking."

"Not really but kind of. And no, I wasn't drinking." She blows out a frustrated breath. "What happened last night wasn't fair to you, Regan, and I'm really sorry for that."

"Are you…Are you sorry it happened?"

Lina peers at Regan, searching for a sign of what's going through her mind. She doesn't regret what she believes happened, but she absolutely regrets how it happened. She gives herself a mental kick to get her words out of her head.

"I'm sorry for how it happened." Lina fights a smile. "I'm not sorry for what happened, and I'm kind of excited to get the memory back."

"So this has happened to you before?"

Lina scratches the side of her neck. She'd love to exit this conversation, but there's no way out. "Yeah. Not in that context, but yes." She winces as the memory of sleeping with Luciana jabs her conscious thoughts. "It's hard to explain."

Regan nods, seeming to contemplate the situation. "And you'll let me know when you get that memory back?"

"You'll be the first to know." Lina smiles a genuine smile and shifts in her chair, causing a ripple of pain from her sore ribs. Grimacing, she points at her torso. "Can you fill me in on what happened here?"

Regan cringes. "Bit of an incident between my elbow and your ribs."

"You're gonna need to give me more than that."

"You kissed me again. And I kissed you back." Regan blushes again, and Lina feels compelled to kiss that blush away. "As much as I wanted to keep kissing you, I knew you weren't really there with me, so there was some playful struggling in your bedroom. I guess I got you kind of hard, huh?"

Despite the heaviness of the events and the conversation, Lina finds herself laughing. Regan, after a hesitant beat, joins in. When their laughter dies out, the troubled weight oozes back in.

"I'm sorry," Lina says, and shakes her head at Regan's attempt at protesting. "This is a lot." She gestures toward herself. "I'm a lot."

"I know," Regan says simply. She stands up and stretches. "I need to go home and get some real sleep before my shift tonight."

"Oh. Okay." Lina chews the inside of her cheek. In spite of the waterfall of negative thoughts and sensitive emotions, she realizes she doesn't want Regan to leave. The thought jars her and she stands upon recognizing it. "Yeah. You should go get some sleep."

"I plan on it." Regan closes the small gap of space between them and places a soft but meaningful kiss on Lina's mouth.

Before she can stop herself, because there's a part of her that definitely does not want to say what comes out of her mouth,

Lina sputters, "You don't want to do this. I'm too damaged for someone like you."

Regan takes a step back, her eyes never leaving Lina's. "I think I should be the one to decide that." After squeezing Lina's arm, Regan walks past her and disappears into the daylight.

CHAPTER TWENTY-TWO

It took Lina a magnificent amount of strength to admit to her therapist the events that took place on the night of July 4th. Or, as Carolyn said, "You're brave, and I'm proud of you." The truth is, Lina knew she had to come clean, and so she did. She doesn't want to put more stock in it than that, even if Carolyn made it seem like a big deal.

Over the course of Lina's therapy session the day after everything happened, she learned that she had, in fact, dissociated. It was a hard pill to swallow—it might still be stuck in her throat several days later—but giving the experience a name has helped Lina move through her embarrassment and anger about how she handled herself. Or, sorry, no—how her body needed to protect her. She didn't have control over that dissociation, which irritates her, and there's no guarantee it won't happen again, which makes her feel even more damaged. But on the plus side, she's coming around to the fact that it wasn't her fault.

That, and calling Regan that night was actually a "wonderful first step," as Carolyn said.

That, and the fact that in the aftermath of The Great Fireworks Dissociation, Regan has been far more amazing than Lina feels she deserves.

She may be coming around to that, too. Slowly.

At Carolyn's encouragement, Lina took a few days off from work. In the moment, it didn't seem like a good idea. Why would Lina purposely give herself more time to overthink everything about that day? She assumed she'd drive herself crazy, but the opposite has happened. Just like Carolyn predicted (who gave her therapist the right to be so damn smart?), Lina felt her body loosening up, breathing more deeply, feeling more anchored. She begrudgingly started journaling, which has been a struggle and a release all at once. Nothing feels as though it's snapped back into place, but everything feels just a little bit easier, a tiny bit less threatening.

* * *

Two days before Lina goes back to work, she's enjoying as much of the sunshine as possible. The previous three days were gloomy and restless, with sullen cloud banks playing tag in the sky. Today, however, is pristine and gorgeous, not even unbearably hot. Lina's taking advantage, and after her morning workout, she treats herself to a quick swim before trudging back through the sand to the deck.

She opens the sliding door and grabs her phone from the kitchen counter, intent on texting Regan, just like she has every morning since July 4th. When she returns to the deck and makes herself comfortable in an Adirondack, she sees two missed calls from Caitlin. Before returning the calls, Lina rubs her damp hair and shuts her eyes. She hasn't spoken to Caitlin, or Mallory, in over a week, and while she's not entirely sure she's ready to be lectured about that, she knows the longer she puts it off, the more dramatic it will be, so she makes the call.

"Nice. So you are alive."

"Of course I'm alive. I've been busy."

Caitlin snorts. "Busy doing what? Working?"

"Are you going to be a rude dick, or will you calm down so that I can actually talk to you?"

There's a pause on the other end of the phone. "Okay. I deserved that. I'm sorry."

"She's still pissed you're not here!" Mallory yells in the background.

"I can tell," Lina says, shaking her head. "Caitlin. I need you to get a grip. I'm not coming back for a while yet."

"I *know*," Caitlin says. "Let's put aside my inability to accept the fact that you're not coming back until April, okay? Tell me what's going on with you. You sound different."

Lina smiles. She can't get anything past Caitlin, and while it's sometimes annoying, it's also kind of amazing to have that kind of bond with someone. "Some things have happened."

Caitlin lasts a full five seconds into Lina's purposeful silence before exploding. "And? Come on, Lina, spill!"

"Let's get the not-great stuff out of the way first." Lina sits up straighter, bracing herself. She told Carolyn that Caitlin is the only person she feels comfortable enough with to own up to her mental health struggles, and if she doesn't start now, she'll keep putting it off. "I've been dealing with some things. Some struggles. Problems." She grunts, unable to find the right word. "I've been having a hard time."

"Okay, I'm listening," Caitlin says, and her gentle tone is enough to propel Lina forward with her confession.

"So, I have PTSD." She waits for Caitlin to congratulate her for finally saying it out loud, but the other end of the phone is quiet. "I guess it helps that I'm accepting that. Anyway, it—the PTSD—has been really bad. Bad in ways that I wasn't expecting to ever deal with." Lina casts her gaze out to the ocean, calming herself with the predictable pull of the waves. "I've had a lot of nightmares. And, I don't know, I've just been feeling bad. Not like myself."

"You haven't sounded like yourself."

"Yeah. But I couldn't explain what was going on with me. I still can't, not completely. But I'm starting to have a better idea." Lina pauses, not wanting to dig into the next part, but she promised Carolyn she'd try. "The Fourth of July was particularly bad for me."

"Oh shit," Caitlin whispers. "You called both of us that night. We were—fuck, Lina, we were at a picnic, and it was so loud. I didn't even think about why you'd be calling."

"It's okay. It's not your fault. I'm not your responsibility."

"Yeah, but I'm your best friend. I should be there for you."

"You can't always be there, Caitlin. And that's life. It's okay."

"I'm nodding. Okay. Go on. Tell me what was so bad about that night."

"The fireworks," Lina says, then laughs. "It all comes down to the fireworks. It got so bad that I called someone to come over and be with me."

"Oh, please don't tell me you called that married doctor. What the hell was her name?"

"Luciana, and no, I didn't call her. I called Regan."

Caitlin's quiet for a couple seconds. "Who exactly is Regan?"

Lina fills Caitlin in on Regan, reminding her that she did in fact indirectly tell her about Regan a couple phone calls ago. Lina confesses to having gone out with Regan, and even mentions the surprising pull she feels toward her. Caitlin's silent throughout Lina's explanation, speaking only after Lina says, "And that's Regan."

"Mmhmm. Interesting."

"Don't be mad."

"I'm not *mad*, you idiot. I'm excited. But I'm also a little pissed you weren't filling me in along the way."

Lina kicks her feet up on the bench. "I was never sure of what to say, Caitlin. I didn't know anything was going to come of it, and I still don't know if anything really will. I mean, let's not forget how fucked up I am." She winces, hearing Carolyn's voice in her head yet again. "Or that I have shit to work through. Beyond that, she's not my type."

"What? What does that mean?"

Lina hesitates, mistakenly giving Caitlin room to jump back in with her argument.

"Oh, wait, let me guess. She's emotionally available and healthy, not married, and mature? Right, Lina. Right, definitely not your type."

"I wasn't referring to any of that, you asshole."

"But am I wrong?"

"No. You're not wrong. She is all of those things." *And more*, Lina thinks.

"Okay, fine. She's definitely not your type in that sense. Check that off the list. What does she look like?"

"Nothing like Barrows."

Caitlin laughs so hard she can't speak for at least a minute. "So she's *really* not your type."

"That's just it, Cait. She's not. She's—she's not, like, butch. Oh my God." Lina presses her hand against her forehead. "I can't explain it. She's not super feminine. She's kinda…middle of the road."

"Like Mallory?"

Lina pictures Mallory and Regan side by side. "Sort of. But different. More androgynous. Tomboyish." She blushes as a fragment of a memory floats back into her mind. Beneath her clothing, Regan's body is anything but androgynous.

"Are you trying not to say that Regan's not femme enough for you?"

"No," Lina says immediately. "Not at all. I think I thought that at first, maybe? But she's gorgeous, Cait. Sporty."

"Oooh. A sporty lesbian. Big fan of that. Send me a pic."

"I don't have one." She wishes she did.

Caitlin huffs. "Well, get one. Wait! Wow, Lina. So we're talking hot butch-on-butch action?"

"I just said she's not butch."

"Close enough! This sounds sexy. But do you actually expect me to believe that you give up control in bed?"

"Remind me when it was that you and I slept together? Exactly never. You have no idea what I'm like in bed."

"Oh. I'm suddenly very sorry I brought this up."

"Good timing, because I'm going to kindly ask you to hand over your phone to your girlfriend now."

"Cop-out." Caitlin yells for Mallory and hands off the phone.

"Hey! Wait a second. Okay, she's gone. How did it go? Is she pissed about the Regan thing?"

Lina feels calmer instantly. She loves Caitlin, but there's something about her friendship with Mallory that feels different in a wonderful, refreshing way. Mostly, it's that Mallory doesn't stress Lina out in the well-meaning way that Caitlin has a habit of doing.

"She took it pretty well."

"Good. And how are you taking it?"

"I'm trying to let it happen," Lina admits. "But it's not easy. I've never dated someone like Regan. I don't even know if we're dating. But still. She's so different."

"And that freaks you out?"

"Yes! I'm used to knowing what women want from me. With Regan, I don't know what she wants—or I have a sense, maybe, and it feels nothing like my past."

"Isn't that a good thing?"

Lina laughs. "Apparently. I still don't know what to do with it. With her. She just takes me as I am. What's the catch?"

"There is no catch, Lina."

"There has to be. There always is."

"Can I go out on a limb here?"

"Yeah, of course."

Mallory clears her throat and Lina fully expects to hear her "teacher voice" come through the phone. She smiles when she hears her assumption was correct. "Regan's different, and therefore confusing to you, because she actually cares about you. She's showing you that and you want to push it away because you're not used to it. You're comfortable with women who like to push and pull. Regan's not doing that, so again, you want to run because it's unfamiliar and uncomfortable."

"Jesus," Lina mutters.

"Shall I go on?"

"Yes. Please."

"Great. You've been with women who need you, Lina. But not in healthy ways. You gravitate toward women who need you to be the one steady, loyal thing in their lives, because everything else about their lives is unpredictable or unfulfilling. You've become comfortable with being the person who gives the support. You're the rock. And now you've run right into someone who can be everything you've spent your adult life being for other people, and you don't know what the hell to do with that."

Lina scans through her previous conversations with Mallory. There have been quite a few, even some that have gone deeper and more personal, but the way Mallory is seeing Lina right now still seems shocking. And shockingly accurate, she can admit. "Wait. How do you know all this about me?"

"I pay attention." Lina can hear Mallory's smile in the way her tone shifts out of her teacher voice. "Plus, Caitlin has told me a lot. I just put all the pieces together."

"I can't say you're wrong about any of that," Lina says. "I wish you were, though."

"Can I say one more thing?"

"No sense in stopping now."

Mallory laughs. "I know your big thing is that you feel like you don't deserve anyone good in your life, because you think you're damaged. Don't even try to argue with me, because I've heard you say it. It's time to let that go, Lina. Throw it out into the ocean. Don't let your past keep you from what sounds like an incredible present."

Lina leans her head against the chair and shakes her head. "I feel like you're saying all the things my therapist wants me to say for myself."

"Too much?"

"No. It's probably exactly what I needed."

"Good. Then go throw some old, burned-out feelings into the ocean. Or maybe just go kayak or something." Mallory laughs. "I'm not a therapist, I have no idea what you should do right now."

The non-therapy-therapy session is interrupted by Caitlin announcing that Mallory's phone time is up. Lina spends the next ten minutes getting updates about Caitlin's job and coworkers. She does her best to laugh at the right times, but Caitlin doesn't hesitate to point out a particularly funny story about Barb Brewster, famed colleague who has a massive crush on Lina, that Lina didn't seem to find humorous.

When she's finally off the phone, she realizes how much she misses having Caitlin and Mallory right next door. This TDY was necessary, as was the distance that came with it, but Lina is starting to feel flickers of missing home.

She glances at her phone, remembering that a text came in while she was talking. Sure enough, it's Regan, sending a simple and sweet message that sends a trickle of warmth through Lina's chest and into her heart. She taps out a response right away, and before she can second-guess herself, darts inside and throws on shorts and a T-shirt before grabbing her keys and jumping into her Jeep.

About fifteen minutes later, Lina pulls into the parking lot of OBX Hospital. Her heart is jumping excitedly in her chest, and she's not sure if it's from the anticipation of seeing Regan or the anxiety of making this kind of gesture. Either way, she accepts the feelings and walks into the hospital, heading straight for the ER.

It's a slow day with an empty waiting room, and the triage nurse greets Lina with a bright smile. "How can I help you?"

"I'm actually looking for one of your nurses. Regan Murphy. Is she available?"

The nurse's smile gets even wider. "She just might be. Let me page her."

Lina steps aside and waits, trying to calm herself in the process. She runs through every possible reaction Regan might have. She tries to focus on the positive ones.

Too soon and not soon enough, Regan pushes through the doors and walks right over to Lina. Her eyes are dancing with the smile that's hidden behind her mask.

"This is a nice surprise," she says, guiding Lina out into the lobby. "Got tired of lounging in the sun?"

"Nope, I'm actually enjoying my down time. But you said you were starving, so…" Lina holds up a paper bag with a turkey club from Publix; Regan mentioned them on their date, swearing up and down that no better turkey club exists.

"Is that what I think it is?" Regan grabs the bag and opens it, inhaling deeply. "Oh, it is." She looks up at Lina. "This is the best thing that's happened to me all day. Thank you so much."

Lina feels her cheeks flush. "It's not a big deal."

"Nope, don't do that." Regan pokes Lina's shoulder. "Don't downplay doing something random and wonderful for me. Just say 'you're welcome, Regan.'"

"You're welcome, Regan." Lina grins, feeling a second wind of confidence. "But truthfully, this was a selfish act."

Regan tilts her head and studies Lina. "Is that so?"

"Yes." Lina drops her voice. "I wanted to see you."

"Hmm. I like the sound of that." Regan pulls her mask down so Lina can see her full, wide smile. "You're off tomorrow, right?"

"Yeah, it's my last day off. Are you off?"

"I am." Regan grins. Lina marvels at the way her lips curve and how utterly kissable they are. "Can I have you for the day?"

Lina fumbles through several responses, some over-the-top flirty that she's used in the past, others that are too bold for Regan's straightforward question. In the end, she settles on: "Yes."

"Great. I'll pick you up at eleven. Wear something cute and comfortable."

"I can do that."

"I know you can." Regan lifts up her bag. "I have to go appreciate every single bite of this sandwich now. Thank you again. You truly made my day." She eyes Lina, silently coaching her response.

"It was my pleasure." On impulse, Lina reaches out and grabs Regan's hand, squeezing it twice before dropping it and walking out of the hospital.

CHAPTER TWENTY-THREE

Lina sits on the bottom step of the deck's stairway, poking absently at the screen of her phone. It's 10:58 a.m. She didn't want to wait for Regan inside—truthfully, Lina's not used to being the one who's picked up for dates—so she's biding her time on the step, trying to be casual in her waiting even though she's been sitting there for fifteen minutes.

Surprisingly, she had a nightmare-free night of sleep. That might be because she tossed and turned most of the night, distracted by a mixture of excitement and nervousness about the outing today. Letting Regan take control, even in such a minor way as planning a day for them to enjoy together, is something Lina has never done before with a woman. Perhaps that's because most of her previous relationships have been clandestine; she actually can't remember the last time she went on a real date with a woman. She's always been so certain that she would be the plan maker, the creator, the one in charge.

And yet, there's something about Regan that lets Lina slip into the back seat, and while she doesn't understand it, she's at least starting to like it.

A car pulls into the driveway at 11:00 on the dot. Lina looks up, and her eyes nearly pop out of her head. She stands and knows she's gaping, but she absolutely cannot help it.

From the driver's seat, Regan grins and waves as Lina, still stunned and enthralled, walks slowly toward her.

"You like?" Regan asks when Lina finally reaches the passenger side.

"Are you kidding me right now?" Lina runs her fingers over the body of the vehicle, touching it as though it's pure gold, which to her, it is. "Where did you find this?" She shoots Regan a sharp look. "Wait a minute. Have you had this all along and you've been hiding it from me?"

Regan laughs, her eyes shutting and her head dropping toward her chest. Lina feels the shuffle of warmth spreading through her body.

"No, it's not mine. It was my grandfather's originally, and now my dad shares it with my uncle. I pulled some strings to borrow it for the day. So," she says, grinning at Lina. "Do you like it?"

"It's incredible," Lina whispers, taking in the pristine Jeep CJ5. It's bright blue, a splash of color on the sandy driveway. She tours the outside of the vehicle, gawking at the unblemished surface. When she makes her way past the driver's seat, she stops and looks at Regan, who's watching her with an amused smile. Before Lina can second guess herself, she leans in and pulls Regan's head toward hers. The kiss starts sweet but deepens quickly, sparking a murmur of suppressed desire. Regan runs her fingers through Lina's hair, scratching gently as her touch drifts down toward Lina's shoulders.

Caught between wanting to take this kiss and this woman inside vs. going for a ride in this amazing Jeep, Lina pulls back, giving Regan a toothy grin.

"That was quite the kiss," Regan remarks, her fingers still light on Lina's shoulders. "I guess I should bring this baby around more often."

"That would be cool, but I don't want to make out with the Jeep." With a wink, Lina jogs around the front of the vehicle and launches herself into the passenger seat. "I believe I'm all yours for the day. Whatcha gonna do with me?"

A throaty laugh comes from Regan as she turns the ignition and the Jeep comes to life. "You'll have to wait and see. But first—milkshakes."

"Milkshakes?"

"Do you trust me?"

Lina stares at Regan, all too aware of the pleasurable tension flowing between them. Regan blinks at her, the picture of innocence.

"Yeah. I trust you."

"Excellent answer." She backs out of the driveway and slides her sunglasses down from where they were holding back her buoyant curls. "First stop: John's."

Little more than a minute passes before they pull into the tiny parking lot next to John's. Less than ten minutes after that, Regan has them on the road again and Lina is taking delicious sips of her chocolate mint shake.

"I can't believe," she says between sips, "that you went with plain vanilla. Is that some kind of clue about your personality?"

"Nope! I just really like vanilla, and when I find something I really like, I stick with it." Regan casts a not-so-surreptitious glance at Lina. "For the record, *I* can't believe you've been here since April and you haven't walked less than a mile to the best shake spot in town."

"There's a lot I haven't done." Lina looks out the side of the Jeep, watching people prepare for their short trek across the street to the beach.

"Then it's a good thing you're with me today. I plan on showing you some of the best places on the island."

"I'm all yours." Their eyes meet after the words echo through the car, cutting through the breeze and humid air to hover in their double meaning. Regan's slow smile illuminates dark, lonely parts of Lina's heart.

As they cruise down Beach Road, Regan points out some landmarks and houses that she favors. She points a steady finger when they pass American Pie, making Lina promise that they'll stop for ice cream another day.

"Okay, we're going to head all the way down to Hatteras, but we'll make a few stops on the way there and on the way back." Regan pulls into the parking lot of a gas station. "Now's your chance to grab any necessary drinks or snacks. And yes, this is a test." Regan smiles proudly and leans back in her seat, gesturing for Lina to run into the store.

The arctic blast of air conditioning smacks Lina in the face upon entry. She scans the aisles, mentally planning the best attack for acquiring refreshments. With practiced speed, she winds through the small store, grabbing her favorites (pretzels and red licorice), a couple protein bars for good measure (she doesn't know exactly how far away Hatteras is, but Regan made it sound like a journey, so it's best to be prepared), and a pack of gum. After collecting two bottles of water from the cooler, Lina doubles back and eyes up the rack of potato chips. She remembers Regan describing a very specific flavor and… Yes. There it is. Lina grabs a bag of spicy dill pickle flavor, tries not to gag, and heads toward the register.

At the last minute, she spies a king-sized KitKat bar and doesn't give herself time to second guess. She adds it to the pile, pays, then heads back to the glorious CJ5, which is sparkling in the sunshine.

The driver is also sparkling, but in a different way. Lina's pretty certain she's the only person who can see the way Regan radiates happiness and peace. As she gets comfortable in the passenger seat, she steals a couple glances at Regan.

"Whatcha lookin' at?" Regan asks as she pulls back onto the main road.

"You." Lina hesitates. "Don't laugh."

"Never."

"You have this…I don't know. An aura? I sound fucking ridiculous." Lina laughs nervously. "There's just something about the air around you. Okay, yeah, I'm going to stop because this sounds—"

"Amazing," Regan interjects, casting a quick look over at her passenger. "Tell me more."

"Seriously?"

"Yep. We've got lots of time." She turns onto NC-12 S and gestures with one hand toward the two-lane road. "And hardly any traffic. But you might have to yell because it gets kind of loud in here."

Lina wastes some time by watching the scenery blur past as Regan picks up speed. It's not that she doesn't want to keep talking, she's just terrified about what might slip from her lips. Eventually, the silence wears thin.

"You're not like anyone I've ever known before. I hate how cliché that sounds, but it's true." Lina wipes her palms on her shorts. "You have this calmness that just kind of…comes with you everywhere you go. It's soothing."

"Say more."

Lina rolls her eyes. "That wasn't enough for you?"

Regan reaches over and rests her hand on Lina's knee. Lina stares at her hand for several seconds before slowly slipping her fingers through Regan's. The simple touch, delicate and assured, settles Lina's nerves.

"That," she says, pointing at their intertwined hands with her free hand. "That's what I'm talking about. How do you do that?"

"How do I hold your hand?" Regan's voice is teasing, and Lina rolls her eyes again.

"Are you enjoying making this harder for me?"

"Kind of." Regan squeezes Lina's hand. "Just tell me what you're feeling."

"That's a loaded statement."

"It doesn't have to be, Lina."

She's right, of course, and Lina takes a mental step backward. The startling simplicity of the connection she feels with Regan has been there since the moment she first saw her, and while she can feel it evolving into something bigger and more important, that original "this person is significant to me" feeling persists.

"You calm me down. I didn't even think it was possible to experience that with someone. But you have this way of making everything seem quieter. Even if my brain can't respond to it, my body knows what to do." Lina shakes her head and keeps her eyes focused on the passing sand dunes. "Usually people ramp me up. But not you."

Regan's quiet for a moment, seeming to take in Lina's words. Eventually, she says, "You know what I really like about you?"

"No, I honestly don't."

She laughs as she squeezes Lina's hand again. "You're real, Lina. You are one hundred percent who you are, and I don't think there's been a moment since I met you that you've tried to hide yourself from me."

"I've wanted to."

"Oh, I know. I can tell. But there's something about this"— she releases Lina's hand for a moment to gesture to the space between them—"that keeps you from hiding."

Lina rests her head against the headrest and loses herself in Regan's words. Part of her is scrambling to analyze the meaning behind it all, but another, usually quieter part, is pushing that analyst down, telling it to kindly shut the fuck up for five seconds. The silence between them is comfortable; it stretches along with the miles, their hands still clasped together.

"Ready to explore some wildlife?" Regan finally asks as she slows and turns off NC-12.

"Absolutely. Where are we?"

"Pea Island. We're going to check out the Salt Flats Trail, but I want to come back another time, later in the day, and bring you kayaking out here." Regan bites her lower lip. "If you want, I mean."

"I want."

The smile that blossoms over Regan's face sends sparks shooting in all directions within Lina. She decides, in that very moment, that her new main goal in life is to make that smile happen as many times as possible.

The Salt Flats Trail is a little rugged, but Lina loves every moment of it. Regan points out various shorebirds, and Lina watches her eyes light up when she finds a cluster of blue crabs scuttling across the sand. When they reach a particularly secluded area, Lina grabs Regan's hand and pulls her back.

"This is incredible," she says, pushing Regan's sunglasses up so she can see her eyes. "Thank you for bringing me here."

"The day has just begun, ba—" Regan cuts herself off, flustered.

Lina leans in and presses her lips against Regan's, picking up that heated kiss from the driveway. Regan steps forward, closing the space between them, and Lina wraps her arms around Regan's waist, pulling her as close as possible. The humidity surrounding them pales in comparison to the heat rising from their kiss.

Time passes—Lina has no idea how much, and she could care less because kissing Regan is sensational—and Regan is the one to break the kiss. She playfully shoves Lina back.

"Do not distract me from the incredible agenda I have planned for us."

Lina offers her a cocky grin. "I wouldn't dream of it. Lead on, tour guide."

* * *

Down in Hatteras, Regan takes Lina to the lighthouse, and like good tourists, they pay admission and take the tour. The views are beautiful, a hallmark of the Outer Banks. Lina could happily continue staring at the lush landscape leading to the ocean, but Regan has other ideas, and pulls her back to the CJ5. She promises it'll be worth it.

"You ready?" she asks, a glimmer of excitement in her eyes.

"I've been ready all day." Lina dangles the bag of spicy dill pickle chips from her fingers. "But are you ready for this?"

"Oh my God!" Regan snatches the chips. "You remembered?"

"I know my memory sucks for some things, but other things, I never forget."

Regan's expression changes into something far less enthusiastic, and Lina would give anything to take back her words. Since that's impossible, she tries the next best thing.

"I do remember some of that night, you know."

A nod, but Regan won't meet her eyes. "Yeah, I get it, it's fine."

"It's not fine." Lina twists in her seat and touches Regan's chin, guiding her to look up. "I can't promise it won't happen again, but I *can* promise that I won't have sex with you when I'm in a fucked-up mental place."

Regan lets out something like a laugh-sigh. "Okay."

Lina bites the inside of her cheek. She has no idea how to make this right, so she chooses to let out the truth and see how Regan takes it.

"I told my therapist about what happened. She said it's actually pretty normal, and she's surprised it hasn't happened to me before. I mean, it has, but not in that context. It's kinda like what I was telling you earlier, how you're different, and I feel so differently with you. Things are happening to me that I've never experienced before."

"Is that bad, though? Like, did I make it happen?"

"Regan, no. Not at all." Lina leans forward, trying to close the distance between them. "It happened because the fireworks took me to a really shitty place. And then you were there, and I wanted to be close to you, but my brain had other ideas. You didn't make it happen. My bitch-ass brain did."

There, a laugh. A small one, but it counts. Lina breathes a sigh of relief.

"Will it happen every time? Assuming *that* happens again?"

Lina lifts one side of her mouth. "Are you asking me if I want to have sex with you again?"

"What? No. Yes? Okay this just got awkward."

"Regan. I very much want to have sex with you again." Lina watches a blush spread over Regan's rounded cheeks. "If you want to, that is."

Those deep, shimmering blue eyes finally settle on Lina. "Oh, I do."

"Even with the possibility that I might dissociate during it?"

Regan nods. "Fancy word, but yes. Even with that possibility. At least now I think I'll be able to recognize it happening, so that helps."

"See?" Lina says, running her fingers over Regan's still heated cheek. "That's how you're different."

"I care, Lina. I care about you. And if that's what makes me so different from your past, then I officially hate your past."

They stare at each other, taking in the gentle shifts between them. After she leans over for a quick kiss, the devious glimmer returns to Regan's eyes.

"Now. I asked you if you're ready like ten minutes ago. Are you still ready?"

Lina lets her eyes linger on the sloping lines of Regan's face. She wants to wind her fingers through her blond waves. She wants to brush her lips over every centimeter of Regan's mouth and trace kisses over her jaw. She wants to—yes, she wants to do so, so much more.

But for now, she wants to see that smile on Regan's face.

"I'm so ready."

CHAPTER TWENTY-FOUR

Lina pushes the newly labeled samples further down her table and suppresses a yawn. She slept like a rock last night, but being here, at work, staring at blood and urine samples can't compare to the excitement of being around Regan. And truthfully, she's still riding high from yesterday. Being with Regan is new, fresh, unknown—surprising at every turn. *Regan* is surprising at every turn, and Lina finds herself leaning into it rather than fighting an urge to run away. She still can't put her finger on it, but whatever it is about Regan that makes her so unlike anyone Lina has ever known is quite possibly the most magical thing Lina has ever encountered.

The memories of the previous day are bright, outlined with sunshine and salty air. After touring the Hatteras lighthouse, Regan drove them to a secluded beach and, to Lina's utter delight, let her drive the CJ5 on the sand. Lina was sure her face was going to crack in half due to the size and stretch of her smile. The wind had kicked up, and as they rolled along the beach, Lina sucked in as much clean ocean air as she could, feeling tiny latches unlock inside of her with each breath. By the time Regan convinced her they needed to head back, Lina's limbs were loosened, unburdened. She helped Regan prep the CJ5 for getting back on the road, then, surprising them both, caught her in a long, passionate kiss that would have led them directly to a bed had there been one nearby.

After a casual dinner down at Art's Place, Regan dropped Lina off in her driveway. They stared at each other, neither seeming to want to break the beauty of the day or push it past its precarious limits. Lina wanted to take Regan inside; she wanted to show her exactly what she was feeling and how strongly she was feeling it, but she was also scared shitless that she was going to fade out and disappear. She didn't want to do that to Regan, and she wasn't sure she could handle it if she did. So, after a somewhat chaste kiss in comparison to the long, thorough kisses of the day, Lina went inside by herself.

She regrets that decision. A lot.

Lina grits her teeth and scans the lab. She usually enjoys work, but this is the last place she wants to be today. She cannot get Regan out of her mind, and while that's not a bad thing, it is highly distracting and definitely not helpful when Lina's trying to focus on work. She also knows Regan is off today, so there's no chance she'll randomly run into her, which takes the spark out of the workday.

She tells the other lab tech that she's taking a short break. Once she's in the hallway, she takes out her phone and sends a text to Mallory.

I think I'm falling for her.

Lina stares at the bubble of sent words. Did she really type that? She continues to stare in disbelief until Mallory's response comes flying in.

I KNEW IT.

Lina snorts, watching the dots float on her phone.

Do not run from her, Lina. Don't do it. Promise me.

Lina taps out a quick reply before heading for the bathroom across the hall.

I can't promise but I know that I don't want to run.

The bathroom, as always, is weirdly warm in comparison to the cool, sterile atmosphere of the rest of the hospital. Lina feels sweat dimpling her upper lip as she walks into an empty stall.

Chatter surrounds her as she sits down. Usually this bathroom is empty, but today it seems to be the popular hangout spot. Lina half-listens to the conversation filling the room.

"So is he going to be okay?"

"I don't know," a woman says. Her voice gives away her distress. "My parents haven't heard from his captain today. I keep replaying the conversation in my head, trying to find an answer."

"I'm sure he's going to be fine. Don't let yourself think otherwise."

"How can I not, Gina? He was right there! The bomb went off forty feet in front of him! He's obviously not okay."

Lina inhales sharply and presses her hand against the wall of the stall.

"Okay, okay. I hear you. But forty feet away is better than being right there, in the place where it went off. Right?"

The woman's voice trembles when she speaks. "You don't get it. You never do."

"I'm sorry, I—"

"My brother was in the exact place where a suicide bomber decided to off himself. My brother, who is serving this country. You never understand, Gina."

The bathroom door bangs as someone leaves, either Gina or the other nurse. Lina doesn't know, and she's not sure if the silence is because both women have left, or because her brain has been shrouded in dense, black fog.

* * *

Afghanistan, three years ago

Lina looked up from her notebook to watch Brit pace the tiny space between their beds. She was half-dressed, a sight Lina was normally stoked to see, but today, Lina just wanted Brit to put her clothes on.

She was certain Brit hadn't noticed, but Lina was well aware that things between them had shifted in the wake of Candice Barrows's return to base. While Brit was even more interested in having sex with Lina, Lina felt herself fading into the background, sometimes even just going through the motions to make Brit happy—or at least satisfied. She wasn't as obsessed about the outcome of their pseudo-relationship. She was wasting far less time daydreaming about how they'd manage a long-distance relationship once this deployment ended.

Instead, Lina's thoughts had become wholly consumed with Candice: when she would see her, what Candice might say to her, if they might possibly find themselves alone in a situation where—

"Stop," Lina said, realizing too late she'd said it out loud.

Brit stopped her pacing and angled her head toward Lina. "You know I need to do this in order to get mentally ready to face a mission."

"Yeah, yeah, I know. Sorry. I was talking to myself."

This earned Lina a sweet but cocky grin from Brit, who paced her way over to Lina and pressed her hands on her thighs. "Talking to yourself? Better knock that off, Latch. We don't want anyone thinking you're losing it."

Lina searched Brit's face, looking for some emotion to connect to. As usual, she was met with an unreadable expression that only shifted, and barely, in the cloak of night. On impulse and still searching, Lina leaned in and kissed Brit, who immediately stepped back, eyes wild.

"What the fuck are you thinking?"

Right. It was the middle of the day. Anyone could saunter into their room at any time. Lina knew the risks, and then some.

"Sorry," she mumbled, pushing off the bed.

Brit caught her arm and held her in place. "What's up with you lately?"

Lina kept her eyes focused on the floor. She rummaged through the myriad thoughts and feelings tumbling inside of her and pulled out one that needed to see the light.

"Why are we doing this?"

The air shifted immediately. Brit dropped her hand from Lina's arm and took two steps back. "You want to have this conversation now, Latch? Really? You have the worst timing."

"There's no good time to have this conversation, *Lock*. So let's just have it."

Brit blinked, probably caught off guard by Lina's uncharacteristic response to her predictable avoidance. "Okay. Fine. You know I can't give you what you want."

Sure, Lina knew. And sometimes she cared, sometimes she didn't. Brit was like a drug—Lina kept coming back for more temporary moments of pleasure while knowing the caustic risks of partaking. And yet, there were all of those words Brit liked to dangle in front of Lina, bait to keep her hooked.

"Are you even willing to try?" Lina cringed internally at the slight whine in her tone.

"You make me want to try." And there it was, the trademarked Brit-response. "But we both know I'll end up hurting you." Paired with another hammer hit, also predictable. "Can't we just have fun while we're here and not worry about what happens next?"

It wasn't atypical, this kind of perspective coming from another soldier. There were so many unknowns—deployments, TDYs, location assignments, injury, death—that the urge to live for the now was hard to avoid.

"I don't want you to go," Lina blurted, surprising herself.

Brit shook her head. "I don't have a choice. And it'll be fine. It's just another mission."

Lina slumped back onto her bed. "You keep volunteering, Brit. You do have a choice."

"It might seem that way to you, but it doesn't to me. This is part of my job. I have a responsibility to go on these missions. Besides, this one's only for a week." She grinned at Lina. "Think about how much I'm going to want you when I get back."

Her words stirred Lina's arousal and she reached for Brit, who walked into her arms. Hugging was usually safe during the day, but Lina knew Brit's internal timer was already ticking.

"Stay with me," she mumbled into Brit's chest. "Just this once."

"I can't." Brit gave Lina a final squeeze before pulling away and returning to her side of the room to finish checking her gear. "Not this time."

* * *

Several hours later, Lina joined a group of soldiers heading off base to venture into one of the nearby towns. Lina didn't normally go off base—it freaked her out—but she needed a break from her overlapping thoughts. Plus, Brit had disappeared, promising to be back by 2100 hours so they could spend the night together before she left the next morning at 0500. The distraction seemed perfect.

Actually being off base wasn't as great as it had sounded in Lina's head. It was *not* a distraction or a break; there were too many civilians making too much noise. She couldn't stop scanning the area. When she heard a man whistle loudly, she whipped her entire body around so fast that she collided with another soldier.

"Damn, Ragelis. Chill out." The soldier nudged her, and they continued walking.

But Lina couldn't chill out. She was on high alert the entire time, and the amount of relief that filled her upon returning to base was palpable.

She was so relieved that she let her guard down, slightly, and hung around near the entrance to base, chatting with the soldiers she'd just spent an hour ignoring. They were all so caught up in their jokes and banter that none of them noticed the growing crowd across the street.

Out of the corner of her eye, Lina saw a group of soldiers jogging from the base entrance to the other side of the road. She clocked their movements, wondering what was happening, but returned to the conversation in her group. Something pulled her attention away a second time, and it was then that she noticed the familiar head of red hair bobbing across the street.

What happened next was fast, loud, and chaotic. The blast of the suicide bombers came with shrieking and screaming. The air filled instantly with panic and thick smoke. Lina wiped at the air in front of her, trying to find a way to get across the street. She was distantly aware of her fellow soldiers springing into action. Her feet, however, were cemented into the ground.

Brit. She gasped, her lungs filling with acrid smoke, burning flesh. *Move.* She tried again to lift her leg and was dumbfounded by the amount of weight holding her down. *You have to get to Brit.* She cried out, a guttural, animal-like sound. She needed to move.

Another soldier sprinted past her, yelling commands. Lina grabbed at her hips, her chest. She was weaponless. How was that possible? She was never without a weapon. Wait, yes. She patted her cargo pocket. Her knife.

More time wasted away as Lina wondered how she would face this terrible and terrifying—not to mention incredibly dangerous—situation with her fucking knife. Was she going to slash away the smoke? Stab the already dead suicide bombers?

Run, her internal voice commanded, and with it, the shackles released. Lina took a tentative step forward, finding movement possible, and gritted her teeth. Just as she was about to haul ass across the street, a firm hand grabbed her arm and yanked her backward.

"Lina." That couldn't be right. What was that voice doing so close to her?

"Lina," it repeated, louder and stronger. "You're safe."

* * *

The trembling is what brings Lina back. She blinks, trying to make sense of her surroundings. She's hot, way too hot, and yet her ass is frozen. And her head, oh my God, her head is pounding in a way that cannot be healthy.

A tentative touch to the floor reveals that there's tile beneath her. And it's cold to the touch, explaining the glacial status of her butt. She looks to her left and comes face to face with a standard toilet. Okay, yes. She's in a bathroom. Check.

Lina struggles to her feet, moving too quickly so she has to take a break halfway through rising to shut her eyes against the rush of blood to her head. Once she's completely upright, she shakes out her limbs, trying to get the trembling to subside. It refuses.

With a shaky breath, Lina opens the stall door and peers into the greater part of the bathroom. Miraculously, she appears to be alone. She has no idea how long she spent curled in an upright fetal position on the floor in the stall where she last remembers emptying her bladder and listening to—

Oh. The memory clicks in. Lina feels her body taking up a new, heightened tempo of shaking. *Don't*, she thinks. *Don't remember.*

She forces herself to the sinks, and after washing her hands, throws several handfuls of icy water into her face. The sensation brings back enough of her common sense to help her out of the bathroom. Instead of returning to the lab, Lina hightails it out of the hospital, not stopping until she's in the safety of her Jeep.

There, and before she so much as puts her key in the ignition, she calls her therapist. Carolyn doesn't answer—she's probably tending to another client—so Lina leaves a message.

"Hi. It's Lina. Can you please call me back? I don't know what just happened to me." She hears the frantic sound of her own voice and shudders. "It wasn't like before. I don't know what to do. I—" Lina hesitates. She can feel tears, real tears, building behind her eyelids. "The bombing. It all came back to me. Please call me back."

Against every noise of good judgment in her body, Lina starts her Jeep and begins the drive back to Kitty Hawk.

CHAPTER TWENTY-FIVE

She's not sure how long she's been crying, but the pile of used tissues next to the bed indicates quite a bit. The tears won't stop. They're on a mission of their own, undeterred by Lina's chastisement, her attempts at distraction, even her emergency session with Carolyn. She swore she'd never cry in front of her therapist, yet there she sat, crying for approximately fifty minutes of the hour-long session.

With Carolyn's patient guidance, Lina's been able to put together the horrific memories of the suicide bombing that took place during her last deployment. It's not that she didn't remember that it happened—how could she forget?—it's more that she didn't *want* to remember, and by pushing the memories down, she put her nervous system into a state of suppressed panic. All along she thought it would be better to shift and avoid, when apparently she's needed to face and digest.

She hates it. She truly hates it.

Lina rolls onto her stomach and buries her face in her pillow. These are the feelings she's been trying to hold at bay, and now that they're here, she feels suffocated by them. The regret, the sense of failure, the fractured responsibility, the astoundingly painful sensation of not having done enough—one feeling would be enough, but when all of them arrived at once, it's no wonder she broke down the way that she did.

She turns her head so she can look out the window. The dazzling blue of the sky reminds her of Regan's eyes, and she realizes she misses her. Acutely. Lina lies still, staring out the window, wishing she could erase every ounce of pain from her body.

She's startled by the sound of a knock. As she continues to stare at the brilliant sky, she hears a second knock, this one louder and more insistent. Lina closes her eyes, hoping the knocker will take the hint and go away, but a third knock comes, and along with it, the sound of her name in a newly familiar voice.

"Lina. I know you're home. Come answer the door."

Lina pushes herself off the bed and trudges through the house. She might recommend to the homeowner that he get a soundproof door.

When she opens the door, she finds Regan, just as she expected. But what she didn't expect was the immediate response of her body and the release of yet another round of tears.

Lina's hands fly to her face, trying to put a barrier between her vulnerability and Regan, but Regan gently grabs her hands and pulls them down. She searches Lina's face, her expression calm and kind. Then she puts her arms around Lina's shoulders and tugs her closer, holding her tightly.

"Don't disappear on me," Regan says.

Lina hiccups in response.

"I mean it, Lina."

"I didn't mean to," she says, pulling away slightly to scrub her hands over her wet face. "I just—I didn't want you to have to see me like this."

Regan doesn't say anything. She pushes Lina's hair off her face, then cups her cheek. Lina leans into the touch despite the fact that she feels like a soggy mess.

"Can I come in?" Regan finally asks, a note of humor in her voice.

"I mean, since you're here…" Lina tries to smile. She closes the door behind Regan, then goes to sit next to her on the sofa. She lets her instincts take over and rests her head on Regan's shoulder.

"You do realize you've been missing in action for four days, correct?"

Lina closes her eyes. "Honestly, no. I didn't know it had been that long."

"Yup. Four long days. I was about to completely freak out when Erin kindly reminded me that I know where you live."

"She's a good friend."

Regan laughs, and Lina's head bobs with the shake of her shoulders. "She's all right." They sit together for some time, Regan's arm wrapped tightly around Lina's waist. Eventually, she asks, "Will you tell me what happened?"

Lina lets the silence reclaim its presence as an answer. It's not that she doesn't want to tell Regan. Well, okay, maybe she doesn't want to. Or she does, but she's afraid to. Nervous. Worried it will change the way Regan sees her, and, shit, Regan already knows she's damaged—broken—difficult—going through some challenging things, whatever, but it's still—

"Lina," Regan says gently, breaking through the hailstorm of Lina's worrying. "You don't have to. But know that you can."

"It's a lot." Lina clears her throat. "But basically, I blacked out while I was at work and then I had a bunch of old memories come up and…they're a lot to take in."

"That's a good start."

Lina tries to laugh, but the sound comes out cracked and hoarse. "I don't want you to see me differently."

"Oh, Lina. You can't control how I see you, and neither can your past. Haven't you figured that out yet?" Regan sits up and turns so she's facing Lina. "But for the record, I see you as an incredible, strong, determined woman. I know you have faults. And I know you think you're broken." She strokes her thumb over Lina's jaw. "But you are so much more than the things that hold you back."

Lina swallows back the fresh bout of tears that are threatening to reveal themselves. "I don't deserve you."

"Maybe you don't. Maybe you do." Regan shrugs. "I think you do, and what I say goes, and that's that."

The urge to kiss Regan is powerful, but Lina's too preoccupied by the teary, blotchy state of her face and the fact that she's not quite sure when she last brushed her teeth.

She clears her throat again, hoping a strong voice will help her be courageous. "You really want to know? The weight I carry?"

Regan nods. "I do. But only if you want to tell me."

It isn't easy, walking Regan through the ins and outs of Lina's relationship with Brit. But she does it. She explains how they met, how they first hooked up, how their connection was fragile and seemingly dependent on their proximity to one another. Explaining Syria isn't too bad, but the moment Lina utters the word "Afghanistan," she feels her throat start to close up.

Regan's hand on her thigh brings her back into the present. "Do you want to stop for now?"

Lina leans against the sofa cushions and reaches for Regan's hand. "Yeah, of course I do. But I also want to just get through it, get it all out."

She plows back in, recounting the way she and Brit reunited in Afghanistan. She purposely avoids any mention of Candice because that story simply doesn't need to be told (yet, or ever, she's not sure). Lina details her own confusion about what was going on between her and Brit, and she dovetails right into that final conversation before Brit was to leave for her mission.

"We weren't fighting. It was just a discussion, but she never wanted to have that specific conversation—she refused to actually *talk* to me about where our relationship was going. I assume that's because in her head, it was going nowhere." Lina stares at the ceiling. "I really didn't want her to go on that mission. I had a weird feeling about it. But she'd made up her mind, and I knew she couldn't back out. So she packed up and told me she'd be back in our room at 2100 hours so we could—" Lina breaks off and her face heats up. "Is this weird? Me talking about being with another woman?"

To Lina's surprise, Regan laughs. "I've never been under the impression that you're a virgin."

Lina fake-gasps. "That sounds like you think I'm a slut."

"No, not at all. But I'd be kidding myself to think that you haven't been with women before me." Regan raises her eyebrows. "You do know I've had sex before you, right?"

"Obviously." Lina doesn't love knowing that, but Regan's gorgeous, unbelievably kind, and two years older than Lina, a little fact that Lina secretly loves. Anyway, it's not like she's been saving herself for Lina.

"Anyway, enough about our promiscuous pasts. I knew Brit would want to, uh, be together that night."

Regan wiggles her eyebrows, and Lina rolls her eyes.

"She took off, and I was in my head about her not wanting to have that damn conversation, so I went off base with some other soldiers, which, for the record, I rarely did. It always freaked me out." Ironic, Lina thinks, that the real danger was much closer to home. "When we got back, we were hanging out close to the entrance of base. I remember seeing Brit cross the street, and I should have—I wish I had paid more attention to that. It was weird. It didn't make sense."

Lina keeps her tight hold on Regan's hand. "It happened really fast. The suicide bombers. They just showed up, did their thing, and threw us all into chaos. And I lost every ounce of my military training. I couldn't move. I couldn't do anything. I stayed right there while one of my best friends died, just fifty feet from me."

The silence arrives again, broken only by the wind carrying voices and squawks from seagulls through the open windows leading to the deck. Lina feels Regan stroking her hand and she's thankful for the small touch that's keeping her grounded in the present.

"It's not your fault, Lina."

They're familiar words, but they sound different coming from Regan. Lina nods.

"Thank you for telling me," Regan adds. "For trusting me."

"I do trust you."

"I know. And I'm really, really grateful for that."

Lina turns so she's looking at Regan. She was worried she'd find worry, panic, disgust, annoyance—anything bad, really. But instead, it's just Regan smiling at her, nothing but familiar kindness and warmth shining from her eyes.

"Can I ask you something?"

"Yeah, of course."

Regan drops her voice to a whisper. "When's the last time you showered?"

Lina laughs. "I don't want to answer that." Her hand flies to her mouth. "Don't ask me when I last brushed my teeth."

"Okay, here's an idea. You ready?"

"Always."

Something shifts in Regan's expression, and Lina takes it in and holds it tight. "You shower, brush your teeth, get dressed. And then we'll go catch the best part of the golden hour in the best place to catch it. Deal?"

"One question."

"Go."

"Will you kiss me after I brush my teeth?"

Regan grins. "You're not going to be able to *stop* me from kissing you after you brush your teeth. So get a move on it."

* * *

By the time Regan and Lina get to Jockey's Ridge, the brilliance of the day has started to give in to the promise of a stunning sunset. Lina's excited to share another memory with Regan, in this magical place where she found her, until she catches sight of what Jockey's Ridge is.

"Are you serious?" She throws her hands against her hips and gives her best menacing look to Regan.

"Oh, totally. Look." Regan points, and Lina follows her finger. "See all those people? They know what's up."

"Who in their right mind would voluntarily climb a gigantic sand dune?"

"More people than you'd want to believe." Regan tugs on Lina's hand. "Let's go. I'm not going to miss the sunset, and neither are you."

The trek itself isn't too bad, but Lina hates every grain of sand she climbs over. Regan fills the walk with chatter about her family, which ends up being a useful and interesting distraction.

"I told my mom it was a terrible idea to put the twins in sailing lessons, but she's determined to make them into these bratty, yuppy little jerks. It's working."

"Wait a minute. I didn't know you had siblings."

"Oh, well, they're miniature monsters. Except for the youngest. She reminds me a lot of myself as a kid. The other two, though? I refuse to take genealogical ownership over them."

"That sounds like something my best friend would say." Lina smiles against the pang of missing Caitlin.

"Yeah? Well maybe you'll introduce us someday." Regan casts a quick look at Lina before refocusing on the sandy incline they're ascending.

"She'd like that." Lina reaches for Regan's hand. "I would, too."

Regan goes silent for a stretch of steps before saying, "I really like you, Lina. Like, a lot. Just so you know."

Lina stops and tugs Regan back to her so their noses are touching. "Good. I really like you a lot, too."

"Hmm." Regan sniffs. "You brushed your teeth." She glances at the sky. "But we're limited on time, and I will not let your mind-blowing kisses make us miss the sunset." She gives Lina a quick, not entirely innocent kiss before pulling her back into their climb.

A few minutes later, Regan announces they've arrived. Lina looks around at the groups of people, then turns her gaze to where the sky dips down to meet the bay. It's a beautiful sight, one she might have missed entirely if Regan hadn't come into her life.

Regan rolls out the blanket she brought, sits down, and pats the space next to her.

"Now we wait," she announces once Lina's seated next to her.

They don't have to wait for long. The sun is already starting to fade out, leaving the sky painted in cotton-candy pinks and sherbet oranges.

"Tell me more about your family," Lina says, keeping her eyes on the sky.

"There's not a whole lot to tell. My mom remarried Dirk, who isn't as big of a tool as his name implies. I'm not a huge fan, though. They have three kids, one boy and two girls. The twins are Farrah and Jeter, and yes, I'm serious. Opal came as a surprise for my mom's forty-second birthday. She's pretty cool, but she's still young."

"Wait a minute. How old is your mom?"

"Oh, that." Regan laughs. "My parents had me when they were sixteen. So they're fifty-four now. Dirk is a younger man, much to my dad's disliking. Opal is twelve, and the twins are sixteen."

"I'm gonna need to know how old Dirk is."

"It's scandalous, so brace yourself. He's thirty-eight."

Lina takes a couple seconds to regroup before blurting, "He's the same age as you?"

"Gross, right?" Regan smirks. "They're happy, so whatever."

"And your dad? Did he remarry?"

"Nope, he's a lone wolf, and he seems to like it that way. He and my uncle live next door to each other. I'm much closer to them than I am to my mom."

Lina peels her eyes from the sky to look at Regan. There's so much more to learn about her, and Lina smiles, feeling the excitement stirring inside of her. She wants to know everything there is to know about this woman.

"Stop staring at me," Regan whispers. "We're at the height of the golden hour, Lina, and I don't want you to miss a thing."

Though it pains her to do so, Lina moves her gaze from Regan back to the sky, which truly is astounding. They sit in familiar, gentle silence as they watch the sun paint deliriously beautiful designs across the sky. As the sun sinks, people around them erupt into cheers and applause, but Regan and Lina sit silently, safe in their bubble of excitement and wonder.

Finally, Regan pulls Lina to her feet and before she picks up the blanket, she pulls Lina close and kisses her slowly and thoroughly. Lina grabs on to the buzzing that's circulating every inch of her body and melts into the kiss, wondering where the hell Regan came from and why it took her so long to get here.

"Lina," Regan says, her voice a quiet hum. "You can't punish yourself forever, especially for something that you had no control over."

The buzzing subsides just a bit as Lina rolls Regan's words through her mind. They coat her brain like a well-worn winter blanket, quieting the constant noise. Lina leans her forehead against Regan's, unable to find words that could possibly explain what she feels.

CHAPTER TWENTY-SIX

Fort Bragg, present day

Everything seems different at Womack now. The sounds, the smells, the sights: Lina feels like an intruder, like she's finally seeing the place for what it actually is, but she's not even supposed to be there to take it in. It's only been thirty-six hours since she left the sanctity of her borrowed home in Kitty Hawk, but she can already feel the difference in herself. And she doesn't like it.

A group of lab technicians huddle around a computer screen behind Lina. She can hear pieces of their conversation, not enough to get a grasp on what they're discussing, but the animation of their voices suggests some groundbreaking discovery. Lina snorts. More likely they've discovered traces of drugs in a blood sample and can't wait to burst someone's bubble.

She scratches the back of her neck. The panicky feeling she'd just started to shed in Kitty Hawk has come back, not quite full force, but strong enough to make her uncomfortable. She's sure it's due to the sudden change in schedule—the orders came abruptly and without fanfare—along with the change in location.

Two weeks. Lina breathes steadily, repeating the words in her head. *Two. Weeks.* That's all she has to get through before she can hightail it back to Kitty Hawk. They put her up in a hotel that's perfectly fine, but she misses the ocean views.

She misses Regan.

Lina sits up straight, the thought jolting her. She has to call Regan as soon as she leaves work today. Lina's been vague in her texts, but it feels gross, like she's hiding something. That thought is quickly overlapped by an aimless idea of trying to go back to Kitty Hawk for the weekend. And *that* thought is cleanly interrupted by a manicured hand landing on the lab table, directly in Lina's line of vision.

Bold red nails tap, then inch toward Lina's arm. She stares at the progression and pulls her hand away before contact can be made.

"I was wondering when I'd see you again."

The voice that briefly had an atomic effect on Lina now falls flat, listless, against her eardrums. Lina looks up into Luciana Alvarez's coppery eyes and feels nothing. She straightens her shoulders, a surge of pride making its way through her body.

"I got reassigned," Lina says with a friendly smile. "How have you been?"

If Luciana is surprised by Lina's distinctly non-flirtatious communication, she doesn't show it. Or perhaps she simply doesn't care.

"Lonely," she remarks with a slow wink. "How long do I have you for?"

The words chafe against Lina's pride. She wonders, briefly, if Candice was like this, too—overt about Lina's specific value to her. She pushes that thought down. Candice was different. Luciana is in a class all her own.

"I'm here for two weeks," she says, choosing her words deliberately.

"Hmm." Luciana splays her fingers on the silver table then sweeps her hand closer to Lina, who immediately leans back. "Did you get coy while you were away?"

"Hardly." Lina stands to put more distance between them. "It's nice to see you, Dr. Alvarez, but I have work to do. Maybe we can catch up later." She winces, worrying Luciana will read into that.

Too late. Lina watches as Luciana's eyes light up. "I'll hold you to that," she nearly whispers before turning and walking out of the lab. Her hips have extra swing in them.

Lina shakes her head, wondering how the hell she keeps getting herself into situations like this.

* * *

"So you got reassigned to Fort Bragg, and you didn't think to tell me this until you've already been there for two days?"

Hearing it out loud makes it even worse than it's been sounding in Lina's head. She rubs the back of her neck and stares down at her phone, willing Regan to understand.

"Lina…" Regan's voice crackles a bit through the speaker. "I thought we agreed you wouldn't disappear on me."

"I didn't disappear. Well, okay. I kind of did."

"Not kind of. You totally did."

"But it was out of my control," Lina points out.

"The orders? Yeah, I get that. But actively deciding not to tell me until you've already been there, again, for *two* days? That's a choice."

"I'm sorry." Lina hesitates. She knows what she wants to say, but she's not sure her mouth will cooperate with her. "I—I'm not used to this."

Regan is quiet. If Lina strains, she thinks she can hear her breathing. She leans toward the whispers of the sound. "I'm listening," Regan finally says.

Lina nods even though Regan can't see her. "You know I'm really close to Caitlin, right?"

"Yes."

"Okay. She's the only person in my life who keeps tabs on me. No one else checks in, or wants to know where I am or what I'm doing. Or, I guess, *how* I'm doing. It's been a long time since I had someone in my life other than Caitlin who I have to answer to."

"Whoa," Regan says immediately. "You don't have to answer to me."

"No, I know, that came out wrong. I'm not sure how to say it."

"Can I try?"

"Please."

Regan clears her throat. Lina pictures her in her scrubs, standing in one of the many hallways of OBX Hospital. In the middle of Regan's workday isn't the best time to communicate, but the longer Lina put it off, the worse she felt.

"You're not used to having someone care about you. I mean, yes, Caitlin cares about you. But in a different way than I do."

Lina leans over the round glass table in the corner of her bland hotel room. She slides her arm out and rests her head on her arm. Antsy, she pokes the side of her phone. "Yes."

Regan laughs. "That's your response? 'Yes'?"

"Well, you're right. It is different."

"Can I go out on a limb here? Just say what I'm thinking?"

"Of course," Lina says, sitting up. "Please."

"I know we haven't defined anything between us, and I'm okay with that. If that time comes, we'll get there together. But, Lina, I've told you how I feel about you. In case you forgot, I'll remind you: I really like you. I care about you. And additionally, I want to know that you're okay. I don't need you to tell me your every move, but if you have to suddenly go to another part of the state for two weeks, I'd like to know. Right away, that is."

Lina rolls Regan's words through her brain. She can't find fault with any of them, even if she does get stuck a bit on the "if that time comes" piece. For some reason, she feels her throat tighten when recalling those words.

"I'm sorry."

"You already said that." Regan laughs a little. "Just don't do it again, okay?"

"I won't."

"I believe you. Now, tell me again why you can't come back to Kitty Hawk this weekend?"

Lina sighs heavily and recounts the story to Regan. It's nothing glamorous; she's simply needed at Fort Bragg through the weekend, which will free her to leave and return to Kitty Hawk the following Friday instead of having to wait until Monday. It's not a bad deal, but Lina feels a slight ache in her chest at the prospect of being away from Regan for two weeks.

"Gotcha," Regan says once Lina's finished her explanation. "Hey, I have to get back to work, but can we make sure we're on the same page before we hang up?"

"Yes." Lina nods again.

"How about...Ugh, I can't believe I'm about to ask you to text me."

Lina can hear the embarrassment in Regan's voice. "Tell me what you need, Regan. I told you, I'm not used to this. So just tell me."

"And you'll do it?"

Lina grins, knowing that teasing tone well. "I make no promises."

Regan laughs, and Lina wishes she was there to see the way her cheeks rise so high they look like they're going to swallow her beautiful blue eyes. "Okay. This is what I want. Send me a good morning text every day, and if we're able to talk at some point during the day, let's do that, even if it's just for two minutes."

"That's it? Damn, you're easy."

"Really? Let's ramp it up then."

"Didn't you say you have to get back to work?"

Regan laughs again, this one deeper and playful. "Lucky for you, I do. Can't wait to get that good morning text tomorrow."

"If you're lucky."

Lina smiles at her phone long after Regan's hung up. She promises herself to follow through with what Regan's asked for, and tacks on a mental reminder to stop being an idiot.

CHAPTER TWENTY-SEVEN

The calendar hanging in the lab informs Lina that she has only three days of this monotony before she gets to return to Kitty Hawk. While she's been tempted to bring in a Sharpie and X out the days she's been here, she's remained respectful of the calendar that does not belong to her and has X-ed out the days in her head instead. It's not the same, but it'll do.

As she scans the list of samples on the computer, her mind floats over to how awesome she's been. Though she refused to promise, Lina has made sure to text Regan every morning. She's even tried to vary her texts, sometimes being funny, sometimes cute. Once she aimed for sexy, and Regan's response was a mixture of surprise and humor. Lina didn't go for sexy again after that one.

The scent of Luciana Alvarez's perfume kicks Lina out of her Regan daydreams. She's managed to successfully avoid any and all advances Luciana has attempted, but she's worried about a Hail Mary now that Luciana knows Lina's time at Fort Bragg is coming to a close.

Sure enough, the lovely doctor strides with purpose toward Lina, who watches out of the corner of her eye. There's extra determination in that confident walk. Heads turn as Luciana makes her way through the lab and stations herself in front of Lina's computer.

"Dr. Alvarez," Lina says in greeting. "What brings you to the lab this morning?"

"You," she says simply, not bothering to hide her intentions. Normally, Lina would be incredibly turned-on by such boldness, but today, she's almost disgusted.

"Do you have something in particular you'd like me to do?" Lina kicks herself internally, hearing the double entendre.

"Oh, I do." Luciana bats her eyelashes. "Come over tonight."

"I'm afraid I can't." The words aren't hard to say, but Lina's still not used to saying them.

Luciana raises an eyebrow. "Is that so?"

"I have a commitment tonight." To a burger with extra bacon and pickles plus a side of fries with extra ranch and barbeque dipping sauce, but Luciana doesn't need to know those specifics.

"One that's more enticing than this?" She gestures to herself, subtly enough so that others don't see it. Hopefully, anyway.

Lina fixes a stoic expression on her face. "It's been great working with you, Dr. Alvarez. If you'll excuse me, I have samples to run."

Fifteen minutes later, Lina's heart is still racing, stuttering in disbelief. She's never been one to turn down a gorgeous woman. Never. It's not in her DNA, or at least that's what she assumed about herself. She marvels at the fact that knowing Regan is looking forward to seeing her when she returns to Kitty Hawk is more than enough to make Lina completely uninterested in a very attractive woman who leaves zero room for question about her desires.

Then again— "Been there, done that," Lina mutters to herself as she pushes through the doors leading into the hallway. Her previous romantic encounter with Luciana wasn't exactly one to write home about. The old Lina would have been perfectly happy with the meaningless, somewhat decent sex, but the ground beneath her feet has shifted.

She finds a quiet, empty spot in the hall and leans against the wall. She feels weighed down today, more tired than she has been lately. There was a nightmare last night—nothing as bad as some of the previous ones, but enough to leave Lina on edge today. The noise in the lab was pressing against her nerves, further agitating her.

She's taken Carolyn's advice and started giving herself breaks instead of blindly pushing through the difficult moments. Now, in the hallway, she closes her eyes for a moment and lets herself do nothing but breathe. Once she feels more centered, Lina takes out her phone, intending to text Caitlin. Instead, her finger hovers over the group text she has on silent. She barely pays attention to this particular group text because it's composed of a group of Army guys she works out with in Jersey. Since she's been in North Carolina, there's been no point in reading the texts. But now, something must be happening. She watches as texts come in, one after another in quick succession, before she opens the thread.

Lina's head hits the wall as she reads through the messages. There's no way what she's reading is true. Considering it's a bunch of guys, though, she can't imagine they'd be lying.

There it is, in black and white, from the guy who owns the gym they all go to: *Steve told me himself. She served him with papers last weekend, moved out right away. We gotta support him.*

A laugh escapes from Lina. Paired with it is a brisk internal ice bath, one that leaves her skin chilled.

So she finally did it, Lina thinks. *Candice finally left him.*

She lets the reality sink in, waiting for a reaction from her brain or body. But there's nothing.

* * *

New Jersey, two years ago

Lina gasped, reaching for whatever was closest to her. It could have been a pillow, but maybe it was a body. Either way, she needed something to grip.

"I'm here," Candice said softly, pulling Lina into her arms. "And you're here with me, at home. You're safe, Lina."

"No," she mumbled, burying her face in Candice's neck.

"Yes, shhh."

As Lina came through the murkiness of her nightmare, she felt the light touch of Candice's hand on her back, the other massaging her neck. She tried to relax into the touches of the woman she loved—the very woman she had tried so hard *not* to love—but her body remained rigid, stoked by the terror that haunted her every night.

"Do you want to tell me about it?"

Lina shook her head. They both knew she wouldn't, and yet Candice continued to ask. There weren't any words anyway— they were both there, they both saw it happen. Candice hadn't seen the moment of impact, but she was there for the aftermath. She was there to pull Lina back when she tried to run across the street to save Brit, who was already dead. She was there when the second bomb, a much smaller one, went off, which certainly would have killed Lina had she been able to run instead of being yanked back by her superior.

But more than that, Candice had been there afterward. After the devastation was cleared, after the bodies were pieced together, after the bodies were laid to rest. After their feet hit American soil once again. Neither of them had meant for it to happen, and they'd had to be more secretive than ever. But Candice was there when Brit was not. Candice was there, Lina assumed, to make sure that Lina was not completely alone.

And miraculously, Candice was still there. They'd been back from Afghanistan for nearly six months, and their relationship— affair—felt deeper, more permanent. Lina was attached to Candice; she hated being away from her, felt empty without her. And she marveled that Candice kept coming back, kept sneaking away and spending the night. She was tricking herself into believing that Candice needed her as much as she needed Candice.

It was a nasty trick, considering that Lina was very aware that Candice was still married, and had never once mentioned the possibility of getting divorced.

Lina pulled back to look at her lover. There was strength in everything Candice did, and Lina found herself pulling from that strength more than she'd like to. She hadn't found her way back to herself after losing Brit; she hadn't closed the door or even peeked into the room to see what debris remained to sort through. Being with Candice precluded the need to do that. She was a distraction, a rather lovely one, and while they didn't talk about what had happened, Lina found comfort in simply knowing that Candice knew. That she'd seen it, too.

That she, too, had lost a friend.

"What do you want to do today?"

Candice laughed a little and patted Lina's arm. She sat up in bed. "I have to get home."

On cue, the pit dropped into Lina's stomach. It was the same every morning—and not even *every* morning, as the nights they spent together were unscheduled and infrequent. If they got one night together per week, that was a miracle. But Lina waited on tenterhooks for each text, each call, each moment.

She sat up, too. Candice was already out of bed, getting dressed. Lina blinked at the clock. Not even six a.m. She had no idea what Candice told Steve about the nights she never came home, and frankly, she didn't think she wanted to know.

Some things—perhaps too many things—were better left unsaid between them.

Before she left Lina's bedroom, Candice perched on the edge of the bed and reached for Lina's hand. She intertwined their fingers and squeezed.

"Lina, I think you need to see someone."

Lina's breath caught in her throat. "See someone? You mean date someone?"

Candice shook her head, her blond hair swinging. "No. I mean a therapist."

Lina's limbs turned to cement. She wanted to turn away from Candice but couldn't bring herself to do so. "No thank you. I'm fine."

"No, Lina, you're not. Look at me." Begrudgingly, Lina met Candice's sharp blue eyes that did not miss a thing, let alone something Lina tried desperately to hide. "You experienced a traumatic loss. I see you suffering. You need to work through this with a professional."

That was about the last thing Lina wanted to do. Besides, she had Candice.

"I can't always be here for you," she continued, as though reading Lina's mind. "Please think about it."

One loveless kiss later, Candice was gone, leaving Lina to flop back into bed and throw her arm over her eyes.

Two short weeks later, Lina would look back on that moment as a warning. Candice wasn't one to mince words, and it was true: she couldn't always be there for Lina, especially when she called off their romance and threw herself back into her marriage. It didn't take long, a month at most, before she came knocking on Lina's door and they fell into another messy, detached, back-and-forth affair. Neither wanted to use language to identify the bond between them, but there was an unspoken reliance, a heavy dependency built from their time in Afghanistan. Each time Lina told herself she could live without Candice, she was fine for approximately five minutes before she was certain she had stopped breathing and would never breathe again.

After Candice retired, Lina assumed they could pick up more naturally. After all, the main thing (as she considered the marriage a secondary issue) keeping them apart had been taken out of the picture. But aside from a handful of encounters leading up to an intensely connected two-month period after Candice actually moved out of her home, leaving her husband behind, Lina was wrong. A year passed, and still, she refused to let go of Candice, who continued to come back on her own unpredictable, sporadic schedule.

The final detachment came unexpectedly, after Lina had convinced Candice to go away with her for a week. That week, away from the prying eyes of soldiers and a husband from whom she was supposedly separated, was bliss. Tucked away in the woods of upstate Pennsylvania, Lina watched Candice unfold and open herself. They seemed to grow even closer each day, though Candice never reached the point of being able to fully reciprocate during sex. There were moments that teetered toward her reciprocation, and Lina hooked herself on those precious moments, believing one day—maybe once the divorce actually happened—Candice would be able to fully engage with her.

Time had passed, but the bond that had locked them together was still there. By that point, Lina had been meeting with Carolyn for over a year, a fact she'd told Candice in passing and never mentioned again. She wanted to appear stronger for Candice; she had a strange feeling that her grief mingled with survivor's guilt was something that kept Candice at arm's length. Lina perceived her weakness, her damage, as the hurdle Candice could not or would not jump over. And if that was the case, then Lina would try to fix it.

Besides, she rationalized that the nightmares were the only problem. Candice understood her quirks, her need to have her back to the wall, her dislike of loud, sudden noises and crowds of people. Lina didn't have to explain anything to Candice. She almost felt normal around her.

When they returned from their trip to Pennsylvania, Candice went dark for an entire week. It wasn't uncommon for her to distance herself, but zero communication for seven full days was abnormal. With each passing day, Lina's anxiety increased to the point where she was unable to leave her house. She knew something bad was coming. The delay was, truthfully, nearly killing her.

It ended with a text. A short, emotionless text: *I'm committed to my husband. Please don't contact me again.*

Lina doesn't remember much about the days and weeks following that text. She purged Candice from her system as much as possible, but the roots were tangled and deep. She felt a deep resentment coupled with abandonment—she had given herself to this woman, been open and real with her in a way she'd been unable to do with anyone before her, and Candice had packed their time up and left it on Lina's doorstep. No note, just emptiness paired with the unspoken phrase: "I won't be needing this anymore."

The loss, grand and silent, broke Lina in a way she hadn't realized a person could break.

One short month later, Lina was standing in the driveway of a home in Kitty Hawk. She'd begged an old Army friend for help getting a TDY as far away from home as possible. North Carolina was far from being on the opposite side of the country from New Jersey, but it would have to do. She'd spent the eight-hour drive bandaging her busted heart.

But the truth was, she was still bleeding.

CHAPTER TWENTY-EIGHT

Kitty Hawk, present day

Hurricane season, as Lina understands it, primarily occurs from September through November. So she's understandably stunned when the lab techs at Womack start talking about an incoming system, and it's only the beginning of August. During her last three days on base, it's all anyone is talking about. Lina's not necessarily afraid of the storm—she's dealt with her share of bizarre weather during deployments—but she's not thrilled about potential damage to the house she's still working on in Kitty Hawk.

That's the reasoning she repeats to herself on the drive from Fort Bragg to the barrier islands. Yes, *that's* the reason she's breaking speed limits to get back to Kitty Hawk before the storm makes its presence known.

When she hits the stretch of US 64E known for speed traps, she slows down and calls Caitlin.

"Well, hello, Staff Sergeant. What kind of trouble are you getting into today?"

"That's actually why I'm calling—to avoid getting into trouble."

"Oh God," Caitlin groans. "What did you do?"

"Nothing, nothing. But I was driving too fast, so I figured talking to you would slow me down."

There's silence, then Caitlin says, "I feel as though I should be offended by that statement, but I'm not sure why."

"Don't overthink it. I have news."

"Oh? You know I love news. Hit me."

"Guess who's finally getting divorced? For real this time."

Again, silence. Lina can only imagine the things Caitlin's preparing to say.

"Lina Ragelis. Do *not* tell me she contacted you."

While Lina may not remember that precarious span of time after Candice officially ended things, for good, Caitlin certainly does, and she's never hesitant to remind Lina about it. The ferocity in her voice is warning enough.

"She didn't, and no, I didn't contact her. It came through the gym text."

"That group text is so weird." She's not wrong. Lina often sends Caitlin screenshots of the absolutely bizarre things the gym guys talk about, sometimes (it seems) forgetting that she's in the thread. Plus, they out-gossip any woman Lina's ever met, which is both entertaining and informative. "But seriously? It's really happening?"

"Yep." Lina's been checking the text a little more frequently to gather information. Sure enough, Steve announced to his friends that he signed the papers, and the divorce is finally going to happen. There's been no rumblings about the cause, and Lina's thankful for that. She doesn't need to know.

Actually, she doesn't even *want* to know.

"And I'm fine, by the way."

"Yeah, you know, you sound fine. I wasn't expecting that."

"Me either."

"Might it have a little something to do with a much more appropriate woman in your life?"

Lina scoffs. "You wish."

"Don't be coy with me. Mallory showed me the text you sent."

"She did not."

"She most certainly did," Caitlin says, pride and maybe a smattering of arrogance in her voice. "So you're falling for her, huh?"

"Put Mallory on the phone."

"Ooh, so sorry, she's not here!"

"I hate you," Lina grumbles. "I was going to tell you, but now I'm going to pretend I never sent that text."

Caitlin laughs. "Too late for all of the above. When do I get to meet her?"

"Never."

"Bullshit. You're on your way to her now, aren't you?"

Lina glances around her Jeep, wondering if Caitlin bugged it before she left Jersey. "Why would you think that?"

"Because I watch the news, and I know there's a hurricane situation coming right your way, and the Lina I know and love wouldn't want someone she's falling for to be alone for such an event."

"Have I mentioned that I hate you?"

"Yup. But we both know that's not true. Seriously, though, Lina. You're not going to fuck this up because of Candice, right?"

Though it pains her to hear the question asked, Lina knows it needed to come out. "I'm not. I really am done with all of that, Cait. I promise."

"From the woman who never makes promises."

"Only ones I can keep, and I assure you, this is one I can keep. There will be no contact. I blocked her number, remember?"

"Yeah, but," Caitlin says softly. "There are other ways she can contact you. And I really, really don't want her to."

"I don't think she will." And it's true. Lina has no reason to believe Candice would make a move now. They may be tethered for life, but the string has gotten longer as time has gone on—long enough that Lina has room to move all on her own.

"On that note," Lina says, flipping her turn signal. "I'm about an hour out and I need some time to decompress."

"Say hi to Regan for me."

"I still hate you."

"Love you too, bye!"

* * *

When Lina pulls into Regan's gravel driveway, she doesn't rush to get out of her Jeep. She takes a few minutes to collect herself and send Caitlin a text, letting her know she's safely back in Kitty Hawk, at least until the hurricane comes through. Caitlin gives her a thumbs up and a thumbs down in response, a perfect mirror to Lina's crooked humor.

Once she's feeling moderately confident, Lina climbs the stairs to Regan's porch. It's her first time seeing the small house, and from the outside, it seems exactly like somewhere Regan would be. It's a stilted home with room for two cars to park underneath. When Lina reaches the top of the stairs, she finds herself in front of a screened-in porch that is far bigger than it looks from the driveway. The house itself is painted a cheery yellow with equally bright green trim. It screams happiness, really, and Lina laughs a little as she opens the screen door.

She knocks, but the door is opening before she can finish a second rap. Regan stands before her, one hand on her hip, wearing an oversized white T-shirt and dark green gym shorts. She's barefoot and smiling.

"I was wondering how long you were going to sit in my driveway." She opens the door wider and motions Lina in.

"I figured since I showed up unannounced, I'd give you some time to prepare yourself."

"That's assuming I saw your Jeep pull in."

"And you did, didn't you?"

Regan grins and reaches for her. "Yes. Come here, please."

Lina wraps her arms around Regan and holds her tight. She breathes in her now-familiar scent of vanilla and lemon. Her lips brush against Regan's neck, eliciting a low moan.

"Happy to see me?"

"You could say that." Regan pulls back and looks Lina up and down. "I'm sure you hear this all the time, so I kinda don't want to say it, but…You look incredibly hot in uniform."

For once, those words don't send Lina running in the opposite direction. Instead, she draws Regan back into her arms and kisses her, trying to communicate how much she's missed her for the last two weeks.

"Is that your way of saying thank you?" Regan asks, a little breathless.

"Yes." Lina looks around the living room where they're standing. "Are you prepared for the storm?"

"Of course I am. I've lived here my entire life."

Lina raises her eyebrows. She's not used to hearing that hard tone from Regan.

Regan looks down and nods, a flush creeping across her cheeks. "Sorry. It's just—is that why you're here? To protect me?"

Lina rocks back on her heels. She has to think for a moment; she wants to be certain she's being truthful with her response.

"Partially, yeah. That's my nature, Regan. I want to know you're safe." They both smile, hearing Regan's words repeated in Lina's voice. "But I also missed you and couldn't wait to see you."

Regan's blush deepens as her smile returns. "That's what I was hoping for."

"So can we ride out the storm together?"

"Absolutely," Regan whispers, bringing her lips to Lina's once again.

Several hours later, dusk has fallen and brought with it the beginning of the rain. Lina, having showered and changed into shorts and a T-shirt, follows Regan around the house as she points out all the ways she's prepared for the storm.

"It's an early one," Regan acknowledges as they return to the kitchen. "Are you sure your house will be okay?"

"I hope so. I talked with the owner, and he didn't seem concerned." Lina shrugs and scratches her cheek. "If there's damage, it just keeps me here longer. And I'm fine with that."

A flurry of emotions float across Regan's face. Lina struggles to identify any of them, pulling Regan into her arms instead of asking.

They sway together in the kitchen, the cacophonous sound of pouring rain surrounding them. Lina puts her hands on Regan's waist then slides them under her shirt, spreading her fingers out over the smooth skin. Regan gasps slightly, leaning closer.

Lina shuts her eyes, commanding herself to stay in the moment. She's been daydreaming about this, about touching Regan, for weeks. She wants nothing more than to show her how she feels, but she's worried her brain has other plans.

She feels Regan's touch as she works her hands from Lina's back to her shoulders, slips her fingers under the sleeves of Lina's T-shirt, and strokes the skin there. Regan hums lightly as she moves her hands down Lina's arms and lands them on her hips.

Their lips meet in a kiss that begins softly, quickly accelerating to one filled with need and desire. Lina feels herself pushed back against the counter, and she grips Regan tighter. Their kiss deepens, teeth nipping. Regan draws her tongue over Lina's bottom lip, and Lina groans, sucking Regan's lower lip into her mouth.

Suddenly, Regan pulls back. Lina watches the light reflect in those luminous eyes.

"We do need to talk, Lina."

"I know." She clears her throat, surprised at how hoarse she is. "And we will."

"But not right now," Regan breathes. "I don't want to talk right now."

She takes Lina's hand and guides her to her bedroom.

Once Lina has removed Regan's clothes, she sits back on her heels on the bed and takes in every inch of her body. Her broad shoulders and the delicate curves of her torso that lead to narrow hips. Large, full breasts with the glimmer of steel winking from both nipples above a flat stomach. Regan's body is a study in artful contrast, and Lina is enamored with it.

"You are sensational," she says, leaning over Regan. Her left hand strokes the side of Regan's breast. "Absolutely beautiful."

"Kiss me. Now."

Lina grins as she meets Regan's mouth, reigniting the fiery kiss from the kitchen. Her hand explores Regan's breasts and pierced nipples, drawing gasps and groans. Just as Lina moves to place her mouth where her hand is, Regan stops her.

"We're doing this the right way this time," she announces. Her hands tug on the bottom of Lina's T-shirt. "So this comes off now. And your bra."

Lina obliges, stripping both items and tossing them to the floor. She watches Regan's expression shift as she takes in Lina's bare chest. A flicker of darkness dims Lina's vision. *No*, she thinks. *Stay here.*

She lowers herself so that she's lying on top of Regan, and their chests press together. The feeling of skin-on-skin contact is a secret pleasure of Lina's. She closes her eyes and focuses on that silky, sultry feeling. Soon, Regan's hands are on her back, then her sides, then sliding between their bodies. When she captures Lina's hardened nipple between her thumb and finger, Lina cries out.

"Sensitive," Regan whispers, wiggling so that she can get her mouth on Lina's nipple. She works magic there. Lina's body responds with a fury, desire and fire surging through her veins. Regan's tongue and teeth lick and tug. Lina finds herself grinding against Regan's thigh, riding into the pleasure as much as she can.

Regan releases her and sits up. "I'm feeling very naked."

Lina grins and strokes her fingertips over Regan's abdomen. "That's because you are."

"You need to be, too." She points at Lina's shorts. "This isn't a one-way street, Lina."

Lina quickly obliges, surprised and wildly turned-on by the edge of command in Regan's voice, something she wasn't expecting but finds she very much likes. Once she's suitably naked, she kneels over Regan.

"Fuck," Regan says, her voice reverent and adoring. "Look at you."

Lina looks down at her body, seeing nothing spectacular. But then she looks at Regan and watches her see her, and Lina flushes. No one has ever looked at her with such unbridled desire.

She has to look away; it's wondrous and sexy and almost too much. Lina gazes at Regan's naked body, tracing her finger down her torso, over her hip bone. She wants to fuck Regan. Badly. She wants to be deep inside of her. But something silent holds her back.

"Lie down with me," Regan says, and Lina does. They lie side by side, kissing and gently touching. Each time Regan touches a different part of Lina's body, the dark flame flickers, threatening to take over. Lina does her best to fight it, but her worry intensifies as the minutes tick by.

"Lina." It takes her a moment to open her eyes and look at Regan. She finds nothing but warmth and yearning in her eyes. "Stay with me."

Lina flinches, waits for the inevitable avalanche of memories. She stills. Nothing comes. Regan continues looking at her. Lina swallows the lump in her throat. She will never understand how Regan can be so patient with her, but she promises herself that she will never take it for granted.

"I'm here," Lina whispers. "I'm here."

Regan nods and when she kisses Lina, the gentleness has evaporated. In its place is a woman who very much knows what she wants, and what she wants to do to Lina.

"Oh my God," Lina says. She grips the sheets with both hands. She's dying to open her eyes and look at Regan, but she's worried that she'll instantly come if she does, and she's not ready for that release yet.

Regan's tongue is working absolute magic on Lina. Her fingers, too, arching and hitting right where Lina needs them. The sensations are enough to make her brain swim in a haze of overwhelming pleasure. Every stroke, every thrust: Lina feels Regan everywhere. She leans into the feeling, letting her body rise and fall. As she does, an ivy-covered door in the shadowy corner of Lina's mind unlocks, creaking open slightly. It's just enough to shine a bolt of light, to clear a path Lina has forgotten or maybe never seen. *This,* she thinks, *this is where I belong.*

The thought collides with the sensations purring through her body and they slam into a blissful punch of sensual pleasure. Lina feels her hips arching off the bed. She squeezes her eyes shut and rides out her orgasm, loving the fact that Regan's mouth is riding it out along with her.

She grips Regan's shoulders and tugs her up the bed so that she's lying completely on top of Lina. Lina holds her tightly. She's still shuddering with waves of pleasure.

"No one's ever taken me like that," Lina finally says. Her eyes are still closed.

"What? No one?"

"Never."

Regan brushes the hair from Lina's forehead. "I think you've been sleeping with the wrong people."

"Should have been you all along."

"Hmm." Regan shifts so her thigh is pushing against Lina's center. She gasps and swats at Regan, who laughs and repositions herself. "You weren't ready for me until now."

At that, Lina opens her eyes. Regan's gazing at her intently. All Lina can do is nod. When Regan kisses her, however, the rest of her body springs into action.

She has a very sexy, beautiful, patient, kind, thoughtful woman to make love to.

In seconds, Lina's flipped them so she's back on top. Regan rolls her eyes.

"You do realize you can't always be in control."

"Hey," Lina says, biting Regan's nipple. "Didn't I just let you have your way with me?"

"Yes. Now get used to it."

In response, Lina slides three fingers inside Regan, who gasps and thrusts her hips down. "I think this is going to have to be a give-and-take situation, Regan."

"Yeah," Regan hisses. "Sounds good to me."

Lina alternates watching Regan's expression and watching her fingers slide in and out of her. She arches her fingers and changes the tempo. Regan groans loudly and pushes her body toward Lina, urging her fingers deeper. They move together, moans echoing against the pounding rain, until Regan cries out and floods Lina's fingers.

"Fuck, yes," Lina breathes.

"Your mouth," Regan says. "Now."

Lina grins as she shifts her position and obeys the command. She luxuriates in the taste of Regan. Her tongue circles and stripes, again responding to the sounds coming from Regan. It's not long before she yells, "Fuck, Lina!" and unravels yet again.

The rain is picking up speed, but the room Lina and Regan are lying in is a cocoon of warmth, safety, and sex. Lina's body aches, but she feels an unfamiliar vibration making its way through her limbs. She feels… Alive. Renewed. And completely, utterly infatuated. Even as she lies next to Regan, she's replaying every moment of the evening. She stares at Regan. Still, she wonders where in the world this woman came from, and what she did to deserve any moment of time spent with her.

Regan looks back at her. They're suspended there, watching each other, thoughts and feelings strung delicately and silently between them.

"Are you still with me?"

Lina hears the worry, the edge of fear, in Regan's voice, and she hates that it's there. She hates that she put it there. She presses her lips against Regan's forehead and strokes her cheek. "Completely."

"And, um, during?"

It's right then and there that Lina promises herself that she will do everything in her power to never, ever make Regan have to wonder or worry about her for the rest of her life.

"Yes. The whole time. All of the times."

"Good." She sounds relieved, even though her smile is tentative. "That's good."

The words stumble over themselves, creating a linguistic pile-up on Lina's tongue. She swallows them back down. There will be another time, more time. Not now.

But someday.

CHAPTER TWENTY-NINE

R.E.M. blasts through the house, Michael Stipe's unmistakable voice filtering into the rooms. Lina nods along with the music. She has to remember to tell Mallory that she's really been killing it with the playlists lately.

When Lina returned from Regan's house after having holed up with her for two full days, she was worried she'd find damage from the hurricane that had been downgraded to a tropical storm. Fortunately, just one shutter had fallen to its sad, battered death, and Lina had no trouble fixing it.

The lack of damage has allowed Lina to return her focus to the inside of the house. After going back-and-forth with the homeowner, she's decided to go ahead and refinish all the kitchen cabinets. It's a task that sits very, very low on her preferred list, but it's higher up than retiling the bathroom, so the cabinets have won.

Lina glances at her phone, then opens the calendar app to double check her work schedule. There's been no word of having to return to Fort Bragg. She knows it'll happen again at some point, but she's hoping not for a while. Being back at OBX Hospital feels good, comfortable—and not just because Regan is there. That's simply an added bonus.

When the image on her screen changes abruptly, Lina nearly drops the phone but recovers in time. With a grin, she accepts the call. Keeley's face fills the screen.

"Latch!"

"Hey, Key. Where the hell have you been?"

"Oh, you know." Keeley grins wickedly. "Wait, actually, you don't."

Lina rolls her eyes. "Yeah, that's why I asked."

"New boyfriend, new job." Keeley moves the phone, and Lina gets an uncomfortably close look at her nostrils. "More sex than work, but who's counting, right?"

"So things are going well?"

"So good!" She moves the phone back to a normal distance and wiggles her eyebrows. "Seriously, though, everything is really good. How's my favorite crash test dummy? Still roughing it at the beach?"

"Yup." Lina walks onto the deck and flips her phone around to show Keeley the ocean. "Just look past all the sand."

"I'm honestly itching just knowing it's there. Okay, Latch, look. I have very limited time, but I wanted to see your face."

Lina turns the phone back to her face and waves. "Here I am."

"You look good. Better." Keeley gasps. "You got laid, didn't you?"

"What? No." But Lina knows she's blushing, and her eyes are probably doing some lovesick dopey thing that Keeley will assuredly *not* miss.

"Holy sugar snaps! Who? Tell me!"

"Maybe one of the hotties from the brewery."

Keeley's eyes light up. "The hot blond nurse? I knew it."

"You knew no such thing."

"Oh, Latch. I so knew it. You, however, were so in your head about Lord knows what—you weren't seeing the way she looked at you."

Lina goes back into the kitchen—it feels like it's a thousand degrees outside—and sits down at the counter. "She was looking at me?"

"Oh yeah. Big time. That chemistry was crystal clear. I bet the sex is amazing." Keeley cackles with laughter, clearly proud of herself.

"But don't you think she's a little…I don't know…masculine for me?"

"Does it matter?" Keeley wrinkles her nose. "Are you attracted to her?"

"Yeah. Definitely."

"Okay, and do you like her?"

Lina smiles. "I do."

"And is she good to you?"

"Beyond."

Keeley shrugs. "Then who gives a hoot? Honestly, I think you need to be with someone who's more your speed—it's not like any of your exes were a good fit for you, right? Stop fixating on labels, Latch." The phone flies close to Keeley's nostrils once again. "The sex is so hot, am I right?"

The sound of a door opening and slamming saves Lina from having to answer, and Keeley hurries a goodbye with a promise to call back soon. She disappears from the phone screen as suddenly as she appeared, and Lina stares at the black screen, replaying the last bit of the conversation.

It's her thing, and she knows it. Call it a hang-up, a fixation on "type," whatever: Lina has never, *ever* dated a woman who isn't way over on the feminine side of the scale. She's never even been attracted to a woman who falls under the tomboy, almost androgynous label—which is definitely where Regan lands. Until, that is, Lina takes off her shirt and doubled-up sports bras and reveals Regan's hidden, incredible, undeniably feminine and large breasts.

She toes the floor as she thinks. Or, more accurately, obsesses. So many of her past flings (because truthfully, has there been anything she can call a real relationship?) have been based on primal, instant physical attraction. Sometimes feelings and attachments shifted as time went on, but everything was originally centered around that hot, intense, "gotta have you" feeling when she looked at another woman.

And Regan... Well, Regan is different. That steamy slap of attraction wasn't the first thing that Lina noticed. It's not even what pulled her in. There was something else about Regan that made Lina want to be close to her, and when the attraction caught up with the rest of her feelings—that's when the fire took root and spread.

Lina pushes herself back from the counter and grabs her screwdriver. Thinking about how intense that attraction has become will either land her in her bed by herself, or on the phone, asking Regan to come over. Plenty of time for that later.

For now: the cabinets.

The cabinets are assholes. It's taken Lina about an hour to figure that out, and now she's too far in to abandon the project.

She rubs the spot on her hand where she's just evicted a splinter. Truly, the cabinets are unruly, self-possessed assholes. She grumbles and makes her way to her phone, needing different music to get through the rest of today's work.

"Much better," she says as Queen replaces Soundgarden.

Lina loses herself in the music. "Somebody to Love" fades into "Under Pressure" which slides into the opening notes of "Don't Stop Me Now." It's exactly what she needs as she launches an attack against the kitchen cabinetry.

When a lesser-known song ends and opens the stage to "I Want to Break Free," Lina drops her screwdriver. The first eighteen seconds of the song fill the room, and she takes them in with each of her breaths. By the time Freddie Mercury lets loose the opening words, Lina has picked up the screwdriver and repurposed it as her microphone.

She loses herself in the song, dancing wildly and singing at the top of her lungs. The words run through her, landing with satisfaction, surprise, and purpose. It's not the intended meaning of the song that draws Lina in, but rather the way she, too, wants to break free and fall in love.

Or, actually, maybe she's already doing the falling in love part.

All that's left is to fully, truly, purposefully break free.

From herself.

"I can't get used to living without, living without, living without you, by my side," she yell-sings, feeling the weight of the words and how true they've become. "I don't want to live alone."

When she spins around, still very much in her karaoke superstar moment, Lina drops the screwdriver once again.

Regan's standing there, just inside the sliding glass door from the deck, watching with a bright smile on her face.

"Oh," she says, holding up her hands. "Please don't stop on my account."

Lina narrows her eyes at Regan and stalks over to her phone, hitting pause. The house lapses into silence.

"What have I said about your terrible habit of sneaking up on me?"

Regan bats her eyelashes. "I knocked. Several times. For some reason, I guess you couldn't hear me. Though, really, I'm shocked that the door was unlocked to begin with."

Fully charged by both the song and her need to touch the gorgeous woman in her kitchen, Lina closes the distance between them and takes Regan in her arms. She kisses her long and hard, pouring her feelings into the movements of her mouth.

Breathless, Regan pulls back. "I'm beginning to think you like when I sneak up on you."

"You know that's not true." Lina searches Regan's eyes, a thought jabbing her suddenly. "Are you checking up on me?"

Regan shakes her head immediately, though Lina wouldn't be surprised if that were the case. Their communication has been sparse in the week following the tropical storm; Regan's been helping her dad and uncle fix some damage at their houses.

"Nope. I missed you and I wanted to see you. The performance was a nice bonus."

Lina focuses on the feeling of Regan's hands slowly caressing her hips as she studies her. Regan's ocean eyes reflect back the words and feelings Lina's still keeping tucked down and safe. Her smile is filled with the kind of light and life that people chase after their entire lives, and Lina feels undeniably lucky that she can see that smile whenever she wants.

With a start, she realizes that it's true. She doesn't *want* to get used to living without Regan.

"Lina," Regan says, her voice hushed and tinged with desire, leaving Lina wondering if Regan really can read her mind. "Take me to bed."

Several hours later, Lina lies on her back in bed. Regan's lying next to her, one leg thrown possessively over Lina's. Lina watches Regan idly trace the swell of her breasts and her body hums with want, even though she is over-the-top satisfied. Regan's instincts in bed continue to thrill her. She never thought she could meet her lovemaking match, but Regan is proving her wrong.

"What's this scar?" Regan's hand has traveled to Lina's bicep and is stroking the raised skin.

"Childhood injury. My cousin scraped me with a stick."

"Ouch." Regan slides her fingers to the top of Lina's shoulder. "And this one?"

Lina lets out a low laugh. "Basic training. Keeley and I did some stupid shit back then."

"Keeley," Regan says, leaning up on her elbow. "Your battle buddy."

"That's her." Lina holds out her previously injured hand for Regan to inspect.

"Does she know about us?" The question is lazy, backed up by nothing but curiosity.

"Actually, yeah. I told her today."

Regan peers at Lina. "And what did you tell her?"

Lina makes a face, remembering the conversation. "Honestly?"

"Always, Lina."

"That we slept together."

"Ah." A little sound, packed with a desolate punch that hits Lina right in her gut.

"Regan," she starts.

"No, it's fine. I mean, that's the truth."

Lina braces herself, waiting to feel the shift as Regan gets out of bed. She holds her breath. Nothing happens. She risks turning her head to meet Regan's eyes. Unsurprisingly, Regan's watching her, waiting.

"I want more than just sex, Lina," Regan says without preamble. "And correct me if I'm wrong, but I don't think I'm the only person in this bed that feels that way."

Lina bites back the terrible urge to make a joke about a threesome. "You're not wrong."

"I know." And with that, Regan rests her head on Lina's shoulder once again.

There, again. The way Regan is nothing like anything, anyone, Lina has ever known. She recognizes the importance, the gravity of this. She also sees the memo in flashing lights.

If she wants something more than just sex with Regan, she needs to say it. She needs to be open and honest, and not be dodgy or noncommittal.

This is all up to Lina.

She knows, too, with unavoidable clarity, that Regan will not wait forever.

"I'm hungry," Regan murmurs. "Can we get pizza from Cosmos?"

"I thought you'd never ask."

When Regan moves to get out of bed, Lina tightens her hold and wraps her body fully around Regan. She breathes in the lemony scent of her skin. She trails her fingers over the painful softness of Regan's arms, her back, the sides of her thighs. Whatever yearning Lina thought was sated spreads through her, fresh and demanding. She shifts and pulls Regan over so she's lying on top of Lina.

"Pizza?" Regan asks, her voice teasing as their naked bodies begin a new rhythm.

"Not yet," Lina responds, sliding her hand between them until she hits the spot she wants and knows Regan needs.

CHAPTER THIRTY

"Are you sure I can't bring anything?"

"Positive. But tell me again what you're wearing? We can't show up looking like twins again."

Lina chuckles and squeezes her phone between her shoulder and ear. There was an unfortunate incident the week prior when Lina met Erin and Regan at OBX Brewery and had shown up wearing an outfit nearly identical to Regan's, which Erin had enjoyed far too much. "Jeans and one of your old basketball T-shirts."

Regan gasps. "You little shit. How?"

"You may have left it here last week." Lina counts down from ten, waiting for the correction.

"And what? Gone home topless? You totally swiped it from my clean laundry pile yesterday, didn't you?"

"Guilty. Can you blame me for wanting a little part of you to sleep with when you're not here?"

"Lina," Regan says. Lina can hear the smile in her voice. "When was the last time we spent a night apart?"

She knows the exact date, but there's no way she's going to tell Regan it was thirteen days ago—the night before Regan showed up in time to catch Lina's karaoke performance. Though words haven't come from either one of them, and Lina still knows it's up to her to start the conversation, something else shifted between them that night. Maybe it was the pizza, or the way Regan fell asleep with her head in Lina's lap while they watched old episodes of *DeGrassi* together after dinner. Or maybe it was Lina's silent but obvious need to be as close as possible to Regan, as often as possible.

She could exist without her. She's well aware of that. But why should she, when she doesn't have to?

"What are *you* wearing?" Lina asks, deftly changing the subject.

"Well, obviously not one of my basketball shirts," Regan grumbles. "And now I have to change. Be ready in ten."

When Regan picks Lina up exactly ten minutes later, she leans on the horn instead of coming up the stairs. That was another lesson they'd recently learned—when in a time crunch, do not meet each other anywhere near a bed.

"Nice outfit," Regan remarks as Lina gets in the car.

"Thought you might like it." She leans over and kisses Regan. "I like your shirt."

"Don't even think about it." Regan shoots her what Lina can only assume is meant to be an intimidating look. It's eclipsed by the adoration shining from her eyes.

They arrive at Erin's parents' house and make their way around to the back. Lina scans and makes note of familiar faces. Her pulse quickens when she realizes there are some new people in the backyard. Regan slips her hand into Lina's, and her heart rate slows.

"Come on," Regan says, tugging Lina's hand. "Erin's mom is really excited to see you."

Lina snorts, knowing exactly why Erin's mom is so excited to see her.

The cookout unfolds much like the one Lina attended earlier in the summer. Once again, Erin's mom ruthlessly destroys Lina and Erin in a game of cornhole. Foolishly, Regan and Lina agree to take on a newly formed team of Erin and her mother. It does not go well for Lina and Regan.

"We need to practice," Regan says afterward. She's standing with her back to the sound, her hands balled against her hips. "That was embarrassing."

"Hey, you're the one who thought it was a good idea to take on Erin *and* her mom." Lina shrugs. "I just went along with it to support you." She scans the horizon behind Regan then double checks her watch.

"Are you expecting someone by boat?"

"Just some pirates." She grabs Regan's hand. "Come with me."

"Oh God, Lina, am I your offering?"

"Nah, you're too mouthy. They'd give you right back."

Regan laughs and nudges her shoulder against Lina's. They walk to the spot where they sat together so many weeks before. The chairs are there, as though waiting for them. Or, more accurately, waiting for Lina to get her shit together.

"This looks familiar," Regan says as she sits down.

"Well, I'd think so, considering how much time you spent here as a kid."

"That's not what I meant and you know it." Regan stands up and pulls her chair closer to Lina's, then sits back down. She places her hand over Lina's. "That's better."

"Much," Lina says, turning her head to gaze at Regan. She watches her take in the beauty before them.

"You were so closed off," Regan says, almost to herself. "That night," she clarifies. "When we sat here and I told you things about myself, hoping you'd tell me about you."

"I tried."

"You did." She nods. "I know you did. And you still are. I do know that, Lina."

A funny sensation in the back of Lina's throat catches her off guard. She clears her throat immediately, hoping that scares off the threat of unexpected emotion.

"Regan," she says softly, and waits for Regan to look at her. "This is way more than just sex to me."

Regan laughs but it sounds forced. "Yeah, I know."

"I'm serious." She waits until Regan's features relax. "Please know that there is so much I want to say, but I still don't have all the words."

Regan blinks, then nods.

"Parts of me will always be broken," Lina continues. She clears her throat again. "And I know I can be a lot. I know I'll never be the perfect girlfriend." To Lina's surprise, she doesn't stumble over the word. "I come with a lot of baggage, but I promise you, I'm always working on it."

"I know," Regan says, her voice a trace above a whisper.

A dull, almost-forgotten internal siren blares a warning. Lina takes a deep breath. She doesn't want warnings. She doesn't want any of that anymore, because if she keeps listening to it all, she'll never find anyone like Regan ever again.

And more importantly, more detrimentally, if she keeps listening to her internal system, wired with panic and fear, she'll lose Regan. For good.

"Be with me," Lina finally says, her own voice hushed.

Regan is quiet, her eyes locked with Lina's. She lifts one shoulder in a half-shrug. "I *am* with you."

"No, Regan. Be with me. More than sex. All the feelings. The commitment. You and me, and life. Be *with* me."

Regan stands up and pulls Lina up with her. She wraps her arms around Lina and holds her tightly. As they embrace, Lina watches the sun slip down the sky, settling into a depth beyond the horizon. The sound is bathed in bold reds and vibrant oranges. She doesn't want to look away, but the most true, most beautiful thing is not the sunset, but the person in her arms.

Lina pulls back and looks at Regan, waiting.

"Yes, Lina. So much yes."

"Yeah? You'll do this with me? Even though it won't always be easy, and I'm—"

Regan presses her thumb against Lina's lips. "All the yeses in the world. Yes. You're everything, Lina." Regan kisses Lina then, and a new rush of feeling bathes them in the heat of the late August night.

EPILOGUE

Seabrooke, New Jersey, four months later

"What is this?" Regan's voice is a mixture of horror and shock. "Are we in Antarctica?"

Lina comes behind Regan and wraps her arms around her. "This, my love, is something we Northerners call 'snow.'"

"What in the world…" Regan continues to stare out the bedroom window, transfixed. "You do realize I've never seen snow like this before in my life."

"Well if I didn't before, I certainly do now." Lina kisses the back of Regan's neck. She knew the storm was coming and prepared for it, hauling Regan to the grocery store the day before in order to prepare. They may only be in New Jersey for a week, but this storm will have them stuck at home for a solid two days. Lina's not complaining; there's nowhere she'd rather be.

Regan leans back against Lina, arching her neck for better kissing access. "Have I mentioned lately how much I love it when you call me that?"

"Once or twice." Lina smiles and spins Regan around. "You're not sick of it yet?"

"I never will be." Regan brushes her lips against Lina's. "And before you ask your next question, no, I'm not sick of you yet, either."

Lina cups Regan's cheeks in her hands and brings her back for a longer, more thorough kiss. Her hands travel down Regan's arms, pivoting to splay over Regan's breasts.

"You're obsessed," Regan says between kisses.

"It's not my fault you like to hide them under so many sports bras." Lina ducks her head to kiss a trail over Regan's bare chest. "Just give me a couple minutes," she says before locking her mouth over Regan's hardened nipple.

Regan gasps, then gently pushes Lina away. "Nope. I'm not going to be late for breakfast with your best friend and her fiancée just because you're obsessed with my breasts. Let's go. In the shower." Regan swats Lina's bare ass.

"Fine, but you should know that New Jersey is having a water crisis, and—"

"If you think I'm not getting in that shower with you, you're mistaken."

Regan brushes past Lina, who grins and enjoys watching every step Regan's naked body takes toward the bathroom.

Lina holds Caitlin's hand up and inspects the ring. She has to admit, Mallory picked an exquisite ring that screams *Caitlin*. She's still a little miffed she wasn't given a head's up about Mallory's plan to pop the question, but the reality is, Lina's been a little...consumed with Regan.

She watches Regan now, smiling as she and Mallory pore over a complex French toast recipe.

"You love her."

Lina startles and glares at Caitlin. "Shut your mouth."

Caitlin shrugs, dangling her ringed finger in front of Lina's face. "Love is in the air, Lina. Don't fight it."

Lina grabs Caitlin and drags her out of the kitchen, away from the other two pairs of ears in the house. Well, three, but Pepper, who is neck-deep in her food bowl, doesn't count right now.

"Just because I love her doesn't mean I have to ask her to marry me." The words come out in a heated tumble.

Caitlin raises her eyebrows. "So you admit it. You love her."

"Yeah. Obviously."

"And you've told her that?"

Lina glances at Regan, who's laughing with Mallory. "She knows."

"Lina." The warning tone is very familiar, and Lina rolls her eyes, knowing she can't escape this conversation.

"Maybe I haven't exactly said those words, but she knows."

Caitlin taps her chin with her finger. "I did hear you call her 'my love.'" Lina nods. "That doesn't count."

"Oh for fuck's sake." Lina drops onto the sofa. Caitlin follows. "Just let me do it on my own timeline, okay? I feel it, I think she knows it. That's good enough for now."

Lina waits for the response, but nothing comes. She turns her head and finds Caitlin studying her.

"Okay."

The surprise kicks Lina far into the cushions. "What?"

"Okay." Caitlin shrugs and pats Lina's knee. "You'll figure it out. Oh, but for the record, Mallory and I both absolutely adore her, so if you fuck this up, Lina, you're not only going to lose the best thing that's ever happened to you, you're also going to hear about it for the rest of your life."

With that, she gets up and rejoins Mallory and Regan in the kitchen, leaving Lina to silently and privately stew over the remaining challenge of vocally acknowledging her feelings.

* * *

"I won't miss the snow," Regan says as Lina drives out of New Jersey. "But I do like your town. It's cute."

"It can be claustrophobic."

"Can't any town? Especially when you have a lot of history there."

Instead of answering, Lina hands Regan her phone. With a nod, Regan scrolls through Spotify. Soon, Fleetwood Mac comes through the speakers.

"What playlist is this?"

"It's called 'Don't Be a Dick.'" Regan laughs. "Caitlin gave me very strict instructions to play it as soon as you asked for music."

"Of course she did." Lina can't fight her smile. She knew Caitlin would insert herself into their drive back to North Carolina, but creating and sharing a playlist? That's new, and sneaky. Lina has to admire the effort.

And of course, the particular Fleetwood Mac song that's playing happens to be "Everywhere." Lina shakes her head. She knows exactly what the rest of this playlist will sound like.

Sometime after Elvis Presley's "Can't Help Falling in Love" fades into Taylor Swift's "You Belong with Me," which is surely Mallory's contribution, and Billy Joel's "Tell Her About It" gives way to Katy Perry's "Unconditionally," Lina can't take it anymore. She checks her rearview mirror, then yanks the Jeep onto the shoulder of US-13.

"Holy shit," Regan exclaims, glancing around. "What's wrong? Are you okay?"

"Yes. Very okay." Lina unbuckles her seat belt and pushes herself over the console. With her hand around the back of Regan's neck, she pulls her close and kisses her fully. She's almost distracted by the ever-present electricity between them but stops the kiss before she gets carried away.

"Lina," Regan says, a bit breathless. "What's going on?"

"I love you," she blurts. "Regan. I love you. So much."

Regan watches her, never once taking her eyes off Lina's.

"And I didn't want another mile to pass without telling you," Lina adds.

Regan's face breaks into a grin. "I love you so fucking much."

"You do? Really?"

"Oh my God, yes. I told you, back in August." Regan strokes Lina's jaw. "You are everything, Lina."

She lets her head fall into the safety net of Regan's palm. "I don't want to be without you."

"You never will be." Regan kisses Lina's cheek. "My heart is yours."

Lina brings their lips together, sealing the words. She feels a new lightness as she pulls back onto 13. Regan, and her heart, and all the incredible things that make her so *Regan*: she loves Lina, too.

And for once, there's not a single worry inside Lina, begging her to think it's all a lie.

More miles pass, the two women sneaking glances at each other until Regan grabs Lina's hand and holds it tightly after pressing her lips to Lina's once-wounded palm—the very spot that Regan bandaged up so many months ago.

Regan shifts in her seat, still holding Lina's hand. "Okay, but who really made that playlist?"

"Definitely Caitlin, with a side of Mallory." Lina shakes her head. "Welcome to my life."

"There's nowhere else I'd rather be."

Lina looks over at Regan, her love, very possibly the love of her life, and feels a contentment she's never known existed.

And right there, somewhere in the middle of Virginia, for the first time in her life, Lina Ragelis lets her heart lead the way.

Bella Books, Inc.

Women. Books. Even Better Together.

P.O. Box 10543
Tallahassee, FL 32302

Phone: 800-729-4992
www.bellabooks.com